MEET THE UNFORGETTABLE CHARACTERS OF
VERDICT AT MEDICINE SPRINGS

FRANK WOODSON: He was a good man who was done a bad turn, when all he wanted was to head home to the woman he loved. But turnabout is fair play, and the man he'd taken a fall for was fair game. . . .

CLETUS KANE: He went from breaking the law to making his *own* law, in the town he ruled with money and murder. And heaven help any man who dared defy him. . . .

NANCY MERRILL: She was the love Frank Woodson had to leave behind. She kept his memory alive in her heart as long as she could—and in the child she bore him long after that. . . .

Praise for R. C. House's
Trackdown at Immigrant Lake

"R. C. House is a writer of consummate skill, with both a deep love for and an intimate knowledge of the American West and its history. . . . Destined for a place on everyone's Fifty Best list for generations to come."

—Loren Estleman, two-time Spur Award–winning author of *King of the Corner*

JED PARKER: Once, he'd been Frank Woodson's best friend. Now he wore a badge in the service of Woodson's worst enemy. Torn between two determined men, he could pledge his allegiance to only one. . . .

HUGH KELSO: A big-hearted cowboy, he'd seen hard times of his own. He taught Frank Woodson how to trust again—and reminded him what friendship was all about. . . .

TOMMY O'FALLON: The burly Irishman had his own score to settle with the man Frank Woodson was dogging—and he was a valuable ally when fists and lead began to fly. . . .

More Praise for R. C. House's
Trackdown at Immigrant Lake

"*Trackdown at Immigrant Lake* crackles with excitement. From start to finish, this book draws a reader into the vortex of the action. R. C. House creates memorable characters and you'll be sorry to see them go when the last page is turned."

—Fred Bean, author of *The Last Warrior*

JOHN TWO BEAR: He was a Sioux Indian settler who lived at peace among white men—until he ran afoul of Cletus Kane, and was forced to run for his life. . . .

HELEN TWO BEAR: She was daughter to John, desired by Kane, and destined to fill a special place in Frank Woodson's life. . . .

More Praise for R. C. House's
Trackdown at Immigrant Lake

"R. C. House is a writer who deserves more recognition. . . . With the death of Louis L'Amour, there is a need for somebody to fill the vacuum in the genre. One of the established writers who will claim his share of the range is undoubtedly R. C. House. *Trackdown at Immigrant Lake* moves rapidly and has some surprises."
                    —Don Coldsmith, Spur Award–winning author of the
                       bestselling Spanish Bit Saga

Books by R. C. House

Verdict at Medicine Springs*
Ryerson's Manhunt*
Spindrift Ridge*
Requiem for a Rustler*
Warhawk
Trackdown at Immigrant Lake*
Drumm's War (with Bill Bragg)
The Sudden Gun
Vengeance Mountain
So the Loud Torrent

*Published by POCKET BOOKS

VERDICT
AT
MEDICINE
SPRINGS

R.C. HOUSE

POCKET BOOKS

New York   London   Toronto   Sydney   Tokyo   Singapore

This book is a work of fiction. Names, characters, places and incidents are products of the author's imagination or are used fictitiously. Any resemblance to actual events or locales or persons, living or dead, is entirely coincidental.

An *Original* Publication of POCKET BOOKS

POCKET BOOKS, a division of Simon & Schuster Inc.
1230 Avenue of the Americas, New York, NY 10020

ISBN: 0-671-87244-3

First Pocket Books printing August 1994

10 9 8 7 6 5 4 3 2 1

POCKET and colophon are registered trademarks of Simon & Schuster Inc.

Cover art by Dan Brown

Printed in the U.S.A.

✦ 1 ✦

1868

Frank Woodson's hands and wrists ached from gripping and kneading the arms of the wood chair that was the defendant's seat in Batavia's makeshift courtroom. The sweat from his palms was slick against the polished surface as he continued to work the wood, his knuckles bloodless with tension.

His face was a slab of anxiety and agony, the strain of these unfounded charges printed all over it, his mouth bone-dry and sour.

His old identity gone, he was a shell, a bag of bones looted clean of energy and spirit. The ordeal had left his lips cracked; wetting them with his tongue only made them sore. He found it hard to build tears to moisten his tension-parched eyes.

Woodson only half heard the words raised against him from the witness chair, and out of the mouths of the prosecutor and Judge Thaddeus Chase. If he had heard the prosecutor's name, he had forgotten it.

He tried to shut out the words, not wanting to hear any more of the false testimonies and lies leveled against him. Each bit of evidence, circumstantial or contrived, was a knife driven deeper into his vitals, the words resounding through the hollowness in him like hammer blows on a coffin lid.

He himself was a spectator, having no say whatever in the farce they called a trial. Resistance—he had learned the hard way from verbal and physical abuse he had endured over the four days since his arrest—was futile. Still he yearned again to scream out what they were doing to a man who had done no wrong. And to Nancy, that dear, sweet, patient girl waiting in Texas to be his bride. And to the children they'd hoped to have who now would never be.

"Nancy," he thought, "my dear God, Nancy! They're doing this to you, too."

He was a captive without escape in a strange land and was headed for prison. The inevitable, he knew now, was only a matter of his tormentors getting through with all their ridiculous sham.

Out of a brain twisted in helplessness Woodson's eyes focused on silly, meaningless things: worn boots, beards, torn pants. Most often it was on the pocked old-man face of Judge Chase, though Woodson's thoughts were miles away with his dear Nancy in Berdan, Texas.

The fine-haired fossil with the gavel seemed only half occupied with the testimony. His mind, too, was probably made up as to Frank Woodson's guilt. Somewhere behind Woodson a clock pendulum thunked with a maddening monotony. He ached to get up and go silence its rhythmic heartbeat. Stopping it might stop time—and these terrifying hours. Now and then a prairie wind outside drummed at the windows like an evil force trying to get in, emphasizing a despair that was eating Woodson's guts alive.

Judge Chase puckered his lips in thought as he now himself questioned the witness, a tired-looking ranch wife in a faded gingham dress. She wore small-sized men's work boots. Woodson's attention centered on her pinched features, pleading with his eyes for her mercy.

"Miz Ames, did you get a look at the man who robbed the Jimtown stage?"

"I surely did, your honor." Her shrewish words were spit out like those of a schoolgirl tattling to the teacher.

"Is he in this room, Miz Ames?"

"He sure enough is. That man right over theyer."

"You're certain."

"Yessir. He had that rag—that one theyer on the table—over his face, and he had a different hat and clothes. But that's the one. Same size. Eyes is the same, and the hair. I seen that scar over his eye when he come up close to take my lavalier. Yanked it offen around my neck like I was a common woman of the street, he did."

Woodson came alert. A surge of indignation forced him to blurt, "Judge, every cowboy I know has a bandanna like—"

The gavel's echo rang through the room, silencing Woodson like a cuff. "Ya'll observe the proper decorum of this court or it'll go harder on ya, young feller." Woodson eased back, feeling the sweat of frustration drenching his armpits.

The Ames woman was but one in a parade of witnesses who had come to the stand to point, pistol-like, the finger of guilt. The man picked to represent him, a nephew of the territorial governor's legislative aide, was new to the law, and he was powerless. Prissy and

3

idealistic, Mr. Delmar Phipps wanted his man to go free, but he allowed himself to be shouted down when he objected to the misuse of the judge's power.

Phipps slumped in his chair and studied the floor when one of the robbery victims threatened him from the stand. Phipps did not again raise his voice in objection.

The shotgun messenger on the Batavia-to-Jimtown stage had been the most embarrassed by the robbery; he'd let a hardcase get the drop on him. He came to give his testimony eagerly, darting scowls at Woodson and at Phipps as if to say, "Mister, I'm going to nail you."

"Maybe I was the only one got a good look at him, judge," the burly guard, Lebeau, said. "Len, the driver, still claims he didn't see it, but when that man Woodson he clumb up on his horse, that mask a his slipped. I got me a real good look at that owlhoot yonder. There ain't no question in my mind. I seen him good. One and the same."

Woodson gasped; Lebeau was lying in his teeth.

Woodson felt himself stiffen when Batavia's sheriff, Dave Beecham, lumbered his way to the witness chair. His gut pinched with nausea in recalling his first look at Beecham's menacing face that day out on the high plains.

The nameless prosecutor pulled back the skirt of his frock coat and jammed a hand into a high-cut pants pocket, his thumb casually exposed.

"Now, Dave, you've been an officer in this town fifteen years, haven't you?"

"Yessir."

"And you arrested the accused there, Frank Woodson, for the robbery of the Jimtown stage?"

"I did."

"Was he cooperative?"

"He was like hell! He wanted nothing more than to get the hell out of there."

"Dave, let me ask you this. You'd know a criminal if you saw one?"

"That's my job."

"How did Mr. Woodson's behavior impress you?"

"You mean how'd he act? Well, he acted like the low-down outlaw he is. He'd've give his left ... he'd've give anything to've gotten the hell out once we had him in custody. His kind are all the same."

"The actions, then, of a common sneak thief."

"All the earmarks, sir."

The evidence piled on Woodson like heavy rocks to keep varmints out of a grave. Nearly everyone in Batavia's courtroom had lost money. Sixteen hundred dollars, as well as the small change and valuables of four stage passengers, the driver, and the shotgun messenger, had vanished after the bandit stepped into the road.

Woodson had been miles away but had no way of proving it. The five-month trail drive north with the crew of the TM Ranch in Texas to the Blackfoot agency in Montana had been anything but a church cotillion. Woodson had been riding alone back to Texas with his $85 in wages buried in his gear. He was crossing the Patchknife Valley, a sprawl of rolling flatlands between two ranges, when the promise of a good life with Nancy vanished with the dust of the posse that took him in.

He had $300 in his name in a bank in Texas, scrimped and saved over four years of hard cattle-chousing work. With the roll he was bringing home he figured to have enough to get married and start his own spread. Woodson's mind's eye swam with the vision of the girl whose father, Tuck Merrill, Woodson worked for. He was thinking Texas couldn't get here soon enough when the bunched-up clot of riders broke out of a swale a mile away and thundered his way.

Woodson eased Lucky's gait, watching the riders draw nigh, first hearing the thud of hooves that grew in his ears, and then the groan and squeak of saddle leathers, the clank of canteens, and the slap of Winchesters and Sharps in under-stirrup boots. He counted eight riders.

Woodson pulled up and got down, waiting for them. Sun glinted off something on the chest of the lead rider, a burly man with a pot gut and a mean face. The gleam quickly took the shape of a badge pinned on the man's shirt.

The distant mountains lay in low profile under a milky blue haze while around him the wind sang a soft song through the grass. As the riders came up he saw they had sidearms drawn. Uneasiness gnawed at Woodson's innards despite the day's serenity.

"Don't go for that six-gun, son," the leader called as they rode up and half circled Woodson and his horse.

"Got no reason to, marshal," Woodson said, mustering a grin.

"Wipe that smile off your face. And it ain't marshal. It's sheriff. Sheriff Beecham."

"Got no reason to go for a gun, sheriff," Woodson repeated, a growing panic stiffening his face. He felt the blood draining from his hands and feet, turning them cold and awkward. Something here would need straightening out.

"What you doin' here?"

6

"Heading home to Texas. Been up to Montan'. Run a bunch of longhorns, five hundred head, through here with a crew four, five weeks back. I'm just a plain old cattle drover, sheriff." His face twitched involuntarily; something nasty was brewing like bad weather.

"I suspected he'd say that, Dave," one of the possemen said.

"Yeah," Beecham grunted. "He's the same size. Same coloring." Beecham lifted himself stiffly out of the saddle and got down, holding his gun on Woodson. "Stand easy, son, I mean to have a look at you." He came up to Woodson, scowling. "You ever hear of the Jimtown stage?"

Woodson tried to be casual despite growing fears that were about to set up a trembling in him. "No, sir, can't say as I have." He weighed his words; somehow the right answers, said with respect, were called for. "Only been through this country once, or should say, twice, 'cause I'm just now comin' back through."

"Where'd you get that scar on your eyebrow?"

Woodson reached up and fingered the hair against the jutting bone above his right eye.

"Had it since I was a kid. Fella shied a sharp rock at me when we were boys." Why, he thought, do my words have to come out sounding weak and apologetic? I've done nothing to be ashamed of.

"Hah," Beecham grunted. "Well, boys, this here's our man. The scar's right, he's the size they said, brown eyes, dark complected. They'll be happy in town about this."

"Hey, wait a minute," Woodson said. "I ain't—"

"You damn well told you ain't. For sure you ain't got the goods on your horse. If you'll kindly tell us where your stash is, I'll tell you it'll go a hell of a lot

7

easier on you in town, son." The possemen had gotten down and now stood by their animals, guns drawn.

"He wouldn't be fool enough to have it on him, would he, Dave?" said one of the posse.

"Well, why don't you check, Charlie? Let's you and me get over out of the way, son. I'll bother you for that hogleg Colt, unless you'd care to go down fightin'."

As Woodson watched in shock, fear numbing him despite the warm sun, the possemen untied his bedroll and shook out the things in his saddlebags. One by one his cartridges, his beans and bacon, his extra clothes, and his little spider for frying meat landed in disarray in the dirt. Lucky turned skittish with the angry action; Woodson struggled to keep him calm. With whipping motions they unrolled his blankets and slicker. His wad of bills flipped into the grass.

"Here's part of it, Dave," a man called.

"Hey, now, look," Woodson said, starting for his money. He was waved back by Beecham's big six-gun.

"Toss me that roll there, Charlie," Beecham said. He riffled through the bills. "I get eighty or ninety dollars here, boys. This ragtag never made that much in his whole life. It's stole money, that's for sure."

"Kept enough to do some hellin' down the line, Dave," Charlie said.

"Or hire a woman," another sneered. He followed it with a lewd chuckle.

"Well," Beecham said. "We seen enough. Leave that stuff there unless some of you fellers sees anything you want. He won't be needing it where he's going. Get him on his horse. I been without a drink for two days and have built one hell of a thirst. The drinks in town are on our friend here."

"Shame for that grub to go to waste," one said, picking up some things.

"I could use that shirt," said another.

"Wait a minute!" Woodson protested. "I told you what I was doing here. You ain't taking me in for no reason at all, are you?"

"Put a cinch on that mouth or it'll go bad with you, sonny," Beecham said. "Just to make it legal, you are hereby charged with the robbery of the Jimtown stage."

In Batavia several of the deputies manhandled him to the livery stable. He struggled against being slammed into a tiny closet off the tack room. "Hey," he yelled, "you can't do this!" A fist plowed into his midsection, cowing him into submission. There was matted straw on the floor. He lay on it for eternities, not marking the hours. At length he was released from the box to be dragged, weak and unprotesting, to the hasty courtroom in the town saloon. There seemed no question he had done the foul deed he was accused of. He was challenged again and again about where he had hidden the loot. He could only respond with what he knew, his innocence.

During the trial he was allowed on the stand only briefly to repeat his story of the cattle drive to Montana and his return through this country to Texas. He was jeered and whistled at and booed. At other times, when he tried to protest from his seat, the judge's gavel pounded and the man holding it threatened him with harsh treatment unless he shut up. Woodson's red bandanna was entered as evidence while the jury leered at him like hungry foxes. Reality was vague and elusive. There was nothing he could grasp and hold onto. This couldn't be happening, he thought.

The jury filed back in. Their chairs scraped shrilly and ominously on the wood floor.

"We have reached a verdict, your honor. We find the defendant guilty as hell!"

Breath was sucked out of Woodson's lungs, leaving him vacant and nearly lifeless. He collapsed in his chair, head hanging. His skin went dry as sun-baked rawhide. His bones had the brittleness of dead branches. The old Frank Woodson was dead; dead as surely as if he had been stood up and executed before a firing squad. The eyes saw and the body moved, but the man who had been Frank Woodson was no longer among the living.

"Frank Woodson, it is the judgment of this court, since you are so damned bullheaded about telling where you hid the money you stole, that you be taken to the territorial prison, there to be confined at hard labor for a period of not less than seven years...."

❧ 2 ❧

The night desk clerk in Brown's Palace Hotel in Jamestown recommended a penny investment in the day's edition of the *Jimtown Jawbreaker* as Cletus Kane came down for dinner. The mid-sized man with the scarred eyebrow and drooping eyelid looked quizzical. All Jimtown, the clerk said, was abuzz with the news.

Kane noted with a quick flutter of his heart the flourishing banner headline in the *Jawbreaker* proclaiming that the robbery of the Batavia-to-Jimtown stage a week before had been solved once and for all. A subordinate deck headline shouted that the miserable wretch who had perpetrated the dastardly crime was at that writing already headed for a hefty stretch behind bars.

Careful lest his actions betray his soaring emotions, Kane casually tucked the paper under his arm and sauntered into the adjoining dining room to order his dinner. A larger barroom and saloon occupied a similar spot at the opposite side of the lobby. Like the hotel's beanery, the saloon could be entered either from the street or from the hotel.

11

Surveying the place, Kane thought contemptuously that this fleabag flophouse bore scant resemblance to Brown's Palace Hotel in Denver. There everything bespoke magnificence and opulence. Jimtown's Brown's Hotel had been built at a time—probably still going on—when wood for construction was either dear or in short supply. The ceilings of the wood-frame two-story structure scarcely reached seven feet. Even Kane, who stood an inch or two under six feet, felt as though he wanted to keep his head pulled close to his shoulders when he stood up. Door frames on the place would have knocked his tall felt hat off if he wore it indoors. As the gentleman of some refinement he considered himself, he did not.

The rooms, too, were small and poorly lighted, even the dining room. Kane strolled in and found a table close to the wall and beneath one of the few coal-oil lamps with shiny, parasol-like shades to direct the light downward. Full night had not yet descended on the street outside. Away from the lamplight, however, the dining room was filled with an oozing gray that suggested total darkness was coming soon.

Light through the glass chimneys focused by the metal collars of the shades played as tiny diffused dancing moons against the field of fancily embossed tin squares that made up the dining room ceiling. With their obvious lumpiness, the walls of the hotel could have been plastered by an itinerant apprentice. Probably some homegrown concoction of burned gypsum, lime, and sand. As an attempt at class to compensate for the hotel's crude architecture, a thin cranberry-colored wallpaper featuring lavish fleurs-de-lis and scroll designs had been poorly pasted over the walls.

Frontier fantasies, Kane mused as he settled himself at his place. Crude imitations of culture where little, if any, existed.

The paper was already dingy and smudged from greasy hands and the hair of diners as they leaned back against the wall.

Accustomed to at least a few of the finer things in life, Kane promised himself that if he ever had anything to do with the establishment of a town or a business in the West, it would reflect class from the foundation up and the walls in. He thought of his nearly two thousand dollars in cash and swag carefully cached near the site of the Jimtown stage robbery. He might very well get involved with the building of a business for himself somewhere in the West.

Maybe even a town of his own. It looked as though he was in the clear now, the money his. But he'd still have to be careful in this part of the country.

Annoyingly, to a man of Kane's tastes, the hotel dining room had but one entree on the evening's bill of fare. Without asking, a tired-looking hag of a woman came out from the kitchen and set the plate of food and a chipped porcelain cup full of coffee in front of him. At least, he thought, surveying the soggy mess and the vapor rising from the brown but otherwise colorless food, it's hot.

He spread his copy of the *Jimtown Jawbreaker* alongside his plate of steaming beef, potatoes, and biscuits heaped with thick brown gravy and pored over the news with grim satisfaction. Almost absentmindedly, as he read, he worked some tendrils of roast beef loose from the large piece with the side of his fork. Despite his misgivings, the flavor and the texture were not all that bad.

13

The headlined article dripped with editorial invective heaped on some misbegotten individual repeatedly referred to as Fred Whitsun, believed to be wanted for questioning for other crimes throughout the West. It was equally lavish in praising to the very heavens the vigilance and determination of the posse of courageous and civic-minded citizens led by Batavia's valiant Sheriff David Beecham. It was their efforts, the writer explained, that brought to swift conclusion the mysterious robbery that had shocked the entire area.

Justice had been equally speedy, the florid report continued. The masked, heavily armed desperado had been quickly brought to the bar, found guilty, and sentenced. Kane grinned in spite of himself, feeling as though the weight of a huge stone had been lifted from his chest. He sensed a rising euphoria at being in the clear. This Whitsun, who was taking the rap for Kane, had been salted away for a good long stretch. The major anguish expressed by the *Jawbreaker*'s editor was that this lowest of the low had steadfastly refused to reveal the hiding place of his loot. The losses due to his foul deeds now would be borne by Batavia's poor, humble, and hardworking souls who had entrusted their life savings to the banking institution in Jimtown via the twice-weekly stage.

The editor closed his long and impassioned essay by suggesting that the courts of justice in this territory were turning namby-pamby. Fie, it said, on a seven-year sentence for this Whitsun. Because of the enormity of the crime and his refusal to return the money, hanging would have been too good for the miserable scoundrel.

His meal finished, Kane set the paper aside. Deep

in thought, he put fire to a cheroot and lingered, puffing it, over a half cup of coffee. The coffee wasn't half bad; his smoke was a fitting end to a meal that had been surprisingly good. His stomach, too, felt comfortable with the warm meal, and his innards were flooded with contentment; it had been a good day. By a sheer stroke of luck and frontier stupidity he had been cleared of the stage robbery. The money was his!

Kane's cultured temperament could have stood some fine brandy. Though he had some in his room, he decided that for now he'd satisfy himself with a whiskey or two in the saloon across the lobby. Leaving the paper, he crossed the lobby to the saloon.

The barroom had more lights than the dining room, the multitude of lamps giving the place a festive air despite the low-slung ceilings. Each light, in addition to its shade, was backed by a large circle of reflective metal bracketed to the wall. Large mirrors had also been placed along the walls to bounce the light back into the room. They had been strategically installed, however, so they couldn't reflect a fellow player's cards. Several gaming and drinking tables stood opposite a long oak bar. Another incongruity of the back country, Kane mused, sidling up to the polished affair. A broad plank on some whiskey kegs would fit better in these rude surroundings.

The saloon had a piano as well. An incredibly thin man with incredibly long fingers and sleeve garters to keep his shirt cuffs pulled above the wrists was working over a tinny concerto. Kane ordered a drink, dashed it down, ordered another, and sipped it, getting himself into the mood of the music and the evening. Kane calculated to have his own quiet celebration.

One poker game with four players was already under

way at a table in the far corner. The only other occupant along the bar was a red-haired, ruddy-complexioned little man who caught Kane's eye, smiled, and tipped his upraised glass in greeting.

Not knowing why except that he was feeling good, Kane, too, smiled and saluted lightly with a brief tip of his glass. He was in no mood, however, to associate with the man.

"Mr. O'Fallon," the piano pounder called, "will you favor us with more of your songs this evening?"

Three new customers strolled in through the bat-wing doors out of the darkening night. Talking among themselves as they entered, they made for the bar. They were local cowboys from the looks of their clothes. The barkeep smiled and poured drinks for the three. He was a big-boned and big-bellied man with long sweeping mustaches and luxuriant sideburns that traced themselves to the roots of his handlebars.

"In a shart while, Mr. Brown," the stubby red-haired man called back, his brogue unmistakable. "Meanwhile, yer talents at the kay-bard is calm to this tired auld soul. Prithee continue."

Kane observed it all, assuming the piano player, Brown, to be proprietor of the hotel. That explained the theft of the Denver hostelry's name. Brown acknowledged the Irishman with a nod and spun back to the keys on his swivel stool. He poised his cadaverous fingers and slid them over the keys in a delicate rendition of "Believe Me If All Those Endearing Young Charms."

Kane ordered another drink and allowed his spirit to be lulled by Brown's talented rhapsody. God, he thought, but that man can play! He has no business here, Kane mused, strumming barroom ballads for the likes of these uncultured boors. Those fingers deserved to be in a concert hall somewhere in the East.

Then he saw why Brown, a man of such talents, had wound up running a bed-and-board dive in a remote windswept corner of the West. Without being summoned, the beefy bartender pulled a quart bottle off the shelves, grabbed a tall and thick glass, and carried it to Brown's piano. A small end table, its top about a foot square, stood at the left end of the piano. The bartender set down the glass, filled it from the bottle, set the bottle beside it, and returned to his duties. With his right hand continuing the melody, Brown made a deft reach for the glass. He downed half its contents and returned his left hand to his music.

Kane shifted his eyes back to his own glass. Such a waste, he thought, already feeling his own liquor; such a waste of a supreme talent.

Movement in the doorway to the hotel lobby caught his attention. A tall woman, with handsome features that looked somehow hardened, stood briefly in the doorway, looking the place over. Seeing the stubby Irishman down the bar close to the piano, she made her way past Kane. As she went by, Kane noted statuesque proportions that she carried with an almost regal air. Her glossy black hair was combed and whipped into an exciting pompadour. The black hair contrasted with a face powdered almost to the white of snow, accentuated by a hint of rouge on her high cheekbones. The same rouge had been liberally applied to her lips.

Kane felt pleasant urgings well up in him as the woman floated by and he smelled the wake of a fragrant perfume. It had been a long time since he had been close to a woman, particularly one with this apparent dimension of charm. He did not delude himself that she probably kept a room on the hotel's second floor as her quarters as well as her place of business.

The woman glided directly to the Irishman O'Fallon's side. Kane, despite himself, felt the bristling spears of jealousy and envy. Probably she was the only available woman in two hundred miles, and even before she walked into the place she was spoken for.

The three cowboys between Kane's and O'Fallon's positions at the bar paid no attention as the woman drifted past them. Over their quiet bass murmurs Kane heard the woman greet O'Fallon sweetly but softly.

"Miz DeLong," O'Fallon responded, his voice coming louder than hers. "What a delate to be after seein' yer agin." To Kane's somewhat woozy disgust, O'Fallon gallantly reached for Miss Delong's hand and, bowing, brought the hand to his lips for a delicate, brushing kiss.

Now that, Kane thought, fuming, is totally out of place. He glanced at the cowboys. They had not seen O'Fallon's kiss of Miss DeLong's hand or probably would have laughed themselves sick.

Kane suddenly decided he wanted this woman. He surely had the money to lure her away from the upstart little Irishman who resembled nothing more than a high-cut hickory stump.

"I hope you'll be singing for us again tonight, Mr. O'Fallon," he heard her say.

"Aye, that I will, and I was only after awaitin' yer presence to honor Mr. Brown's request. It was he as already asked me to sing." O'Fallon's voice was high-pitched. He stepped to the piano, and Brown cut short his floating performance of "Aura Lee."

"I'll sing with yer now, Mr. Brown," O'Fallon said, turning and facing the bar and Miss DeLong, casually propping an arm on the top of the piano. Brown grinned over at the squat little man, waiting expectantly, his long fingers poised over the keys. Brown wore a fine fawn-colored derby perched on the back of his head.

"What would yer like to hear, Miz DeLong?" he said, his eyes on hers.

"Oh, any of them."

Kane observed that her voice was melodic, her words so articulate she sounded as though she had had drama training. A lot of second-rate actresses, he thought, wound up in "the trade."

"Any of them, Mr. O'Fallon. I particularly admired your 'Come Back to Erin.'"

"Then that it shall be. Mr. Brown ... Maestro?"

Brown graced the keys with a few introductory bars of the well-known Irish ballad, working with talent to build to the notes O'Fallon would begin to sing. O'Fallon brought his other hand up to the one propped on the piano and interlaced the fingers. Smiling at Miss DeLong, he tipped back his head.

"Come back to Erin, Mavourneen, Mavourneen, come back aroon to the land of thy birth ..." As O'Fallon's rich Irish tenor filled the room Brown skillfully strummed the keys more softly. His notes lent only a quiet accompaniment to the mellow tones of his guest, whose warm words and inflections now caught and held everyone in the room in their spell, even Cletus Kane.

One of Kane's eyelids drooped from an injury in a brawl that had left a broad scar in the hair of his eyebrow. Now both lids drooped with the quantity of whiskey he had consumed. He deluded himself that he was still very much in control.

As O'Fallon sang Kane gazed down the bar at the DeLong woman, who was paying rapt attention to the music. "Hell," Kane thought, resolve growing in him, bolstered by the whiskey, "she doesn't belong to him." He gripped his glass with deliberation and boldly made his way down the bar to where Miss DeLong stood.

"Pardon me, madam," he said, trying to speak softly and not disturb her enjoyment of O'Fallon's music. "I would be honored, since no one yet has seen fit, to buy you a drink to enhance your enjoyment of the moment and of the evening."

The woman looked at him, a hint of insult growing in her eyes.

"Barkeep," Kane called loudly, and the heavyset man hurried to where Kane stood with Miss DeLong. "Does this establishment stock any good brandy? If so, one for the lady, please, and one for myself."

The bartender, too, in Kane's dimmed perception, appeared to have a short fuse. He was scowling. "No sir, we don't get much call for stuff like that. Whiskey is about it. What you see is what we got."

"Then she'll have one of those."

Miss DeLong spoke up. "I'll thank you, no."

"Barkeep," Kane said in a reminding tone. "A drink for the lady."

Miss DeLong's eyes were on the bartender's. She shook her head with a barely perceptible "no." Thus dismissed, the bartender turned and strode back to a muted conversation he had been having with the three cowboys.

Kane tried again to get Miss DeLong's attention.

"Then perhaps you would honor me with your presence in my accommodations in this very hotel. I still have there a flask of fine Napoleon brandy with a most delicate bouquet."

"Sir, I do not know what kind of impression I have given you, but if you think—"

"I think you've given me the only impression you wanted to give ... a handsome woman here in this establishment ..."

The tightness of the air around the man and the woman at the bar had been communicated to O'Fallon. His singing of "When Irish Eyes Are Smiling" trailed off as he watched the developing events with concern. Aware that O'Fallon was no longer singing, Brown's piano playing also dwindled off to an embarrassed silence.

"Sir," the woman said to Kane, her words knifing into the hushed silence, "I don't know who you are, but I am Christine DeLong, delayed here only briefly to await a stage to Denver, where I am to perform with my theatrical company."

"Of course you are," Kane said, the whiskey urging him not to let up. "All the more reason for us to share several brandies in my lodgings. And then ..."

His ears rang and his face smarted with her powerful slap high on his cheek, close to the drooping eyelid. He felt a grip of iron fix itself to his upper arm, and he was spun around to look down into the glaring eyes of the Irishman O'Fallon.

"From the looks of things, the lady has asked yer not to bother her," O'Fallon grated in a loud growl. The fire rising in his eyes also showed in the growing ruby shine of O'Fallon's cheeks. Kane shook loose of the Irishman's painful squeeze on his arm. Anger, fed by the whiskey he had consumed, roared into Kane like the charge of a maddened bull. He flipped up the same hand and backhanded the stubby little mick with a blow that sent him reeling. Miss DeLong screamed and darted a few feet away from the confrontation to stare in horror at this crude demonstration of frontier savagery.

Knocked off guard by the blow, O'Fallon reeled backward but quickly caught himself on agile feet. Assuming a brawler's pose, he waded back toward Kane, jabbing out a right that caught Kane with a haymaker on the tip of his chin. Scattering glasses and a bottle on the bar with one flailing arm, Kane went down in abrupt and awkward humiliation into the tracked-in dust of the barroom floor.

Groggily his left hand groped along the foot rail to help lift his head up off the floor. His brain still rang with the dull thud of O'Fallon's punch. Round stabs of light as large as stream boulders glanced and darted around the extreme limits of his awareness. The foot rail under his grip at first felt scabby with rust. Then he realized he was gripping crusted manure dragged in by punchers' boots. The insult was too much, and rage rose within him. His right hand, gliding along his leg and past his coat pocket to find purchase on the floor to push himself up, felt in the pocket the bulk of his small hideout pistol.

The roaring anger in him and the disgrace of groveling in the dust of the floor of a two-bit saloon caused the sliding of the hand into his pocket to seem the most natural thing in the world. O'Fallon stood over him, waiting, still poised to fight.

Drunk or sober, Cletus Kane was not a man to stand for such mortification. End it now, once and for all, a calm, calculating voice said, probing through the dimness in his head caused by O'Fallon's punch and the whiskey.

That fast it was out and the trigger sprung, the roar filling the room. The quick dart of smoke momentarily clouded Kane's view of his assailant. O'Fallon belched an alarmed shout at being hit and doubled backward with a lurch to fall against Brown, knocking him off the piano stool.

Alert now, the effects of the whiskey seeming to purge themselves from his system in the heat of the moment, Kane pulled himself up. Hell, he thought, now I've gone and done it. Got to get out of here. His swiftly swinging glance saw only the surprise and shock in the face of Miss DeLong, closest to him at the bar, and those of the three cowboys and the bartender.

Movement in the corner of the room startled him. One of the poker players was on his feet, drawing a gun from its holster and starting toward the bar. Kane winged a shot in the man's direction, not hitting him, but scaring him into dropping the gun and falling into a frightened crouch on the floor. Others at the poker table scattered noisily for cover. Kane waved the short-barreled pistol at the others, his eyes darting between them as he backed to the street door of the saloon.

Out there, the same calm, calculated voice said in his head, there was surely a horse. The law would be on him at any minute. Escape. He was leaving nothing of value in the cheap second-floor room. All he needed was buried twenty miles or so out near the Jimtown stage road.

Kane let the batwing doors swing shut to flap on

their two-way hinges behind him. He picked the best-looking of the three horses tied at the hitch rail close to the door. Swinging up, he kept the little revolver at the ready in case any of those inside tried to come after him.

He urged the horse away from its spot at the hitch rail and galloped off into the inky black of night, only enough light to see the road defined between the Jimtown buildings. Cletus Kane quickly lost himself in the shadowy clots of sage and chaparral at the outskirts.

❋ 3 ❋

Her apprehension grew daily in direct proportion to the tiny, precious life growing deep inside Nancy Merrill.

It was a long, long time before it became clear; Frank Woodson was not coming back to marry her and take up the future they had hoped, dreamed, and talked of for months before Frank rode out with the Merrill ranch trail drive.

When at first Frank was overdue Nancy thought little of it. These things happened. Overdue a few days stretched to a week, then two weeks. She began to lose track of the days as her concern mounted. Then nothing else mattered, not even counting the days. Each day of agonized waiting and watching for him became another notch in time somewhere. They became eras of anguish punctuated by sunlight that let her see and dark in which she couldn't. The dark times were worse; then there was no chance of his coming. During daylight there was always hope.

It had been understood long before the seemingly endless queue of cattle was headed up and started north that Frank would take his money as soon as the cattle broker had issued the letter of credit and head home for Texas. And Nancy.

The other hands, including the trail boss, Mr. Hornblower, figured Frank would have several days' head start on them. Even before the crew left they were joking about it. Frank had taken a lot of good-natured ribbing from Hornblower and the other hands for the ardent swain of Nancy that he was. There was no way in this world that Hornblower's crew would not spend at least some of their hard-earned wages and several days in a trail's-end hurraw in Montana. Frank would miss all that in favor of rushing home to the arms of the girl he'd left behind.

Some of the other hands would not return at all, heading off to other jobs, to homes, or to sweethearts somewhere—just as Frank Woodson had insisted he would burn up the ground between the Montana cattle pens and Texas as soon as humanly possible.

Yet Nancy waited, spending her time at the back of the house or in the yard behind, watching the two ribbons of dust that seemed to stretch to infinity to the north. Daily, through skies sunny or sullen, she planned her work to be around the north side of the ranch house. Her eyes and her being were glued to the vacant, solemn road to the north, that road over which Frank would come riding in. In dreams he rode to her through the night, his handsome features heightened in full moonlight; by contrast, in nightmares he played a cruel hide-and-seek with her, taunting her, always eluding her, laughing evilly as he slipped from her grasp each time she got close to him.

By day, now and then her heart would leap as a lone rider appeared on the road over the rise about two miles distant. She would jump up and race up the lane to greet Frank, only to find it was a drifter, or one of the Merrill Ranch hands who had stayed behind to look after things, or her dad, Tuck Merrill.

Only when she knew that the spark of life swelling deep inside her would begin to show any day did she finally confide in privacy to her mother and father. Tuck Merrill sat in the comfortable, sprawling front room of the ranch, surrounded by all the things that had been familiar to Nancy from childhood, a grim look on his face as Nancy broke the news. She was pregnant with Frank Woodson's child.

She blurted out the shameful tidings. That was the best way. Her mother, Amy, only sat, shrouded in her work-worn apron, kneading her knotted old fingers and listening compassionately as her only child spilled out the awful truth. Nancy was beside herself with emotion in the telling.

An afternoon ride of farewell the day before the cattle drive began. Deep in the woods of the foothills behind the ranch the two young lovers grieved at their first long parting, confessed their undying love for each other, and passions took over as their innocent lovemaking went a step too far.

Nancy's father was a kindly, God-fearing man, and she hadn't known how to anticipate his reaction. He waited a long time before responding. When he did, his strong and fine work-worn face was drawn.

"Well, I got to admit that ain't the best news I've had this day. So be it. Your man'll be back, daughter. It may cause tongues to wag that you'll be married such a short space before you'll come with Frank Woodson's child. But your man'll be here to stick by you, and so'll your mother'n I. Won't we, Amy?"

Amy Merrill's wrinkled moon face wreathed in gray hair swung on Tuck, and for a moment the tension that had tightened there was relieved. "But the Lord forgives all, child. He knows of the love between you and Frank. He'll forgive, and He's the only one, really, who matters."

"And your man'll be back," Tuck said again. "Any day now. Frank'll be back, and you'll marry and take up your housekeepin', and your life'll be good. After while the gossips'll get tired a bangin' their jaws about this and find somethin' else to chatter away about. They don't count nohow."

"It seems dismal to you now, darlin'," her mother said. "But things will look different, much different, when Frank's back. And we love you for confiding your problem in us."

Moved by her parents' understanding acceptance, Nancy jumped up and kissed each of them. Tuck Merrill brightened. "Well, sir, if we've got that out of the way, I've got a sight of chores you womenfolk pulled me in from. By your leave, I'd best be gettin' back to them."

"Yes, Daddy," Nancy said, great tears welling up in her eyes. "It just seemed like the time to be telling you and Mama. You know I didn't do it to be a bad girl. It's just that ... that I love Frank Woodson so everlastin' much."

"I know, dear," Tuck said, touching her lightly and fondly on the head as he used to do when she was a little girl. "Your man is a good man. Ever since he hired on here he's been one of the top hands on the place. If only he'd had a bit more experience, I'd've made Frank trail boss instead of Mr. Hornblower. This was Hornblower's last trip, I'm sure. Frank'll be ridin' point for the crew and the herd the next time the TM brand goes up the trail."

"A fine young man," Amy said, in reinforcement of her husband's statements.

"When Frank come down out the bunkhouse and commenced calling on you," Tuck continued, "I hoped for something good to work up between you. You couldn't have picked a finer fella, I'll say that. I'd stake my reputation on Frank Woodson. I surely look forward to his becomin' one of the family."

Tuck Merrill was standing up, ready to get back to his chores. He reached up with the hand holding his hat, bowed his head ever so slightly, and scratched the back of his neck as he did sometimes when he was thinking, and thinking deeply. His eyes came slowly back up to Nancy's.

"And I'll say this, and we'll be done with it. In no way have you brought disgrace on this home, Nancy Merrill, and I'll defend you to my dyin' day. Regardless of what may be said elsewhere, you and Frank have not brought disgrace on this house."

By way of assurance and confirmation of her husband's words, Amy Merrill rushed to her daughter, caught her in her arms, and pulled her into the ample folds of her well-nourished body. Nancy could feel her mother's frame jerking with emotion.

Stepping back, Amy dabbed at her eyes with a lace-edged handkerchief she always kept in her apron pocket. "Mr. Merrill," she said in a hoarse voice, "you have chores to attend to. And Nancy and I have work in my kitchen. We don't have many hands on this place till the men get back, but what there are of them'll be wantin' to eat on time just the same."

The next afternoon Nancy was working in the

kitchen, again planning and arranging her duties so she could look out the window facing north and keep her vigil on the road for sign of Frank. Movement at the distant rise caught her attention, and with a heart pounding like that of a newly hatched chick she watched as a closed-up bunch of riders walked their horses down the long slope toward the ranch.

With the same heart again shrinking inside her, Nancy realized that Frank Woodson couldn't be among them. He would have broken free of the group and come racing and roaring in, waving his hat and yahooing. Nancy knew Frank; that would be his way.

Well, she thought, maybe tomorrow. Still she watched, and the heart that had filled with some new hope sank again as she identified the lead rider as none other than Thad Hornblower, leading the few remaining hands who had come back from the drive. Frank intended to be here days, if not as much as a week, before Hornblower.

Tuck Merrill, too, had seen the approach of his returning trail boss and the hands, but he stopped off at the house before going out to meet them. He found his daughter in the kitchen, anxiously watching the riders approach.

"Nancy, I want you to stay in the house. I want to talk with Mr. Hornblower first before anything. Now, I'm sure nothing bad has happened to Frank. But let me talk with Mr. Hornblower first."

Nancy watched as her father strode across the hard-packed ground behind the house and started up the road to greet his returning crew. There was an exchange of spirited howdies; aside from the concern about Frank, this end of the work of several years was a time for jubilation. Tuck Merrill had known for some time that beef was bringing top dollar in Montana.

Quickly, though, she saw the jubilation turn to seriousness as her father apparently began to quiz Hornblower about Frank. The other riders clustered close, listening, offering their words of information and question. After what seemed an eternity Nancy saw her father turn from the riders and head for the house while they moved toward the stables to tend to their mounts and to get to the bunkhouse for the first time in months.

"Well, sad to say," her father said when he was back in the kitchen, "they haven't seen hide ner hair of him since Montana. True to his words, he taken his wages right off and commence doubling back on his trail. Hell's fire, he should've been here a good week ago. Hornblower and them had a larrupin' time in Montan' for three, four days before they headed south, and then made an easy ride of it. I just can't figure it."

At the small secretary desk in her room Nancy Merrill touched the end of the pen holder to the corner of her mouth in meditation and wondered how she should begin her letter. Not only how would she begin it, but how would she say what she had to say, and how would she end it?

Now three months old, little Cynthia Frances Merrill was down for her afternoon nap in the ample cradle built by the loving hands of her grandfather, Tuck Merrill, and padded and quilted by the equally loving hands of Amy Merrill. It was a quiet time. Her chores were done, and at last Nancy was writing the letter that had been on her mind since well before the baby was born. She looked at the blank page slightly angled under her left hand. There was, she thought, only one way to start—and that was to start. She dipped the pen point down into the open neck of the bottle, a blotter and a pen wiper close at hand.

TM Ranch, Berdan, Texas

April 19, 1869

Mr. Jared Parker, Deputy
c/o Mr. Mose Laramore
Sheriff's Office
Abilene, Texas

Dear Mr. Parker,

I take my pen in hand this day to introduce myself and seek your aid. I am Nancy Merrill, daughter of Tucker and Amelia Merrill, owners of the TM Ranch here near Berdan. Over a year ago I was betrothed to your close friend, Mr. Frank Woodson.

Soon after our betrothal Mr. Woodson went with a cattle drive of the TM Ranch to Montana. Shortly after the herd was delivered Mr. Woodson began the trip back here alone, not wanting to delay there with others of the cattle drive crew. They reported that, indeed, Frank started on alone as had been planned from the very start.

In all this time Frank has not returned, and there has been no word from him, nor of him. Because of his expressions of love and concern for myself before he left, I cannot believe in my heart that he is electing to stay away from my side.

The others of the trail crew returned, having

seen no trace of Mr. Woodson since he left Montana. My parents and I can only presume that he may have met with foul play.

I know, Mr. Parker, that you and Mr. Woodson have been close friends for many years with your war service together and working and traveling together. You are his friend, and I beg you to contact me and help me and advise me as to what I can do to find Frank. If I cannot find him, my soul will not be at rest until I learn what has happened to him.

Certainly, in your years as a law officer, Mr. Parker, you have needed to find lost men. Now one is lost, and he is a close friend of yours. For Frank's sake, if not for mine, I prevail upon you for help. My anxiety for the man I intend to marry knows no limits.

Yr. Ob'd't Serv't,
Nancy Melissa Merrill

The rolling grassland was dotted randomly by craggy gray rock outcroppings and cutbanks, or clusters of tall trees backed by good-sized woodlots higher up. The trail Frank Woodson rode meandered through this country, dipping, rising, and snaking along, always taking the path of least resistance. It was more of a road than a trail; wagons had worried two wide and dished-out ruts with a center hummock of grass that was trampled and flattened by the horses.

Single one-rut trails, carved by cattle or by horses with men on them, cut in from the sides, flowing down from the back country in the direction Woodson traveled, indicating that he was moving toward some kind of civilization, possibly a town but more likely a ranch. Either way, he had to look for a job.

Out ahead of him, for several minutes now, Woodson had caught glimpses of another rider headed in the same direction, but leading him by a good half mile. Woodson's eyes tightened to a squint of wariness. Seven years of agonized confinement behind the thick adobe walls of a prison had turned around his attitude on life. With only iron bar grilles from which to look out on the precious sunshine of freedom, Woodson had come to mistrusting first.

In the year and a half he had been out, an aimless drifter going from job to job as the season demanded it, he quietly sized up the men he encountered until he could get their measure of trust. Out of it he had made a few friends and figured he was just as well served staying a loner.

Even when trust appeared to be merited, Woodson found he had little time or inclination for elaborate friendships. During his brief encounter with freedom he'd allowed no one to get close to him. He had signed on several places, done his work to the best of his ability, and found reasons to spend his spare time alone. He managed his wages as frugally as possible to tide him over slack times.

He dismissed from his mind the $300 in the bank in Texas. The thought of going back there for whatever reference there might be to his former life was too unsettling. So he said to hell with it and moved on to the next step in reconstructing his shattered life.

Others of the hands at places he'd worked tried to persuade him to go along for a Saturday night of high old times in town. Always he declined pleasantly but firmly. Understandably, he wasn't asked many more times. He picked up the reputation of a quiet loner, a man without a hell of a lot to say, but one who did his share and more; clean and punctual, but still a man who stood apart from the rest.

Always clear in his mind was the face of the man who surely resembled him in build and coloring—a man at least with a scarred eyebrow. Someday, some-where, he swore to himself, he'd meet face-to-face this man who had to be his look-alike. Every time Woodson peered in the mirror he saw a face like the one he'd come to realize must be out there. Often, in his dream of revenge, he gloated over the coincidence that would someday lead him to the real robber of the Jimtown stage, for this man, he was convinced, really existed.

He had a clear track to the man who had set him up for the destruction of his life and everything he held dear. That trail would begin with the lines that age and suffering had etched into that face in the looking glass. Without asking a lot of dumb questions that were sure to bring embarrassing responses and more questions of him, Woodson was content to wait, biding his time.

Somewhere, somehow, out of the blue, he'd encounter someone who had seen the man who looked like him. Woodson would have his first clues, and he'd be on his way.

In his fantasy he'd lived through it thousands of times, in prison and out. In some of his imaginings he found the man and shot him down dead like a dog. In others he rode triumphantly back to Batavia to clear his name, his prisoner riding with manacled hands, head hanging in disgrace.

"Damn if I ain't going to find that judge and that Beecham and rub their noses in it," he thought. Still, the seasoning of seven years behind bars had taught him that he would have to move with caution. In trying to bring down the truly guilty one, he'd make no false steps; in his eagerness to see the right man punished, he must not wind up in worse trouble himself.

Just now the rider out ahead had become aware of someone coming up the road behind him. He acknowledged Woodson by slowing his horse's gait, allowing the stranger to catch up. Woodson felt scorn for the man. How the hell does he know, Woodson thought, that I'm not going to shoot him down in his tracks for the chickenfeed in his pockets, and for his horse and saddle? I waited like that once and got my life shot out from under me for it.

The man had dropped from Woodson's sight down a dip in the land that was marked, from where Woodson rode, by the tops of trees bunched together in a deep ravine-like hollow. When Woodson's horse eased down the sloping road to the place, he saw that the other rider had moved off the double-rutted trail and let his reins go slack. They were tied and dangling from the pommel so his horse could reach down and nibble at the tender grass tops. He seemed to welcome the sight of the man coming up to him. Woodson kept his horse at the same pace, figuring to pass on by with as few words as possible.

"Howdy," the man said, sticking out his hand even though Woodson was still some distance off. Woodson studied the man closely, as he did all strangers. There were no similarities between this man and himself. He breathed easier.

"H'lo," Woodson said guardedly. The man he rode toward was short and stocky with a pleasant face. He was in faded, work-worn range clothes, with the usual range traveler's gear tied behind the saddle. Woodson watched the man's eyes, trying to take some measure of him. The man still grinned, a warm look; his eyes were drawn tight in apparent good nature, and three creases like bird tracks wrinkled the skin at either side of his eyes. Though reserved, Woodson was not altogether antisocial. He rode up to the man and shook his hand.

"You heading this way, mister?" the man asked.

"Guess you know that."

"I'm riding on over to the Tyson spread. Heard he was putting on some hands."

"Heard the same," Woodson said.

"Good, good," the man said. "Maybe we'll work together."

"Possible."

"The name's Kelso. Hugh Kelso."

"Woodson. Frank."

"Proud to make your acquaintance, Frank. Don't believe we'll get there before supper. I was figuring to pull up pretty soon and make a camp. Looks like water out there a couple miles yet. A stream, maybe. Good spot."

"It's likely."

"Be proud to share what little I've got with you tonight. Maybe we could find some fresh meat. Then we can ride in and sign on together in the morning."

Woodson looked Kelso over again, taking the time to study the man. He seemed friendly enough. It would be a simple matter to say he figured to ride as far as he could before dark, catch a few winks, and ride on in to Tyson's alone in the morning. But that, he thought, working it around in his head, might come off as an insult that could taint things when he and Kelso were working on the same crew.

"Well," Kelso said, "what do you say?"

"Ah, I don't know. I mostly go it alone." He eased his horse back to the road.

"I got a deck of cards and a little bit left in a bottle of Old Snort." Kelso followed him, but Woodson got the definite feeling that if he decided to ride on that Kelso would let it go at that.

"Not much of a hand to drink. Haven't played cards in years."

"Well, hell, I got the booze, and you're welcome to some of it, Frank. My card playing's on the rusty side, too." Kelso chuckled, and Woodson took it as a good sign. "We'll rustle up some coffee, fix something to eat, have a belt to settle our hash, if you're of a mind, and play a little two-handed stud for crick pebbles before we turn in. Sounds like a good way to end a day in the saddle, don't it?"

"Yeah," Woodson said. Kelso took that as agreement.

While the sun settled itself into the vast and vacant land to the west of them, Kelso and Woodson walked their horses the distance to where a wide trickle of shallow stream cut its way through this lower part of the grasslands. Stream-fed trees in ragged circular bunches suggested a snug place to camp.

Kelso was talkative without being annoying. He asked few questions of his newfound acquaintance, and that, to Woodson, was just as well. At the stream they made a good camp. Woodson found himself a bit relaxed for the first time since he'd walked away from the thick adobe walls and the iron bars of the territorial prison. Though they put together what little each had for a meal, Kelso managed somehow to take on most of the work. Friendly and agreeable about it all, Kelso was a master at making a camp, and Woodson respected him for it.

It was Kelso who walked out before full dark and plinked off a good-sized rabbit not many steps from the camp. He gutted it and skinned it and washed away the blood in the stream. They sliced long thin strips of Woodson's bacon and wrapped the carcass with it, pinning the bacon with slivers of wood, and they roasted it on a wood spit over the fire, catching the drippings in Kelso's frying pan. They basted the animal again and again until it was done and flavored to a turn by the bacon's salt and seasonings.

The meal was the best Woodson could remember in years, and he polished off his share. After dinner he even broke down enough to have a sip out of the bottle Kelso insisted was "Old Snort," though the label said differently.

The fire was a bed of coals to which they added enough wood to reflect the flame's light off the rocks around them and against the tree trunks and leaves higher up.

Kelso spread a blanket so they could play cards out of the dirt, and Woodson leaned against a great boulder, full of dinner, having a smoke. Sitting cross-legged across the blanket from Woodson, Kelso shuffled the grimy and limp deck. He stopped, holding half the cards in each hand.

"Frank?"

"Yeah?" He grinned at Kelso, feeling comfortable with the man.

"It's none of my business, but you been away, ain't you?"

"What's that mean?" Woodson felt prickly with impatience.

"You done time. Been in the calaboose."

"How the hell'd you know that?"

"And you did it for something you didn't do. You weren't a criminal then, and you aren't one now."

Woodson stared across at Kelso, wondering if he should be angry. He had started to trust again, and now this. He hadn't mentioned his prison stretch to a soul since his release. How in hell, he thought, did Kelso find out?

"Who told you?"

Kelso caught the edge in Woodson's voice. "Now easy, Frank. Don't rile. You told me."

Woodson sensed a brittleness in himself. "I didn't tell you a thing, Kelso."

"Ah, but you did. Tight-lipped, mistrustful. Hell, man, it's sticking out all over you. I ought to know. I've been there myself."

"You went up for something you didn't do?"

"You might say. I went with the Texas cavalry in the war. Hell, my horse hadn't chewed the shine off the bit before I was unhorsed in my first fight. Got cornered by a couple of Yankee cavalry, and I was hustled away and spent the next three and a half years up north in one of their prison pens."

"I did twice that. Seven years."

"Yeah, Frank, and believe me when I say whatever place you were in was heaven compared to being stuck in the open in Yankee country in all kinds of weather. Half the camp was a burial detail for the other half."

"Sounds like you think I was in Sunday School."

"Different set of conditions, but the same damned thing. We didn't think we deserved what we were getting. It was unjust as hell. But it happened. The men I knew, a lot of them, got the way you were when I met you today. Quiet, withdrawn, spoke only when spoken to, and that damned little. Bitter, that's the word."

"I am bitter. Bitter as hell."

"I know. I was the same way. All the time in there we were swearing the things we'd do to the Yankees if we ever got out. When the gates finally opened and they turned us loose to go home or wherever we were headed, we were whipped. There was no anger anymore, just bitterness. Frank?"

"Yeah?"

"How long you going to hang on to it?"

"Hang on to what?"

"The anger, the bitterness, the resentment, the loneliness, the mistrust? You know damned well someday it's going to succeed in eating you up. One day it may even come to a head, and you may really get mad and draw down on somebody. Maybe you'll think you found the man that got you put away. If you wound or kill him, you'll be right back there again. Or hanged. Or the other feller may wound or kill you. Even if that never happens and you stay at playing the lone hand, angry at everybody, believe me, you'll be dead long before your time."

"Huh," Woodson grunted.

"The sooner you cut loose of it and start being a man again—the man I imagine you once were—the sooner life will begin to have some meaning to you. Okay, my friend. Enough sermons. Five-card stud. Ante two pebbles."

✦ 5 ✦

Woodson ambled to the bunkhouse door and opened it, clapping it against the side of the building to let out the night's accumulation of stagnant air. He stood on the furrowed and worn sill step of gray wood, shoved his hands in his pockets, and surveyed the morning. He had slept in his longhandles, but when he got up he squirmed into his Levi's to go open the door. He was barefooted, and his sleep-tousled hair was twisted every which way. He combed at it with his fingers. He felt good about morning and about smelling the fresh, rejuvenated land.

It had rained in the night, giving the ground a bath. The air was free and clean-smelling. The bunkhouse door almost always faced the sun, when there was sun, and that was most of the time in this blessed country. Any unruly weather came from another direction.

Woodson noted that in the few months he and Hughie Kelso had been pards he was starting to take interest in things again. Like this morning. He stood watching the day, admiring it, letting the morning chill seep into the exposed top of his longhandles to sweep out the staleness and wake him up. Behind him in the bunkhouse five men who had gone on a Saturday night tear in town—Hughie among them—still slept. One of them rolled over in his bunk and set up a snore fit to rattle the single window that faced north across from the door.

Woodson sucked in more of the crisp, rain-washed air, remembering the seven years he had lived in the rank, stifling stink of a prison cell. This morning, he thought, was what freedom was all about. He debated putting on his boots to go around back to the jakes. Either way, he'd probably have to wipe his feet before he came back in the bunkhouse because of the thin layer of mud left by the rain. He could take off his boots at the door when he got back and clean them later. He went softly back for the boots and slid into them without benefit of socks. He went out and headed for the outhouse.

Old Ham Tyson was particularly pesky about hands relieving themselves off the bunkhouse stoop and told them so. That might go at other ranches, he said, but it didn't go here. Tyson was equally insistent on a clean-smelling privy, so there was no real reason for a man to avoid it, except for the short walk on a cold night. Tyson left a chamber pot in the bunkhouse, but it was seldom used. A man would prefer to walk the few steps out back to have his relative privacy.

The ranch cook and handyman, Stub Harris, regularly went to work and swamped the place out and sprinkled lime down the three-holer. Even though the smell was tolerable, there was little Tyson or Harris could do about the legion of flies that invaded the place on a hot, sunny summer's day.

Woodson counted it as odd that Harris, Tyson's

cook, should also be the man responsible for the cleanliness of the backhouse. But hell, he thought, that was the way. The same hands that cleaned the privy ladled out the grub in the kitchen.

Tyson had had Harris lay five-foot lengths of broad, rough-hewn oak planks end to end a good footstep apart, from the bunkhouse to the jakes, against such a day as this. They were put there to keep a man's boots out of the wet and mud. After months of exposure the planks were curled and warped at the sides, more resembling tippy canoes than a walkway. In the rain, every step on them caused mud to ooze and sweep through knotholes and over edges, making this handy boardwalk all but worthless.

At the supper table early one evening, with the sun still high in the summer sky—fly time sure as hell as everyplace buzzed with the invasion of the shiny, blue-bellied monsters—Hughie let out an awesome oath.

"Harris!" he yelled from his seat at the supper bench. "Can't you do something about these con-sarned flies? They're down there in the trench of an afternoon bitin' the bejeebers out of my behind while I'm sitting there, and then they come up here at din-nertime and wipe their feet all over my beans!"

By the time Woodson had made his way back over the sloppy planks to the bunkhouse Hughie was awake on the bunk beside Woodson's, his blanket below his armpits, his head propped on his arm, hand supporting his chin. His sleepy eyelids were swollen from what-ever cargo he had taken on during his Saturday night in town. His cheekbones, too, were puffy pouches.

"Mornin', Hughie." Woodson carefully set his boots on the splintered floor so the mud would dry before he cleaned them.

"Judas, don't talk to me about morning."

"You got a head?"

"No, why should I? We just went into town and drank lemonade and played tiddlywinks with some of the ladies from the church."

Woodson grunted and grinned at his pard's discomfort.

"You ought to go with us sometime, Frank. It ain't no life for a man staying cooped up out here seven days a week." He looked around to be sure the others still slept. Woodson's background and problems were something the two shared privately. "You got to get over all that and commence living again."

"Aw, sometime, maybe."

"Found me a swell little gal named Estrella last night. Not too long from below the border. Does a man good to have something cuddlesome once in a while. You ought to try it. Took her and some Old Snort and went for a ride in the moonlight, the two of us on Old Dude out there. Full moon last night, Frankie, and you know what that'll do to a man. Snugglin' up and coupled close as a caboose and a boxcar, and ballin' the jack on down the line. Damned good! Went out on the hill and spread out my saddle blanket in the grass. You know how the air feels late at night like that when it's fixing up to rain. My, that does do a man good. I got it set to see her again Saturday night next. I'm sure she'd find a friend, was you to think a bit about riding in with me."

"Ah, I don't know, Hughie." Woodson glanced at his saddle pard, who now lay back with his head on his pillow, hands clasped on his chest, staring at the ceiling in reverie. Woodson's head dropped, and he stared at his boots, damp with sloppy mud, between his bare feet on the floor, his mind working on things long past.

Once and only once he and Nancy had gone beyond the traditional limits of courtship, aroused by their love on a ride into the wooded hills above Merrill's ranch. Against the hard slipperiness of the thick mat of pine needles under them, all sense of reason flew from their spirits, their breath coming to them in choked sobs. A consuming passion raged into the void as Woodson and the woman he loved each battled to demonstrate the eager power and the ultimate depth of their love. Afterward, while Woodson lay under the soft sun letting his strength seep back, Nancy sat loosely beside him, smoothing her clothes and loudly chanting some nonsensical song. He remembered that experience with a glow, a warm and complete giving of the woman he loved.

On the ride back to the ranch both were contrite, vowing that it would never happen again until they were properly husband and wife. The next day the hands from the Merrill ranch began the drive north that ended in the destruction of everything Frank had worked so hard for.

His thoughts abruptly came back to the Tyson bunkhouse with a stirring in the bed on the other side of him. Vern Griffin, a hand Tyson had signed on the week before, thrashed in his blankets. "Dang it," he mumbled, "you fellers sure start talking early of a Sunday morning around this place." Griffin rolled over to sit on the edge of his bunk in his longhandles. He rubbed his whisker-bristled face and reached for his boots. "What's it like outside, Woodson?"

"Rained in the night," Frank said. "Sun'll be up soon."

"Watch your step on Harris's Grand Promenade on out to the shithouse. Walkin' them planks is like trying to put on your boots standin' up in a hammock." Hughie Kelso was propped on his elbow again, watching them through sleepy eyes.

When Griffin got back from taking his relief he slid his boots off at the bunkhouse stoop, walked barefoot back to his bed, and stretched out. Kelso got up and clumped out, mumbling something about his turn. Griffin rolled a smoke.

"What time do they eat around here of a Sunday?" Griffin was tall and lean, rawboned as a coonhound.

"Pretty quick," Frank said. "Later than weekdays, so the boys can sleep in. Harris likes to get some extra shuteye, too."

"Y'know, Frank," Griffin said through smoke from his cigarette, "when I come here I thought you must be some kin to Cletus Kane over at Medicine Springs. You look enough like him to be his brother."

"Who? Cletus Kane?"

"Big man over in Medicine Springs. West of here. Where I come from last. Worked a spread over there. But it was no good. Worked there a couple of months and got the hell out. It's a trouble town."

Griffin dropped the rag end of his flat, soggy, and stained cigarette paper into a cut-down bean can he kept by his bed.

"Everybody over there has to dance to Kane's tune. He's a blasted robber. Owns most of the land by now, him and his thievin' ways. Kane's money's behind the store in that town, too, groceries and feed and that. Anybody wants anything over there, they got to get it from Kane. And Kane sets the price, no arguments. That or you get your credit cut off at the store. And

48

you know what that can do to a man when the times gets lean."

Woodson's interest was aroused. "You say I look like him?" Woodson heard Kelso stumping back to the bunkhouse, and his thick frame filled the doorway as he worked off his mud-heavy boots.

"In a lot of ways you favor him, Frank. Builds about the same, 'cept you're leaner and he's heavier. Through the gut mostly. You got his walk, and you got Cletus Kane's hair and eyes. And he's got that scar through the eyebrow just like yours. His eyelid droops more, like one side of his head is half asleep most of the time."

Kelso landed heavily on his bunk. "Who?" he asked.

"Griffin was telling me about some guy out west of here," Woodson said. "Said he looked like me."

"Well, Judas, if that ain't enough reason to've got the hell out, I don't know what is, Griffin." It was said in jest, but Kelso's eyes flicked on Woodson, remembering the discussions they had had about the events after the Jimtown stage robbery. Kelso's look at Woodson was dead serious.

"I've known lots of men with scars over their eyes," Kelso said. He jutted out his chin and tossed up his head. "See that?" A ragged white line showed through his stubble of beard on his chin's underside. "I got that taking a nosedive off a horse I was breaking and come down on a rock. I seen just about as many men with a cut like that under their chins as I seen with cuts on their eyebrows."

Several days later, when they were riding alone, Kelso opened up on the subject that had been on his mind since their talk with Griffin that Sunday morning. "Well, I suppose, Frank, that now you're bound and by-God to get on over to this Medicine Springs and have a look at this Kane feller."

"Ah, I don't know. You know I've had my eye out for the real robber for a long time. Seven, eight years is a long time to hold it in, Hughie."

"Why don't you let go of it, Frank? It'll soon be nine years since you went over the road for somebody else's misdeed. What the hell will it prove now?"

"Aw, you're back to that, are you? I am letting go of it."

"Come on. You've changed a lot from the man I met on the trail since we come to Tyson's, Frank. You're different. Better. But you still got a lot bottled up. That's why I said what I said that morning with Griffin. About scars. Just because this Kane may look like you and have your scar, that's got nothing to do with nothing. Even if he is the feller from the Jimtown Stage, what's it going to prove now? Even if you ask him nice to go back over there with you and give back the money, is that going to change the last nine or ten years? You said yourself you figured Nancy had gotten herself married by now. And hell, they won't even remember you back there in Batavia where you got your bum deal. Let go of it and get on with living, Frank. You know damned well you're not going to settle anything with this Kane, if he is the feller, without gunplay. Like I told you, that'll either put you back with a losin' hand in prison or dead."

The two were on horseback, and Woodson's gaze was on the nearby hills, standing clear and stark against a sky going pink with sundown. They were in the country where they had made their first camp on the way to Tyson's.

"Frank, let's ride south when we're through here at Tyson's. We've both got a few dollars. In the spring maybe we can pick up a drive north. I know those towns out of Texas and clean up to the country north by the border. We can have us some larrupin' times, Frank."

"Well, all right. But I'm still for swinging by this Medicine Springs when we leave here. Just ask around a bit, that's all. Have a look at this Kane. I promise I won't do anything, Hughie. Just now it'd do me good to have a look at him."

"Well, I don't like it all that much. I got a hunch you're still aiming to call him out. But hell, if we just pass through there, I suppose it'd be okay. Might make you easier to live with. You'd not be a half-bad man, Frank, if you could puke up whatever it is in your craw. A trip to Medicine Springs might settle it once and for all."

"And if we don't get busy, Hughie, and round up these mustangs in through here and get 'em bunched and headed down to the ranch, old Tyson'll give us our wages and send us packin'."

Kelso grinned at Woodson, and it was a good grin. Woodson wondered how he had been so lucky as to run across a man who could become such a good pard. Kelso was about the only good thing that had happened to him since Nancy.

"You are on, my good friend," Kelso said, bringing his horse's head around and spurring him toward the wooded slopes where they knew Tyson's herd of half-wild horses was headquartering. "Bust a few broncs to saddle, mend a few fences for the old geezer, and head for sunny Texas for the winter."

"By way of Medicine Springs."

"Dammit, yes, by way of Medicine Springs. You don't let up, do you?"

With the horses brought down to tamer land close to the ranch, the hands took turns breaking the really wild ones to saddle. One in particular had succeeded three times in resisting attempts to harness his free spirit, pitching three of the crew into the humiliation of a mouthful of dirt and pulverized horse manure.

The spirited and stronger-than-hell cayuse quickly took on the nickname of Brimstone.

Woodson saw similarities between himself and Brimstone from the time they tried to break his free spirit in his trial and his time in prison. He grew thoughtful. Hughie Kelso had been right; unlike the horse, Woodson's spirit had been broken by the experience. Hughie was also right in that it was time to let go of it. Or somehow make an end to it.

Woodson watched his partner get ready to mount up with that in mind. It was Hugh Kelso's turn, and Brimstone's number had come up again.

When Tyson pulled the rag off the mustang's head Kelso was aboard, toes gripping the stirrups through his boots, his hand tightly wound into the rein. The animal was in the open area of the corral, and that, to the horse, stood for some kind of freedom from all this hazing and penning after a life in the wild and free country.

Brimstone came away from the corral fence for about four steps, remembered the man on his back, and figured to get rid of this one the way he had done the others. His legs stiffened, and he uncoiled like a broken bedspring. The wild stallion did about five of these crowhops with fearsome squeals, heading for the far side of the giant breaking corral.

After about six of his bone-jarring leaps the great horse sunfished in midair, swinging Kelso off balance. When the horse hit the hard-packed corral dirt again Kelso's feet jarred out of the stirrups amid yells of encouragement from the crew hanging around the rim of the corral.

Kelso let out one scream of panic as the brutish horse went again into the air with Kelso's legs flying, clawing to find purchase for his feet in the flapping stirrups.

In midair the horse's back flattened and arched while his hind end swiveled catawampus. Kelso was slammed with evil force out of the saddle, waving for balance with his arms and losing his grip on the reins. The six-tiered corral poles at the far side broke, bent and tumbled like so much straw from the force of the man slamming through, clattering like thunder.

Hugh landed and lay still among the helter-skelter of poles. Brimstone leapt over and trampled the man sprawled among the splintered and jumbled poles in the break in the corral fence. With stirrups and reins flapping he made with the greatest haste for the high country that had long been his home.

Woodson reacted at first with a paralyzed shock from his place on the top corral pole across from the mess Hugh's fall had created. His breath was rammed from his lungs by having witnessed the stunning force of Kelso's fall. Then he collected his wits, jumped down, and sprinted across the expanse of corral, chaps flapping, his boots plowing dirt as he ran. He sailed into a crouch beside Kelso, letting out a choked, hoarse scream.

Hugh Kelso had ridden his last bronc.

❧ 6 ❧

Woodson picked up his wages from Ham Tyson and carefully stowed his gear in his saddlebags, rolling some of it in with his slicker and bedroll. He took his time with the slow, sad chore, remembering that he and Kelso had planned to ride out together. It was the only mournful time Woodson could remember in his adult life. His mother had been long dead when he rode away from his tyrant father in Kansas in 1858 when he was sixteen, three years before he and his Texas pard, Jed Parker, rode off to join the Confederate Army.

There was no mourning, as such, about his time of going to prison. He was only consumed with anger and helplessness over the injustice of it all. That, or he was numb with the shock of things going on around him. Remembering it, and comparing the sensations he now felt about losing Hugh Kelso so suddenly and so frightfully, he knew the tragedy of his imprisonment had not brought grief.

The toll prison took on his emotions was imperceptible. They were shattered from the very start. Because he hadn't been able to tell the court at his trial where he had hidden the Jimtown stage booty, he was sentenced to the additional punishment of being held incommunicado for seven years.

Over seven long years out of touch with the world he'd known, Woodson tried but once to smuggle word out to his home and loved one in Texas. After much hope, the results only drove him deeper into melancholy.

Early in his imprisonment Woodson persuaded another inmate, soon to be released, to take word of the calamity to the Merrills in Berdan, Texas. In his letter he instructed Nancy to give the man bringing the news fifty dollars.

After weeks of waiting word got back to the prison. It wasn't good news. Two days after his release Woodson's messenger was caught with a stolen horse and summarily hanged.

Woodson's letter was found on the man, and that word also got back to the prison's warden and guards. Woodson was hustled off to the pit, a grave-sized hole in the prison yard with a ground-level heavy iron door for a lid. The door only radiated the intense heat down into the pit like a dutch oven, all but roasting anyone confined inside. Three tiny holes in the thick plate provided the only air inside the tiny cubicle. Lesser men had died in there. Woodson barely survived the three-day ordeal.

His three days of suffering and starvation in the pit in scorching August weather took away any thread of hope. Emotional depression yanked at the fiber of Woodson's resistance, slowly unraveling it. Released at last from the pit's extreme agonies, he returned to his cell a spiritless spook haunting some kind of abandoned, vacant structure that had once been Frank Woodson.

There was nothing, nothing at all, that he could trust. This crushing of his spirit stayed with him, even long after his release from this hellhole of a prison.

In two short months Hugh Kelso, with his ready wit and his steady mood of support and encouragement of Woodson, had made himself a part of Woodson's new life. Now Hughie was dead, and that part of him that had grown a part of Woodson was gone, leaving an ache of memory inside him that he could not identify, could not come to grips with; he could not tell which part of him the ache affected most. It seemed to be all over Woodson—head, heart, bones, muscles, and joints.

Hughie had enough in ready cash with what he had coming to him from Tyson for a proper funeral and a carpenter-built pine box. They buried him on a hill not far from the ranch, but up east in the country where Woodson and Kelso had camped their first night together. They were also able to hire a hearse from town drawn by a team of glossy blacks to take him out to his burying place.

Woodson was particularly touched by the simple funeral ceremony. The wind was not howling that day on the hill. Neither was it soft. It was strong enough to whip horses' tails and loose clothing, and to thump and drum around them and occasionally break with gusts that sounded like someone shaking out a blanket. Men screwed their hats down tighter on their foreheads to prevent them from cartwheeling across the high plains.

A preacher came out from town, somber-acting and wearing the blackest of clothing as he waded through the grass up the hill, clutching a thick, gilt-edged Bible to his chest. After the parson spoke some words and recited the Twenty-third Psalm, somebody from town who knew a bit of the bugle stood down the hill out of sight and blew Taps against the wind.

For a long time Woodson's ears would recall the sour, sliding, off-key tones produced when the not-too-talented bugler tried for high notes. But the man was trying, and the emotion of the sad, drifting sound clawed inside Woodson and brought tears.

After the bugle sounded, five or six of the Tyson hands took out their hogleg Colts and fired three volleys into the air at the command of rawboned Vern Griffin, tears streaming down their faces.

The preacher suggested they sing "Nearer My God to Thee," but he managed only one stanza in a booming bass while the hands, most of them alien to church ritual, timidly did their best to go along with it. None of them was at all sure of the words. They were much better at singing to night-quiet cattle when there were no other ears to hear.

They all pitched in and helped finish the grave. They put up a plain plank marker with Kelso's name and the date that Stub Harris had carefully painted on. By common consent they left most of Kelso's gear, including his lever-action, brass-frame Henry rifle, in the stable's tack room to supply less fortunate hands who might come along. Woodson spoke for and got Kelso's hogleg, the same caliber as Woodson's .44. He wrapped it tenderly in a length of soft flannel and stowed it in his saddlebags.

Woodson said good-bye to Griffin and the rest of them in the bunkhouse, all of whom were taking a midweek day off for the funeral and out of respect for their dead saddle pard. Tyson and the cook, Harris, were waiting by his horse when Woodson came out to mount up. Harris's head hung, and he was wringing his big grease-stained apron. Tyson's head was up, but his eyes were moist. His face said that words needed to be said, but he didn't have them.

"I'm sorry about your pard, Frank. Truly sorry," Ham Tyson said. Harris managed to look at Woodson, and then his head dropped again. "You'll be all right, won't you, Frank?"

"Sure, Ham."

"You don't have to leave, you know, Frank. There's plenty of work. . . ."

"I was figuring to move on directly anyway, Ham. That is, Hughie and me."

"I know, son. I just want to know if you'll be all right. Do you need anything?"

Woodson found a smile. "No. I'll be okay, Ham."

"If you ever get back this way, Frank, there'll always be work. You and Hughie were—well, you two were damned good hands. I never seen three men that could get as much done as you two."

Woodson raised one knee, his foot found the stirrup, and he hooked his hand around the horn. "I may ride back through sometime, Ham."

"There'll always be a place for you at our table, son. Right, Stub?"

Harris cleared his throat, looked at Woodson, and said, "Aw, what a hell of a thing to have happen!" Stub turned and ran for the house on his short legs, his pace choppy like that of a spanked schoolboy. Woodson sensed Harris was crying.

"I guess I ain't got the words, Frank," Tyson said. "Not a hell of a lot a man can say at a time like this, except what we used to say down home in Lincoln County. *Vaya con Díos.*"

"*Vaya con Díos*, Ham," Woodson said, the hollowness still strong in him as he swung up and in the movement started the horse off at a walk. Only once did he look back to see Tyson still watching after him, standing where he had been, the thumb of one hand hooked in his belt, the other shading his eyes against the afternoon sun as Woodson headed west. Woodson rode for Medicine Springs, and to put distance between himself and Hughie Kelso's burying place.

For three days Woodson followed trails and roads that pointed west over a solemn, solitary prairie, a benevolent sun caressing him during the day and the stars offering companionship during long, lonely night camps.

Late on the third afternoon he came to a crossroads and for the first time found a signpost indicating that Medicine Springs was thirty miles down the left-hand fork. He camped that night under some trees beside a shallow stream, a setup that sadly reminded him of his first camp with Hughie Kelso—but not enough to disturb him. In the morning, after a scant breakfast, he pulled together his cooking and sleeping gear. As light broke with a gray glimmer behind him he started his horse at a walk over the thirty miles to Medicine Springs.

Thirty miles to Cletus Kane's town. His pulse raced; anticipation tightened his chest as he signaled his horse to take up an easy, mile-eating canter. Glossing over the realities of what it would take to prove Kane's guilt and the people he might have to fight to get to Kane, Woodson consoled himself with the dream of having what might be his man nearly in his clutches.

Hours later his probable destination after years of searching loomed before him as the road took Woodson into the broad, sprawling valley that formed the Medicine Springs basin, a giant hollow between mountains, hills, and low ridges. Nowhere did the pleasant vista of rolling country before him give the slightest hint of evil. He was hardly aware of the long and gradual climb to the grass-covered hills that then sloped away from him into the valley. On the other side low mountains rose, ringing the valley. Shaped like a great horseshoe, its open end faced east, centering on the low pass and the trail Woodson was taking in.

Dunes of fleece clouds kept the sun from becoming too hot. The miles of valley below him drowsed in a warmth that was totally comfortable. The soft wind rising to him from the valley floor further cooled and lulled him.

Over the miles of tree- and rock-studded valley Woodson could see a scattering of ranches in the gently rolling country. Here and there were cattle singly, in small bunches, or herded together by the score. Several serpent-like rows of trees told him where streams cut the great basin. Roughly in the center and at the joining of many twisty roads tracing the land, buildings were bunched together like quail, generally spread along a north-south line, probably marking Medicine Springs' main street.

Again Woodson's eyes roved the scope of the sun-bathed rolling floor before him. It suggested nothing but peace and tranquility. If ever there was a place on this earth that a man might choose to make his home, this would be a likely spot, he thought. Still, nagging in his head were those words of Vern Griffin the Sunday morning before Hughie Kelso was killed: "It's a trouble town."

Woodson nudged the horse's ribs with his spurs, urging him down the sloping trail through the grass and toward the center of the valley. It would still be more than an hour before he'd get there unless he galloped the horse, which would be foolish. His guess was right. About an hour later the road took him to the south end of the town. He couldn't have judged it from the distance when he came over the low pass, but Medicine Springs was not built in the flat portion of the valley. It was in slightly rolling country, adding to the town's attractiveness. The houses and town buildings perched on several levels, lending them charm. The main street, longest in the town and with the most commercial buildings, was built on the central level, with structures on the east somewhat above town. Those to the west were a bit below, but still randomly set in relation to the main stem.

Give Cletus Kane credit, Woodson thought as he walked his horse down the main street toward the center of town. He takes good care of things, or sees to it. A town spirit of some sort was there. Homes and the stores and such were painted, and trees had been hauled in and planted. The town generally had a well-kept look, rare among the many gray and paint-starved towns Woodson had seen.

Homes of the more substantial citizens of Medicine Springs were bordered by low picket fences painted white. Some of the houses behind the fences were two-storied and fringed with ornate spindles and other filigree. Even the lesser homes were occasionally decorated with small flower gardens, bordered by hauled-in and rounded river boulders that had been whitewashed.

Footpaths paralleled the wide and dusty main street past houses and the smaller of the shops as Woodson neared the center of town. There, three steps abruptly went up to raised board sidewalks the full length of the commercial row. Woodson's eyes took in a hash house, a couple of saloons marked by the familiar bat-wing doors, a bank, a post office, a grain and feed store, and a general mercantile. Both the mill and the store indicated ownership and management by Cletus Kane. The store district was also dotted with other businesses necessary to the support of the town.

Medicine Springs was not bustling this afternoon. Still, people were about, busy with errands or just loafing and talking on the broad plank walkway under overhangs and real second-story buildings or false fronts. Now and then a single rider approached him, or a buggy or ranch wagon rattled past. Woodson was impressed and wished Hughie Kelso could have been along to see it. A hitch rail was enveloped by the late afternoon shade across from the hash house. He swung the horse in, found an open spot in the shadow along the rail, got down, and tied up his horse.

Still studying the place, he figured to go over and get something to eat. Then he'd arrange to have the horse put up at the livery stable to be watered and corned and grained and rested in a real stall for the night.

Men and an occasional woman or two moved along the boardwalk as Woodson crossed the dusty, sunny street, their boots and shoes thumping hollowly on the planking. Raised store entrances and the elevated walks kept at least some of the street dust from filtering into the places of commerce. Woodson grabbed an overhang support post and pulled himself up toward the restaurant door.

Next to it was a huge plate-glass window with large and ornate gold lettering, edged and shaded in black, and curving across the expanse of glass—KANE CATTLE COMPANY. It, like the town, was clean and businesslike.

Woodson studied Kane's office window for a moment and pulled at his hat to bring it down to help hide the scarred eyebrow. He had a stubble of beard from nearly four days in the saddle, and he was dusty and grimy from the ride. It was doubtful anyone here would see any resemblance between him and Kane if, as Vern Griffin had suggested, the two looked alike.

The bowl of chili put down before him in the restaurant was one of the best he'd ever tasted, a generous portion he washed down with several cups of coffee. Like the rest of the town, Woodson was impressed that the restaurant, too, was clean, airy, and well-lit from the front by floor-to-ceiling divided glass panes.

Out on the street, his belly comfortably full and warmed by the chili's spice and seasonings, Woodson pulled a splinter from his pocket. He lounged against a post and picked the good beef from his teeth, still enjoying the small shreds he pried or sucked loose. Up the street he saw a sign for the Medicine Springs House. Probably the local hotel, he thought. He figured to take a room for the night after finding lodging for his horse.

He took little notice of the people passing him. They were strangers, as he was to them. To stare at them, trying to identify Cletus Kane, would be discourteous. Though not a drinking man, Woodson figured that he'd clean up at the hotel, and with nightfall he'd stop for a drink at one of the saloons. There he could ask around about Kane and see if he could get a look at the man.

He'd told Hughie Kelso that would be enough, and it would be. Then he could ride on in the morning for wherever the trail might lead. Still, there was that curiosity. There was not a chance in a thousand that Kane would be the man who had robbed the Jimtown stage. Still, he was compelled to find out more about Cletus Kane.

With the good feeling of the chili nestled comfortably deep within him, Woodson squared his shoulders, stepped off the boardwalk, and started across for his horse. Near the horse a woman had stopped on the walk across the way to look in a store window. Woodson's eyes were drawn to her. Something was startlingly familiar about her form, her height, her posture from the back. Woodson dismissed it as mere coincidence, concentrating now on getting his horse properly bedded down. The woman turned to start away up the plank sidewalk, passing nearer the horse and the approaching Woodson. Her walk brought an even greater surge of recollection. Like a flash flood, memory roared back into him at the look of her in profile.

Involuntarily the name rose in his throat. He swallowed it hard, biting his lips against calling out to her.

With never a sidewise glance Nancy Merrill—or at least the woman who had been Nancy Merrill—continued on up the street, oblivious to Frank Woodson a few steps away beside his tethered horse.

In case she might look back and recognize him, Woodson bent low along the far side of the horse and went to work, pretending to check the tightness of the cinch strap. He quivered with emotion.

The tumult of questions bombarding his brain prevented him just now from calling to her, rushing to her. The embarrassment of the prison stretch was too much to blurt out here in this chance meeting in Medicine Springs. There was also that other question that held him back, a question that would have to be dealt with before he could reveal himself to Nancy.

What in hell was she doing here in Cletus Kane's town?

❖ 7 ❖

Memory swirled around Woodson's head like so many colors of paints being stirred together. The darks and the lights were separate but merging slowly into a swirl of the past as well as the here and now, the bitter recollections and the fond ones, his fantasies and his realities so close to each other that he couldn't tell where one left off and the other began.

He hadn't had a drink, yet his brain was numb and foggy with the crowding of his thoughts. He scarcely remembered trying to hide from her. When he was sure she was gone, out of sight, he stealthily led his horse to the livery stable to be bedded down for the night.

At first he took no note of the furnishings of the small room he took at the Medicine Springs House, or if he had gotten change from the desk clerk for the silver cartwheel he tossed him for the four bits night's lodging. His concern was that she might come by outside and see him in the lobby. Just now he couldn't risk a confrontation with Nancy. The shock of seeing her here, in this town, so unexpectedly, was simply too great. He had to order his thoughts over this new development.

In the room, which overlooked the street, he went to the single window, carefully drew back the dingy lace curtain, and studied the street below. Nancy was nowhere to be seen. Some of his composure slid back as he at last checked the room.

Still, his head swam with the shock of seeing her as he settled into the room's surroundings. He didn't have that much to put away. His few possessions easily fit into his saddlebags, and he didn't bother to unpack.

Nancy Merrill in Cletus Kane's town. After all these years, he thought, she must be married. Woodson shook his head to get his thinking back on the right track. The room was furnished simply—a small brass rod bed with ornate bulbs and turnings, a side chair, a marble-topped commode with a pitcher and bowl. The bowl, he saw, had a crack, but it probably still held water. Under the bed he could see the curved and gleaming white porcelain handle of the night pot. On the back of the inside door panel was tacked a card announcing that hot water and tubs were available for five cents at the back of the hotel downstairs. Towels went for two cents.

He brushed and beat as much of the trail dust as he could from his work-worn Levi's. He dug out his clean shirt and a pair of socks from his saddlebags. He also whacked his hat against his thigh to rid it of dust and tossed it on the bed. He headed down for the bathhouse, first checking that he had money in his jeans. He found the two bits change from the dollar he had given the clerk.

The bathhouse was a long shed tacked on behind the first floor and raised several feet above the ground for ventilation. The air inside was hot, as the Chinese attendant kept a fire in a huge cookstove raging fiercely at the job of heating pails of water.

The Chinese grinned at him, handed him a towel, and indicated one of the huge zinc-metal tubs. "You take numbah two, suh," the Oriental said, the grin never leaving his olive moon face, showing most of his teeth when he talked. "Wong Chun bling you watuh." Five or six pails of boiling water on the stove filled the room with moist air and clouded the vision of the place, making it dark and steamy.

"No scard you, suh. Put in cord watuh whire you take off crothes."

A voice came through the deep mist and gray light of the room. Someone occupied tub number one. "One Hung Low says he wun't scald yer. He'll temper the water while you get yourself undressed."

"Obliged," Woodson said. He made his way down to a bench close to his assigned tub. He sat on the bench along the wall and began to worry off his boots. His socks were damp from the day's sweat, and the boots resisted; fighting them, he managed to build a painful cramp in his right arch. Testing the foot gingerly as he stood up, he slid out of his shirt and Levi's and hung them on convenient pegs above the bench. He also shook out his clean shirt to rid it of wrinkles and got his razor out of his pants pocket. He stepped carefully, still favoring the knotted muscles in his foot, across the slick floor to the tub in his bare feet. The board planking was raised above the ground, with inch spaces between the four-inch planks for the air to dry the sodden wood. The place, he thought, was like an oversized corncrib.

He noticed that his hands, to the wrists, were darkened from exposure and dirt. He glanced in the mirror kept on the wall for customers to preen in. From a small V formed by his shirtfront at the base of his neck to his hairline, his head was the same color. The rest of him was white as a pearl.

Wong Chun had filled the tub with convenient pails of cold water. He gradually added water from one of the steaming pails and tested it with his fingers. He grinned again at Woodson, who stood bare at the end of the tub waiting to get in. Wong Chun's eyes were narrowed to slits. It had always puzzled Woodson how Chinamen could see when they grinned.

"You rike it hot?"

"Not partial to leaving my hide in there, no. Other than that, hot's okay."

The tub was full and steaming when Wong Chun rose and bowed to Woodson, still grinning. He backed partway to his stove in the center of the bathhouse.

The zinc tubs were the finest Woodson had ever seen. They were enormous, with rolled edges, the seams carefully soldered and finished. He had been in some with sharp flashing of solder that could rasp a man's skin and draw blood. The back of the tub was a high sheet-metal lip contoured for a man to lean comfortably back against. He could stretch his legs out full length and brace his body on the curved, sloping footrest, all the while being immersed to the chin in the steaming, clear water. He grabbed for the large nugget of brown soap in a waterlogged wood tray on the wall beside him.

Clutching his razor, Woodson eased into the nearly overflowing tub with a relieved sigh. The hot water had an instant calming effect. After seeing Nancy on the street a half hour before, and his long ride into

Medicine Springs, the relaxing bath was just what his system needed.

"If it ain't just right, or if you need more hot or more cold, sing out for auld One Hung Low," the man in the next tub said. All Woodson could make out of the man through the steam was a round and pug Irish head that was red and polished-looking from exposure and the heat of the bathwater. He was nearly bald, but the hair that wreathed his skull was copper-red without a trace of gray. The Irishman had a stub of a lit cigar in his teeth and a half-full flask of whiskey in his left hand. On the floor beside the tub was an ornate shaving mug, a brush propped in it. Beside it lay a good-quality razor with thin ivory handles.

"Care for a nip a the auld monsturr?" the man said, offering his flask. "Improves the bath a hundred purr-cent, I'm here to tell you."

"Naw ... uh, thanks."

"The name's O'Fallon. Tommy O'Fallon." O'Fallon reached across with a dripping and strong-looking hand that was freckled and dense with red hair. At first reluctant, Woodson finally reached out and rammed his hand into O'Fallon's for a firm shake.

"Didn't catch yours."

"Didn't give it. Woodson. Frank Woodson."

"I have not seen the great Mr. Kane but on the one occasion. You would appear to favor him enough to be kin. But I nivurr heard a his havin' any."

Woodson was startled but tried not to show it. "You don't live around here?"

"Been in the town but these two days."

"On business then. A drummer?"

"Not on business but that of a vurry purr-sonal nature."

O'Fallon was obviously an outgoing man, as Hughie Kelso had been, Woodson decided. But his last statement seemed to close the book on what had brought him to Medicine Springs. Still, Woodson decided to try for more.

"But you know Kane? I'm in town myself, more or less, to see him."

"I say I have seen the man. I am learning a great deal about him."

O'Fallon intrigued Woodson. He sounded like a man who might be able to help him in finding out what he wanted to know about Kane. But plainly he must not move in too quickly.

"Then that must be the personal business you spoke of."

"Indeed."

"You say he has no kin? Not married?"

"By the saints no, from what I have seen of the rogue. Likely the woman's not been born as would have him."

Woodson's curiosity continued to flare. He had to get the balding Irishman to open up a little more. At least Nancy was not married to Kane; but to whom then?

"Me, I'm just passing through myself. Heard about this Kane and the strong resemblance we share. Decided to come by and see for myself."

Through the steam O'Fallon eyed Woodson suspiciously.

"Come off it, Woodson. Your clothes and the look of you says you've been on the trail a good many days. No man would ride that long nor that far out of his way in idle curiosity just to see some stranger that looked like him."

Woodson decided to venture farther. "Like you, I have my reasons. And like you, I would call them reasons of a very personal nature."

O'Fallon belched out a sardonic-sounding grunt. "Cletus Kane runs this town with an iron hand. It is a rich and fertile valley, a beautiful land. A man's urge to settle here and earn a livelihood is stronger than the threat of Kane forcing him to conduct all manner of business with Kane's store and feed mill. His ways are legal but heartless. The man has a checkered past, of that you can be sartain. Any man who rides as roughshod over the land as Cletus Kane would make enemies. I have a hunch that's what brings you to Medicine Springs."

Woodson studied the outspoken Tommy O'Fallon again through the thinning haze between them. He could see O'Fallon's face more clearly, even though the light at their end of the room was poor. This was good; he needed to see how the talk was registering in the Irishman's expression. The conversation now had become like a poker game. Each had some cards in the hole but wasn't about to reveal them until he knew what the table stakes were. Woodson decided it was time to bet his hole card. "And I suspect the same of you, Mr. O'Fallon."

The Irishman was silent for a moment. It was as though Woodson had called his raise and O'Fallon was deciding whether to play the rest of his cards or fold.

"I shall be as straightforward as I can with you, Mr. Woodson." O'Fallon leaned out from the tub to talk more confidentially with Woodson. His eyes checked old Wong Chun, busy with his pots of boiling water on the cookstove.

"I get a feeling, Woodson, that we may share a shred of common purpose. My brother was shot and killed nine years ago in a shabby barroom brawl. He was not armed, and he was shot down in cold blood. There were those who said Paddy O'Fallon was hot-headed and goaded his killer into drawing down on him. My brother did have a temper, Woodson, but he would never on his worst day argue past the point of no return with an armed man." O'Fallon leaned farther out of the tub, revealing a dripping, sudsy barrel chest, the red hair rug-like over his pectorals. His voice was a hoarse whisper. "I believe I have tracked the killer of Paddy O'Fallon to Medicine Springs."

"Where was this? Where did it happen?"

"Yer nivirr heard of it. A little place a couple hundred miles northeast of here up in the territory."

"Did it have a name?"

"Jamestown."

"You mean Jimtown?"

"That's what folks around there called it."

❊ 8 ❊

"**I** do believe we have a good deal to talk over," O'Fallon said as the two strolled into the hotel lobby from the bathhouse scrubbed and shaved. "Would you consider that we might have supper and chew the rag a bit?"

The desk clerk acknowledged his two customers with a nod as the pair walked to the front door. Woodson had all but forgotten the possibility of running into Nancy Merrill again.

"Guess I'd look favorably on that," he said. He was beginning to feel comfortable with the stubby, red-haired and red-faced Irishman. For all his fancy shaving gear, to judge by the rest of his outfit, Tommy O'Fallon didn't seem to be living that much higher off the hog than Frank Woodson. His Levi's showed the dust of many a day in the saddle. From the looks of his gray cotton shirt, it had lately come from the mercantile and still bore the wrinkles of folding for shelf storage.

In an attempt at cleaning O'Fallon had quite ineffectively used Wong Chun's damp bath towel to move around the dust on his boots. His appearance changed considerably when he shoved his battered, broad-brimmed and high-crowned hat far down his head at a jaunty angle. Woodson was inclined to forget the bald skull hidden under the hat.

Like Wong Chun's, O'Fallon's eyes nearly closed when he grinned—which he did a lot. The rest of his face turned into a sea of wrinkles with his grin, the product of years of weathering in heat and cold and sun and biting wind and stinging snows.

"They wun't be serving spiritous beverages in the dinin' room," O'Fallon said. "Would you consider stoppin' by the local waterin' hole for somethin' to whet yer appetite?"

Considering it diplomatic, Woodson nodded in agreement.

"I have a bit remainin' of the auld monster in my pocket, but somehow it does not seem polite ner good etiquette to tip it in public. Surroundings, aye, the surroundings. That's what makes a drink a drink."

The Silver Concho across from the hotel was moderately full of other men having a glass of whiskey or two, and layered thick about head level with blue tobacco smoke as Woodson and O'Fallon pushed through the batwing doors.

They made their way to the long bar that took up nearly the length of the big room, a polished rosewood affair of mirrors and small shelves and fancy spools and turnings. It was probably the most ornate thing in Medicine Springs. O'Fallon quickly found a spot for the two of them, leaned comfortably on his elbows, and propped his foot on the rail with the air of a man who had spent considerable time in this position.

The place was abuzz with soft, monotone conversations, the quiet hum broken only occasionally with belches of bass laughter. The Silver Concho was poorly lit, a condition not improved by the quantities of tobacco smoke. That suited Woodson. He didn't particularly want anyone else to recognize his resemblance to town boss Kane.

The big room also smelled heavily—of cigarette smoke and the sweet, ripe aroma from cuspidors full to varying degrees with tobacco juice. They were strategically placed near the bases of ceiling supports to prevent their being accidentally kicked over. The place also smelled strongly of old and new sweat and of fresh manure tracked in on boots.

Woodson noted that four of the spittoons had been appropriated to sit handy to places at a poker table where four men were intent on their cards. All four chewed, pivoting in place frequently to project a brown and glistening gob into the fancy and squat rolled sheet-brass vessels.

A large, heavyset Mexican behind the bar brought them two glasses and, without comment or being asked, filled each half full. O'Fallon threw down four bits. The Mexican, setting the bottle nearby, dug in a pouch-like apron for change.

"You want I leave thees wheesky?" he said, shoving O'Fallon's change at him. His dark cheeks were heavily pocked from some long-ago disease, his features fat, dark, and sagging. "Naw," Woodson said. "One's my limit. What do you say, Tommy?" he asked, addressing O'Fallon for the first time by his nickname.

"Me, I just need one to coat my stomach against the taint of what that place across the street'll serve up. Naw, don't leave it."

The Mexican's benign expression did not change as

he grabbed the bottle and lumbered along the bar to find other needy customers. O'Fallon got right down to the business at hand.

"You seem to be a tight-lipped man, Mr. Frank Woodson," he said after a deep sip from his glass and the resulting sigh. "But like me, you would appear to have more than a passin' interest in our Mr. Cletus Kane."

"A man who I suspect looked an awful lot like me pulled a stage robbery that I went to prison for. I'd like awful well to find him and do something to settle the hash. But I ain't about to shoot from the hip, and I sure don't need to take out after an innocent man. Kane can be as mean as he wants in this town. That's none of my affair. If he turns out to be the one I'm after, and I can somehow prove it, then maybe the fur'll start flying between me and him."

"Ah," O'Fallon said. "The plot thickens, does it? Am I to surmise from the trend of our conversation so far that this robbery took place around Jamestown in the neighborhood of nine years ago?"

Both men were speaking softly to avoid attracting the attention of the Medicine Springs residents lining the bar on either side of them.

"And your brother was killed by a man resembling Kane in Jimtown nine years ago," Woodson said.

"So we may be after the same divil."

"You may be after the devil, Tommy. At this point I only have more to lose in seeking revenge. I've paid the penalty for him. If I were to do anything to Kane, without proof or the law on my side, I would only have to pay more. I'm not ready to spend any more time in one of those places. For what he's done to you, you haven't spent the last nine years suffering the way I have."

O'Fallon sipped his drink, his eyes studying with a faraway look the reflections in the bar's mirrors against the wall. His features softened. "Ah, Frankie Woodson, but I have suffered. In another way. Patrick Francis O'Fallon, my brother, was dearer than the very life to me. We were, in a way, more than brothers. I was the elder, and something in the arrangement charged me with the responsibility ever to be his protector. A fine young lad he was, too. Always a smile that a man could see clear down the street, with never a harsh word for any man. The finest Irish tenor in the entire great American West."

O'Fallon took another sip of his drink, staring again at the bar mirror.

"Unfortunately the child possessed a fiery temper he kept hid most of the time. It would only come out when he felt himself wronged or someone wronged whom he dearly loved or admired. Again, it was Paddy's bad fortune to go up against Kane, or whoever it was killed him, in defense of a friend. Maybe a woman."

"I'm sorry," Woodson said. "I reckon I misjudged. You have suffered. Maybe in your own way you suffered more deeply than I did."

"I did not have the name of the man who shot Paddy O'Fallon. I had but a description. Had I made it a life's quest, I might have found Cletus Kane sooner and dealt with him. As it has been, I have continued my life, always with an ear open for word of someone like him. By pulling bits and pieces of information together here and there I have finally arrived in Medicine Springs to learn more of this Kane, who now seems to be my man."

"There's something else you seem to be ignoring. I resemble Cletus Kane. I was in the neighborhood of Jimtown about ten years ago. Yet you don't suspect me."

O'Fallon broke into one of his broad grins. "True, I was taken by surprise by the uncanny resemblance in One Hung Low's emporium. I was not brought upon this earth last week, Frankie, m'lad. I am a fair judge of men. I was watching for your reaction when I told you of my reason for being in Medicine Springs. Your response was quite normal and unruffled when I disclosed that I was Paddy O'Fallon's brother. No, I have no fears of you. I believe you to be who you say you are. Also, I now believe you were on trial or headed for prison when Paddy was shot. You were a long way from Jamestown. What was the name of the place?"

"Batavia. And my strong resemblance to him and the fact that I was put away for the robbery of the Jimtown stage now gives us both clearer evidence that the man responsible was Cletus Kane."

"I guess I'll be needing another drink after all, Frankie, m'boy," O'Fallon said. "Barkeep!" The big Mexican lumbered back to them, clutching the base of the blue-colored bottle of amber liquid in his big brown fist. "Another round for me and my friend here."

"Now it's my turn," Woodson said, throwing two bits on the bar. This time the Mexican's face was wreathed in a smile that showed most of his crooked, tobacco-stained teeth.

"You want more, señors, you holler for José. I come

running." José slopped the glasses more than half full this time, turned, and rolled back down the bar looking for empty glasses and willing customers. Woodson picked up his glass, already feeling the effects of the first one. Something was beginning to happen, and he was enjoying the new developments. Maybe, he thought, just maybe, with Tommy O'Fallon's help, he'd get to the bottom of this Kane thing once and for all.

The two were leaning on their elbows, shoulders touching because of the crowd that now lined the bar. As Woodson picked up the glass, heavy with whiskey, O'Fallon reached over with his and touched it to the rim of Woodson's. Woodson realized that O'Fallon had been sucking on the "auld monsturr" in the bathhouse before he came in, and the first one in the Silver Concho was taking effect. Though O'Fallon's lids appeared a bit heavy, he was still a man quite capable of holding his whiskey.

"Here's to us, Frankie, m'friend," he toasted. "May we both find the means of ridding our hearts of the bitterness we carry."

Woodson tipped his glass, nodded in agreement, and took a sip.

"Y'know, Frankie, we both have suffered from the evil deeds of our Mr. Kane, or so the sign would seem to point. Around here he would appear to be a mean, conniving son of an owlhoot. Perhaps we have at our hands the means of giving him his comeuppance for past sins without directly putting our own welfare and well-being on the line."

Woodson realized that when Tommy O'Fallon got in his cups he turned profound and philosophical. That, he thought, was better than getting moody and vicious, or becoming a sobbing bag of mush, like some he'd seen. In the midst of his thinking Woodson heard a voice behind him, directed at the two of them.

"Beggin' your pardon, gents." Woodson and O'Fallon straightened up from the bar and turned to face a lean, hook-nosed man with a greasy complexion standing behind them. He wore a black hat, and on his vest a convex circular badge that was pierced with triangles to form a star, and with stamped letters on the rim that proclaimed "Deputy."

"Gents, we have had some foul rustling in our valley. Sheriff Parker is rounding up a posse to ride the miserable thief down. It'll be made worth your while to come along with us on this fine hunt in the morning after that rustlin' redskin. A dollar a day and found, that's what Mr. Kane is putting up."

"And who might you be, sir?" O'Fallon said.

"Deputy Hannibal Wheatley, under Sheriff Parker of Medicine Springs. You're strangers in these parts, ain't you? You wasn't here when I came through looking for possemen earlier."

Woodson nudged O'Fallon to be quiet. "Guess we were over at the hotel in the bathhouse till a few minutes ago. Just spending a couple days in your town, Mr. Wheatley, and then we figure to be riding on. We'd be glad to join your posse, wouldn't we, Tommy?"

O'Fallon gave a bewildered nod.

"Obliged," Wheatley said. "And who might I be addressing?"

"I'm Kelso. This is Mr. Harris." O'Fallon cranked his head around in surprise at Woodson. He got the drift of Woodson's thinking, put on a poker face, and again nodded at the deputy. "At your service, Mr. Wheatley," he said.

"A no-good Indian by the name of John Two Bear has rustled some of Mr. Kane's herd, about twenty head, and departed the valley. Our posse will be charged with bringing him back to answer to a court of law."

"Then he lived here?" Woodson asked.

"He was tryin' to prove up a claim to some of Mr. Kane's land, yes. Figured he could come in here and be good as any white man. Mr. Kane only wanted the squatter off his land. When he finally went, don't you know he run off with part of Mr. Kane's herd? We all in this town figure it's good riddance, but Mr. Kane wants his cows back before we hang the sneak-thief son of a savage. There'll be a meetin' over at the church in about an hour. Then we ride at first light. You gents stayin' in town?"

"Over at the hotel," Woodson said. "You can depend on us. We'll be at the meeting. What did you say the sheriff's name was?"

"Sheriff Parker. Jed Parker."

Woodson hoped his sudden intake of air wasn't noticeable. He battled with recollection, the same stab of shock ramming through him he had felt when he saw Nancy Merrill earlier in the day. The name was so far back in the dim, dead past that for a second Woodson couldn't grasp it, though it was familiar enough to jar him. It was a name as familiar as Nancy's.

Jared Parker; Jed for short. In a flooding rush of memory he saw again the face and build of his best friend from boyhood as they mustered in together at the start of the war in South Carolina and Virginia; their tradition of roaming the fields of carnage to track each other down when the roar, the smoke, and the dust of battle and skirmish ebbed to be sure each had made it through; their almost maddened hilarity of reunion.

The two young Texans served the Confederacy well for four years only to come home disgraced because the cause was considered lost. In the wake of the return Woodson rode out and signed on with Tuck Merrill's outfit and met Nancy. Jed went to Abilene as a deputy under Mose Laramore and began keeping the law. Parker was damned good at his work.

"Huh!" Woodson thought. "What a day for surprises! Nancy and Jed in the same town, so far from Texas." His thoughts swirled. "I wonder if ..." He was seized by sudden inspiration.

"Mr. Wheatley," he said aloud. "Your Sheriff Parker, is he from Texas?"

"You're acquainted with him, Mr. Kelso?"

"I'm from Texas, too. A man by that name had a good reputation there. By any chance would his wife's name be Nancy?"

"I guess you know him. That's one and the same, Kelso."

Woodson went rigid with the shock that traveled along his spine, causing his shoulders to tremble, and he hoped Wheatley didn't notice. Abruptly Woodson brought up his glass of whiskey and tossed the contents down his throat.

✷ 9 ✷

With an hour before the posse meeting at the church Woodson and O'Fallon stepped into the dusk of Medicine Springs' main street and crossed it to the hotel's dining room. The sky had had long tendrils of clouds all day, and now the sun, waving farewell until morning, painted the long strands with flares of magnificence. With salmon pinks and reds and oranges, violets and purples, the luminous brilliance of a Western sunset took a man's breath away no matter how many times he saw one.

O'Fallon's tone, rousing Woodson from his enjoyment of the panorama, was almost accusing. "There's much yet you've to tell me, Frank, m'boy," he said as they strode across the dusty street toward the well-lighted dining room next to the hotel lobby. The eating area had its own entry off the street, as well as an access into the lobby.

"I think I'll have to. You know a great deal about me already. But after what happened in the bar, I owe you an explanation."

"How is it you gave Wheatley trumped-up names? In this town it might land us in trouble."

"That's part of it. Seemed like the right thing. I didn't particularly want Wheatley to run to Sheriff Parker and tell him Frank Woodson's likely to be on the posse. I'll straighten that out with Jed Parker later. As for you, well, Parker very well might give Kane a list of the men on the posse. If Kane did kill your brother years ago, the name O'Fallon might raise an eyebrow—a scarred one at that."

O'Fallon grinned at Woodson's small attempt at a joke. "You've not lost your sense of humor, anyway, Frank. And you're usin' the auld noggin."

Woodson brightened with O'Fallon's remark. Not that long ago Hughie Kelso had chided him for having no humor at all. Between Kelso and O'Fallon he might be on the mend as a human being.

In the restaurant Woodson led O'Fallon to a table in a far corner where they could talk during their supper and not be overheard. While the waiter scurried off for their food O'Fallon got back into it. "All right. For the time being I'm content with being Harris. But you might at layst have dreamed up an Irish name. My brogue'll be a dead giveaway."

"Don't credit these people with too much savvy. Unless I'm mistaken, there's damned few'll think the name Harris isn't as Irish as Hogan's goat."

"And you know how Irish he was."

"I think you should stick with Harris. As I said, if the name O'Fallon comes out, and with my apparent resemblance to Kane, and with you and me seen together, as we probably will be, it could go hard on both of us. As it is, Kane probably knows that somebody went over the road for it, if he did rob the Jimtown stage. The resemblance could still get him smelling a rat. We've got to hold our cards mighty close to the vest."

"Okay, like I say, I follow your line of reasonin', Frankie. But you say you'll have to drop—what is it? Kelso?—when you come face to face with this Parker. What's that all about?"

"I guess we're becoming friends, Tommy. Even if we weren't, we know a lot about each other and why each of us is here. So I'll shoot straight as to what I know and what I've guessed."

"Best under the circumstances. Pray continue."

"The sheriff here, Jed Parker, was my good friend in Texas years ago. We worked together, choused cattle, and drove trail herds as kids. Rode east together, joined the Confederacy, and fought side by side four long years, years both of us wanted to forget. Were you in it?"

"Tenth Ohio. 'The Bloody Tinth.' All of us Irish from around Cincinnati. May have had you in my sights a time or two. But that would have been a tragedy. Would have deprived me of a good friend now."

Woodson looked up from his food and studied O'Fallon's eyes.

"Beggin' your pardon, Mr. Woodson," Tommy continued. "That's long gone by the boards. I'm for forgettin' them years myself. Paddy followed a wanderin' star west, and when the old folks died I worked the farm till Paddy was killed. So I sold out, headed west myself, and used the money to track his killer."

"I had to give up my dream of my own ranch, too. When we got back Jed took on a deputy's badge in Abilene, and I stayed with punchin' cows and brushpoppin'. But Jed and I stayed close. I planned to ask him to be best man at my—"

"Aha!" O'Fallon exclaimed. " 'Twas this Nancy you spoke of to Wheatley, wasn't it?"

"You guessed it. She's here. I saw her this afternoon from a distance. Shocked out of my wits. Wheatley confirmed it. Now I only hope he doesn't go telling Parker there's a stranger in town that knows him and his wife. I don't know how they got together, but it had to be over me ... my being missing. Now, I'll want to take that on on my own terms, in my own time. Probably when I didn't come home years ago, and there was no way I could get word to her, she figured I was dead. Somehow she and Jed got together. They're married."

"And how does that make you feel?"

"Angry, you mean? Jealous? Is that what you're asking?"

"How does it make you feel?"

"None of those things. Not anymore. Strange, I suppose, but I don't know them anymore. Either of them. So much has changed. They're strangers to me now. And yet they're not. My being here is bound to touch off something. I really ought to ride on now and leave their lives alone. But there's you and the curiosity we've both built up about this Kane. Jed and Nancy must have something good between them, so my showing up now isn't likely to destroy it. Then there's me. I won't be able to stay around here long and not come face-to-face with my past."

In the intensity of the conversation and the thoughts bouncing around in his head he had all but forgotten the two or three more bites of meat on his plate. But it was good to have someone understanding like Tommy

O'Fallon to talk with. He was realizing how much he had been able to confide in Hughie Kelso, and now O'Fallon. A man with seven years of solitary, bitter thoughts still in his head sorely needed a compassionate friend.

"But I'm curious enough about this Kane, and about why you're here, to want to stay now and see this thing through. Even if I prove—to myself—that Kane robbed the Jimtown stage, there's no way he'll stand trial for it nor wipe away the seven years I did behind bars for him."

"Aye, and the time may be past for bringing him to justice for killing poor Paddy. It would be a mighty hard thing to prove."

"So, Tommy, what it amounts to is that probably we're both just curious. We're only wanting to get close enough to the man to find out if he's the one we've both had on our minds for nine years."

"Ah, Frankie, but maybe more. He has this town in the palm of his hand. I've learned that since coming here, lad. A man like that has too much power. Power, you know, corrupts, particularly if a man is evil at the start."

"And if he's the one who robbed the stage and who killed Paddy O'Fallon, he's evil."

"Now you follow my line of reasonin', Frankie. Probably neither of us has the guts nor the means to give our Mr. Kane his comeuppance. But maybe, just maybe, if we stick awhile, we can find the chinks in his armor. Since we've no stake in this town, and only our scalps to protect, we might be the tools of his downfall. But, m'boy, you're the one with the problem."

"Which is?"

"Yer former lady friend and love, now Parker's wife. How will you handle that?"

"I don't know. That's why I need to think and talk it out, and why I value being able to talk with you. That's why I want to be on this posse, why I want to be able to observe Jed Parker for a while without his seeing me. He'll be busy and won't be taking particular notice, I don't suppose. He hasn't seen me in ten years and no doubt thinks I've been dead all this time. Besides, it might have looked suspicious if we hadn't agreed to ride with the posse."

"Granted."

"If he notices me, I'll have to face up to it and do some explaining out there. If he doesn't, as soon as we get back I'll go to him and make myself acquainted again. I'll also have to explain to Nancy, but if I handle it right, there's no reason it can't be worked out and all of us stay friends."

"But you miss one important factor, Frankie, m'boy."

"How's that? What have I missed?"

"You say down in Texas ten years ago Parker was a respected lawman."

"One of the best. He left the war wanting to see a better world come out of all that suffering. We talked about it a lot. Four years had brought a lot of changes in us, and in the country. Nothing was ever going to be the same as before. Jed came out different than a lot of them. All the misery and suffering he'd seen drove him to want to see justice and decency become the way of life in the West. He felt he could make his best mark by working to uphold the law, even if it meant going into it with a gun in his hands. He's a good man, make no mistake."

"But the years erode. He *was,* maybe." Woodson, not really knowing what Tommy O'Fallon was talking about, felt a surge of resentment. "You haven't seen him in ten years, Frankie."

"So?"

"The years can change a man. This is Cletus Kane's town, we both know that."

"And Jed Parker's the sheriff. I still don't see what that proves."

"Punch me if you like, Frankie Woodson, but I'm willing to gamble anything I own that Cletus Kane owns your Sheriff Parker, part and parcel."

Tommy carried a modest silver watch in a shirt pocket, attached to a buttonhole by a short and functional rawhide thong. He fished it out and studied the hands. "Would you look at the hour! The gang'll be gatherin', and if we don't want to create a big stir and call attention to ourselves by marchin' in late, we'd best be makin' dust down there."

"Dinner was four bits. You got four bits?"

"And are you thinkin' I'm a deadbeat? Just for that, Mr. Frank Woodson, your money's no good this evenin'." O'Fallon reached into his jeans and produced a silver cartwheel, which he tossed on the table. "This'll handle it. Let's roust, sonny boy."

"You'll . . . we'll need a bottle to take along on this posse if it lasts longer than a day. When it comes to picking one up across the street a little later, then your money'll be no good, Mr. Tommy O'Fallon."

"Ah, Frankie, you're a man after my own heart. Accepted with due grace. One tit always manages to deserve a tat," O'Fallon said as the two of them strode out of the restaurant. "I am well aware what a tit is, but it has often puzzled me about them tats."

"You'll never catch me tattling about that," Woodson said, in good humor from the meal and the general positive trend of the conversation with O'Fallon. He slapped Tommy on the back as he said it, and the two went out the door.

Despite some fears that Jed Parker might not be the same kind of law officer he had been in Texas, Woodson felt good that he had at least one ally in Medicine Springs. And Tommy O'Fallon seemed to be filling the void left by the death of Hughie Kelso.

From far down the street they were drawn to the Medicine Springs Methodist Church. Light streamed through the dark from the open double doors. Horses were tied at the hitch rack, while two buggies and a wagon were parked in the dark of the churchyard, their horses standing in the traces like patient statues. The meeting had not yet begun, and men milled around outside or clustered on the steps in knotted groups of twos and threes, talking. Occasionally a man detached himself from the groups outside, sidled up the steps, and went inside.

Woodson and O'Fallon wordlessly made their way through the groups into the well-lighted church and found seats in a pew toward the rear of the sanctuary. Woodson pulled the brim of his hat low over his eyes, hoping not to be recognized by Jed Parker and not be mistaken by others for Cletus Kane's double. At first he couldn't make out Jed Parker in the group standing and talking near the altar. Then, with a rush of emotion, he saw his old friend and realized that he probably wouldn't have recognized him if he had accidentally run into him on the trail. Here he knew to expect to see Jed Parker. The years had thickened Jed a bit, and his shoulders seemed more rounded.

Jed had affected an abundant and grizzled handle-bar mustache, bushy and full enough to alter the appearance of his face. His hair, once nearly jet black, had gone white in the sideburns and temples and in two streaks down behind the ears. Woodson studied his old comrade-in-arms, wondering if by looking at him he could determine if there had been any change in Jed's determined lawman's attitude.

All around Woodson and O'Fallon were the murmurings of the forty or so men filling the church. They were scattered through the room, but Woodson reckoned it was a large group for this town. If they all went in the morning, this would be a big posse. Woodson could see Jed's deputy, Hannibal Wheatley, close to his boss. Jed turned and spoke to Wheatley, who strode self-importantly up the center aisle to corral the few still lingering out front. Woodson could hear Wheatley barking some words, and the outsiders filed in and found seats. Wheatley closed the doors and was starting back down the aisle when Parker jumped in two quick steps to the altar and the place of attention behind the pulpit.

Jed's voice was strong when he spoke out, and another tremor of emotion jiggled Woodson. All this was like a dream; it had an unreal quality. He hadn't heard that voice in ten years. This was the man who was to have been the best man at the wedding of Nancy Merrill and Frank Woodson. Now for some years—how many Woodson could only guess—Nancy had been Mrs. Jared Parker. The man at the altar was as familiar as the back of Woodson's hand, yet he had become a total stranger, someone for Woodson to shrink from—at least for now.

"All right," Parker commanded to hush the chatter.

"We all know why we're here. Let's get on with it so we can all get home and get a little sleep before we ride out in the morning." Murmurs of approval met this opening announcement.

"This is to be a duly constituted posse of the office of the sheriff of Medicine Springs. Everyone who rides with us in the morning will be judged by that action to be deputized and to act in the best interests of my office.

"I guess most of you know why we're here. By all indications John Two Bear has left these parts, taking with him about twenty head of Mr. Kane's cattle, for which he had no authority. Now one, Mr. Kane wants his cattle back, and two, the offender must be brought back to Medicine Springs to stand trial for rustling."

A man directly in front of Woodson stuck up his hand for attention, and Woodson dropped his head a bit, shielding his face with his hat brim, fearing that when Parker saw the upraised hand he'd also see and possibly recognize Woodson.

"Honus Johnson," Jed called. "You got a question?"

"No, sir, but I got something to say. John Two Bear was my neighbor. Lived on the next place south. Them cattle he took off with was his. Rounded 'em up as mavericks or raised 'em from calves. All due respect, Mr. Kane's got no claim to them steers. It was Kane and you fellas that attend to Kane's business that run John off his land. I didn't come here tonight to sign on with your posse, Mr. Parker. I come here to see that the truth is brought out about John Two Bear."

In spite of trying to shield his face from the direct stare of Jed Parker, Woodson managed a glance around the room. All eyes were on Honus Johnson as he spoke. Woodson suddenly suspected that many of the men were there out of a sense of obligation and not of civic duty. He noted that O'Fallon, too, was sizing up the crowd. He lightly nudged O'Fallon's arm in acknowledgement, and O'Fallon nudged back.

"Honus," Jed interrupted, "I'm glad to have your views, but you're just not in a position to understand the legalities of all this. John Two Bear was squatting on Kane land illegally. As an Indian, he had no right to try to prove up a homestead title even if he had been on open range, which he wasn't. He was clearly and plainly trespassing. For some years Mr. Kane ignored the situation out of sympathy for John's situation. But it's also true that eventually John Two Bear would have to be asked to leave. Besides, there are other places for his kind, and not in Medicine Springs."

Woodson felt a bristling in the audience. Many of the others, along with Honus Johnson, shared a concern for John Two Bear. Johnson had more to say and now got to his feet to say it. "My credit'll probably be cut off at the store tomorrow for speaking up, but I'll say it. Cletus Kane is all wrong on this one. John Two Bear was only trying to be a good Indian and live by the white man's way."

"Now, Honus," Parker said, "you know Mr. Kane doesn't operate that way. That's all a dirty rumor. The only people who ever had their credit cut off at the store or at the mill were poor stewards of their money, and Mr. Kane simply couldn't carry them on the books anymore." Woodson was conscious of a slight murmur running through the crowd; the murmur said many of these men didn't believe that explanation. Parker continued. "As for Two Bear, he finally saw the light and moved on. His crime now is that he took twenty or so head of Kane cattle with him."

"They was his own cows, Mr. Parker," Johnson protested, still standing.

"The law says they were grown on Kane land, even if we don't take into account that their origins were questionable. The man who claims ownership was on that land illegally. They were grown on Kane grass. You're getting the cart ahead of the horse, Honus. We are only here to arrange to bring John Two Bear in to stand trial for rustling. It will be up to a judge and jury to decide what you're standing there debating."

Woodson saw the standing Honus Johnson stiffen in front of him. He appeared to have more to say.

"Slim chance John Two Bear will have in this town with Cletus Kane's rigged jury and bought judge! There, I've said it. I've had about enough of this place anyway. I come on out here after the war and proved up my land. Lived here nigh fifteen year, long before Cletus Kane and his money showed up here. But anymore I don't feel safe, and that's no way to live. If John Two Bear got run off, who's next? I'm of a mind to pull up stakes and go somewhere where they ain't no more Cletus Kanes."

Woodson became aware that a tight, hushed silence had come over the place while Johnson was talking. He looked around him. All eyes were on Johnson. No one was moving or fidgeting in his place.

"I got one more thing to say, and it will really cut my throat in this part of the country, but I'm prepared for it. I don't know about the rest of you fellas, but I'm goin'." Johnson's head swiveled, looking at the crowd staring at him intently.

"Mr. Parker, the real reason that Kane saw to it that John Two Bear got pried off of what was rightly his by his hard work and sweat is that John's daughter, Helen, refused Cletus Kane. John told me so himself."

Johnson lowered himself stiffly into in his place, and Woodson, watching the back of the man's head, saw it quiver in anger and emotion. The air inside the church had turned even tighter than before Johnson's final accusation, which had clearly shocked most in the room. Parker's voice lanced through it sharply.

"I had other things to take up, but this winds up the meeting. Those of you on the west side of the room will ride with Mr. Wheatley. Those on the east side tonight will ride with me."

Woodson felt relieved that he and O'Fallon had chosen to sit on the west side. Jed Parker had one more thing to say, and he said it loudly for all to hear and understand.

"Mr. Johnson, whether or not you came here tonight to be a part of this posse, your presence will not be needed nor welcomed in the morning!"

10

John Two Bear had a three-day start on the posse. Pushing twenty head of beef, or however many he had taken with him, would chew that lead down plenty, Woodson thought as he and O'Fallon lost themselves among the eighteen men being led in the chase by Hannibal Wheatley.

The southern extremes of the range ringing the Medicine Springs basin offered two low passes to get up to the barren badlands country beyond. One led directly south, and one stood off to the southwest. Jed Parker had split the posse, taking his group in a sweep toward the southwesterly pass. Whichever group intercepted Two Bear first would send a rider to the other to bring them hightailing.

Woodson and O'Fallon had agreed after last night's meeting to pass themselves off as long-term saddle pards and stick together for the ride. Since Two Bear's drive out of the basin would have been over open range and away from the roads, Wheatley's division split into small groups of twos and threes to hunt for Two Bear's track as they pushed south toward the notch evident in the hazy high country ahead of them.

Woodson and O'Fallon had talked little the night before of the revelations of Honus Johnson and their effect on the meeting.

"Well, Frankie, m'lad," Tommy said when he was sure none of the other possemen would hear, "whattya you think of the chances of our Mr. John Two Bear once he's apprehended?"

"He'll be railroaded, same as I was. If what that man Johnson said was true, I only hope they don't hang the man. He's going to pay, though."

O'Fallon was reflective. "Aye ... aye. Under the circumstances, a white man stands little chance. A red man's convicted before he's even run to earth."

"Hell, in this country they know how to convict *any* man before he's had a chance to be tried. I'm walking proof of that. That's why this Two Bear doesn't stand a Chinaman's chance. Or an Indian's chance. They mentioned a daughter. She must be with him. What'll happen to her, you suppose? Do you really think they ran Two Bear out because she refused Kane?"

"Ah, Frankie, how should I know? But put your mind to it, laddy. If he's the robber of the Jimtown stage and the cold-blooded killer of Paddy O'Fallon, and the man who's created a fortune feeding off the hard work and misery of others in this basin, what would you think? The man is accustomed by now to getting what he wants when he wants it. Cross him and you pay. The hard way. I daresay our Mr. Honus Johnson is packing his satchel this very morning."

Woodson's only response was to stare ahead at the pass looming up in the distance ahead of them. O'Fallon, he mused, was right. Kane was probably capable of about anything; getting pushy with this Indian's daughter and then making the old man's life a hell was right in character.

By midmorning the group that had been dispersed was slowly drawing closer together as the riders converged on the lower reaches of the pass. Woodson saw Hannibal Wheatley up ahead with a knot of riders clustered around him; they had stopped and were waiting for the others to come up. Off to the side Woodson could see the far flankers appearing behind him and Tommy O'Fallon as they rode in.

"Kelso, Harris," Wheatley called as they rode at a walk toward the group. "Find anything?" Woodson held back, letting O'Fallon ride close to report. O'Fallon got the message that Woodson didn't want to get too close to Wheatley and spurred slightly ahead.

"This basin, your honor," O'Fallon said, "is crowded with sign. I believe you're aware of that. There are fresh tracks everywhere and in all directions, and we found not a fresh plop that wore a brand."

Wheatley glared at O'Fallon's try at a joke. "I know. I know. Sheriff Parker and Mr. Kane wanted us to hunt this way. For my money, the son of a savage won't be tracked till we get to the high country above. It's dry up there, commencing to desert. Full of wormholes for him to hide in. That's the kind of country the 'skins knows. Like John Two Bear. But if we'd've been able to identify a track, it would've just made the job easier. We'd've knowed we was barkin' up the right trail." With his clamped mouth and hook nose and sparking eyes Wheatley resembled some kind of righteous bird parked on a nest.

The other riders had come up now, completing the

posse. They clustered around the deputy, listening and waiting. Wheatley again made the inquiry. "What of sign, Shepard?"

"Bare. Nothin' to go on, Hannibal," the square man with the sweaty face said. "There's cow trails through here like cracks in old leather. You're sure he came this way?"

"Now, Gus, use your head. Would we be out here in the heat chasin' our tails if we knew he'd gone out the east end? If he went that way, he'd've been seen for sartain. There'd've been some report. No, he sure enough come this way, or over west where Mr. Parker's bunch is going."

Wheatley hauled off his hat and rasped a sleeve against his flowing forehead.

"He for sure come this way, south, and took one of the two passes. This is the easier one, and Mr. Parker is thinking that the redskin would probably try to outfox his trackers by taking the tougher pass. That's why Mr. Parker went over that way."

Studying him, Woodson caught the hint that Hannibal Wheatley owned the squint eyes of a tormentor. That damned beak nose, he thought, doesn't take away from that impression. Wheatley was enjoying this chase and would relish seeing John Two Bear get his supposed comeuppance, whether it was lynching on the trail or a bona fide hanging in town. Wheatley was in a lynching mood.

"Well, it sure as hell is gettin' hot out here in the sun standin' around, Hannibal," a man close to the deputy said. "There might be some shade or some trees up in there in the pass, so I say let's get to ridin' again."

"No one's more anxious than me, Sam. I just

wanted to bring the men together. Now that everybody's here, the main aim is to get up to the pass and on out. The trail is generally narrow. Have all you been up that way?"

Better than half the riders raised their hands.

"Well, for those of you who ain't, it's an open trail most of the way up. As it eases out at the crest it commences on to badlands, and it's full of canyons and hidey-holes. He could be back in any of 'em. Gonna be hotter'n four shades of hell up in there. As we get up that way we're going to have to deploy again and search 'em out one by one. It ain't the way I prefer, but it's all we got. Y'all have by now picked your ridin' pards, so I say when we get in there, pair up as you have been and watch for sign. When you find something, backtrack and find me. I'll pull everyone together, and we'll take him. I'm supposed to tell you not to try to take him yourself, but you know how that works. Ain't nobody going to shed a tear if an emergency comes up. Just don't bring in a gut-shot Indian for the town to have to patch up for his hangin'. Over his saddle or straight up, y'all got that?"

There were murmurs of understanding, and Woodson stealthily studied the riders close to him. To all appearances, none of them was buying Wheatley's bill of goods. They had all been at the posse meeting, and Woodson doubted if there were more than a half dozen in this bunch that had the heart for all this. They were along because their credit at the store or their privilege of selling their beef to Kane depended on it. Many were there, too, to see that John Two Bear got at least a chance at a fair shake.

"When we hit the top, fan out and commence searchin'," Wheatley continued. "Come sundown, rendezvous at trail's end at the top, and we'll go into camp. They's a spring not far from there and a fair-to-middlin' campsite. Otherwise, I hope you all brought some rations with you, and if you can't fend for yourself, don't come snot-nosin' to me. Let's ride."

That was a switch, Woodson thought. The night before Wheatley had said the groceries would be provided. Woodson and O'Fallon rode close together over the narrow trail that gradually rose out of the basin and made for a higher country full of buttes and outcroppings. He could already see that the land up there would be fissured with canyons and great rifts, offering John Two Bear plenty of possibilities for hiding himself and his twenty head.

There was no strong hint anywhere. From the sign Woodson could also see that there was an equally strong possibility that the dispossessed Indian and his herd had come this way.

The trail they were on split around a great neck of fluted butte towering over them. Without a word Wheatley signaled about half the posse to follow him and waved the others on. Woodson could see that in the miles ahead the flats between the tall monuments of granite split away again and again, further fragmenting the cluster of more or less reluctant possemen. Without any particular agreement he and Tommy O'Fallon stayed with the bunched group until the very last as others split off down tributary canyons to hunt for sign. It was poor browse country for cattle, but the breed that grew and prospered in here could make it on anything. Though it was hostile and hot canyon country and, as Wheatley had warned, "deserty," the chaparral was thick enough to provide a subsistence for range cattle, however meager.

He glanced at Tommy O'Fallon as at last three other riders with them waved without a word and veered away down the canyon bearing to the southeast. They were on their own again. From the heat and hours in the saddle O'Fallon was as red and polished-looking as he had been almost twenty-four hours before in Wong Chun's bath emporium. O'Fallon became aware of Woodson watching him and glanced back. "Like livin' two feet out of hell, ain't it?" he said. In agreement Woodson made a sweeping motion of his forehead and flicked imaginary sweat from his fingertips.

When their fellow riders had disappeared around a hillside of boulders, some of them as large as a house, O'Fallon rode close to Woodson for a council of war.

"I'm thinking, Frankie, m'lad, that in the interests of continuity of breathing and heartbeat it would be better if we were to separate a bit and make two targets instead of one. Our Mr. Two Bear, if he is up in here, will be well satisfied of pursuit and is probably prepared to shoot first. I'm sure he knows that if he's taken alive, his neck isn't worth more than the price of one of those sick-tailed beeves he's chousing around up in here."

Woodson looked at O'Fallon and only nodded. The canyon was wide on both sides of them and choked with brush, some of it as tall as a man. From the heights over them they would be perfect targets for a long-range rifle. He had no idea what kind of firepower John Two Bear might be carrying.

He reefed on the reins to take his horse some distance from O'Fallon. They were a good twenty-five yards apart. If by any chance either of them was hit, the other could be down and into the screen of bushes in an instant and have a chance of surviving. He also knew that the farther they moved down this canyon, the less chance a gunshot would be heard by other possemen.

But, he thought, feeling very crafty, John Two Bear doesn't know that.

All around them the silence and the heat reigned. In the deathly still brought on by the suffocating sun the fall of the horse's hooves in the soft granite gravel under them and the occasional clang of a shoe against an outcrop of rock rang loud in his ears. Above them the mesas towered two or three hundred feet, their long slopes of decayed rock dotted with growth fighting for life in a precarious environment.

Woodson was dripping with sweat, feeling the salt and the sear of it and the dust working to painfully gall the skin of his thighs and groin as he rocked in the saddle to the horse's slow walk. Even through his shirt he could smell the repulsive odor from his armpits. He felt the shirt fabric clinging to him through the sweat like some kind of second skin. He pulled at the front of it to free his chest and reached around to do the same at his back.

He was alerted to a sinister metallic sound like a weapon being cocked behind him, and the horse's slight shying at the same sound.

"Far enough. Hold it right there," he heard a grunt of voice bellow behind him. He glanced across at O'Fallon, whose ruddy face had gone pale in surprise. O'Fallon had stopped and was slowing raising his hands, not looking back. Woodson, too, dropped the reins with one hand and let the hand behind his back slide skyward.

"Don't worry," O'Fallon said loudly, still staring straight ahead. "We ain't here to do no harm."

Woodson dared not sneak a look behind him, but he sensed the man had stepped out of the bushes as they passed.

"Ride slow. Straight ahead," the voice behind them commanded. "I will be walking, so move easy. Make a run for it and you die in the saddle."

"Mind that trigger finger," O'Fallon said. "We'll do everything you say."

Woodson pivoted his head ever so slightly and then cranked it back to face the trail ahead. From the corner of his eye he caught a glimpse of the dark bulk of a big man standing spread-legged in the deep gravel not thirty feet behind them. The gun held at the ready looked like a big-bore Sharps, maybe a .50 caliber. It was nothing to joke about.

His mind also ran on the warning he had been given again and again where Indians were concerned, or when he was driving cattle through the Indian territories: "Mind your back trail." He hadn't heeded it, and John Two Bear had gotten the drop on him and Tommy O'Fallon.

They had not gone a half mile before Woodson could smell cattle—a characteristic bovine aroma, but overriding it was the rank odor of manure and urine. The Two Bear cattle, however, were quiet, so the Indian must have bedded them in a spot that contributed to their contentment. Ahead he could see the upthrust of land around them come together, but against a broad wall—a box canyon. A cooling breeze drifted down to him from the land they were approaching as the trail began to rise gradually. There was water in here somewhere, Woodson thought; as they walked their horses up this slow rise in the land, aspens, their leaves flickering in the late afternoon sun, began to shade the trail.

John Two Bear obviously knew this country and had picked his spot well. Two Bear also knew that any pursuing posse would have to split up as they probed the scores of blind alleys. There were probably dozens of other spots of grass and trees like this one scattered over the land.

The man behind them walked with a bold, self-assured step. His footfalls in the thick granite gravel made soft, slushy sounds, not the hard thud of a man in boots. John Two Bear was probably wearing moccasins.

The aspens in the moist sloughs on either side of the trail finally gave way to a wide apron of gravel and rock and enough growth for cattle browse. As the trail widened out to this broad fan Two Bear had thrown a rope barricade between two aspens flanking the trail and had tied short lengths of cloth to it. These fluttered in the soft breeze, effectively keeping the cattle back in the box canyon. Two saddle horses and a pack animal were tied at the far end, while the cows—Woodson counted a mere ten—were scattered around the broad end of the open area singly or in twos or threes.

"Stop here," Two Bear commanded as Woodson and O'Fallon neared the rope gate. While Two Bear maintained his menacing distance the rope fell as if by magic. "Ride on," Two Bear ordered. Woodson touched his spurs lightly to the horse's flank, looking straight ahead. In a swift side glance he saw someone standing in the late afternoon shadow of the aspens and holding the loose end of rope.

"Over there. Left. By the horses," Two Bear said.

Woodson could sense that the figure he had seen among the aspens had joined Two Bear, and the two of them followed the riders as they directed their horses to where Two Bear's animals were hobbled. "Far enough," came the voice of command behind them. "Down easy. Don't try for guns." As O'Fallon eased out of the saddle Woodson dropped his reins, grabbed for the saddlehorn, and let himself down to the gravel. He turned and faced the two figures with guns.

John Two Bear was as large as he was tall, towering well over six feet and with shoulders that could only be measured by an axe handle. He carried a converted .50-70 Sharps, and now he held it on the two. His face, naturally dark, was burned black as coffee from exposure to the harsh southwestern sun. His sinister look was only heightened by a tall and wide-brimmed black hat with a black and white eagle feather punching skyward from the back.

The figure beside him was much shorter and slightly built. It could only be his daughter, Woodson surmised as he watched them with growing fear, standing gingerly, waiting for the next command. Dressed for the trail and hard work, the girl wore a coarse gray muslin shirt buttoned at the throat, the collar turned up. Long braids of thick, glossy black hair trailed down past her ears to breasts that pushed amply against the rough texture of the shirt. She, too, wore a tall black hat, the brim turned down to shield her features from the sun.

Her complexion was dark, but lighter than her father's. The features were petite, the eyes flashing. Like the man beside her, she was angry and meant business. The full shirt bloused at a tapered waist. She had a Remington cap and ball revolver shoved into the broad leather belt supporting skintight Levi's. Like her father, the girl wore beaded moccasins. Woodson tried to get a glimpse of the elaborate design; Sioux, he imagined.

Like her father, she held a gun on them, a front-loading double with its barrels docked, the kind used by shotgun messengers on the stages. Both hammers were cocked over sinister-looking capped nipples. The spray from either barrel, at this range, could cut both Woodson and O'Fallon in half at the same time as they stood side by side holding their horses.

"Helen," Two Bear commanded. "Our visitors have no need of their guns. Get them and stow them safely away with our gear."

❋ 11 ❋

Still menacing, Two Bear waved them with his Sharps to the shade of a pair of struggling young cottonwoods while Helen got their six-guns stowed in a place that wouldn't be easy to get to.

"We sit," Two Bear said gruffly, and almost gratefully Woodson and O'Fallon dropped to their butts in the sparse grass under the tree. The shade, after the long hours in the saddle under a scalding sun, was like a drink of water. The smarting of sweat in Woodson's crotch subsided. Two Bear squatted on his haunches, keeping the Sharps on his prisoners, able to cut either one of them down at the slightest false move. Helen drifted back, also keeping her shotgun poised.

Two Bear's eyes and tense posture now reflected that holding prisoners at bay was foreign to him. Helen stood but was also awkward and tense, her soft features carrying a look of apprehension and fear at this new and alien turn of events.

Two Bear forced a gruff tone with the strangers. Woodson gathered that if he had thrown down on a couple of his neighbors from the Medicine Springs

Basin, his manner might have been a bit easier. "Now you tell me," he said. "Why are you here? Parker and Kane, they send you?"

Woodson looked at O'Fallon, who was looking at him, silently questioning each other as to what they'd say and how they'd say it. How do you tell a man holding a gun on you that you have no heart for chasing him? From what Woodson had heard about John Two Bear, he considered him a reasonable man. He took the lead.

"There's a posse out. All through this country."

Two Bear smiled, but the smile was small and fleeting. "Kane and Parker split up their men. I could have figured it. Not a decent tracker anywhere around. So Kane has to go looking for the needle in the haystack, straw by straw."

Woodson was impressed. Two Bear didn't talk pidgin English. He spoke with assurance, as though he had spent much time among whites and worked to acquire the language. Maybe he'd even spent a little time in school.

"Kane's not with them," Woodson said, seeing that slight, knowing smile lift one side of Two Bear's mouth. "Jed Parker and one bunch went over the southwest pass. Wheatley has about eighteen men, us included, up in this country. They did split up, poking down the canyons, looking for sign."

"Kane has others to do his dirty work. But I do not know you men. You are new in Medicine Springs?"

"Was visitin', you might say," O'Fallon said, and Two Bear's eyes surveyed the Irishman.

"And Kane made you ride on his posse?"

"No," O'Fallon said, "but my crony there and me was a bit curious what was going on and what this

110

was all about. That's how we come to be riding with them."

"There's not many that seem to be riding with the posse willingly," Woodson said. "It's like they better do it or get Kane mad at 'em."

Now it was O'Fallon who checked Woodson with his eyes as if seeking permission. "You're acquainted with Honus Johnson, are you not, Mr. Two Bear?"

Two Bear seemed surprised by the formality. "I know him, yes. A good man. A good neighbor. Many years."

" 'Twas him stuck up for you in the meeting last evening. Spoke out so strong, in fact, that he figured he'd run out his string with Kane for sayin' it and was electin' to move out himself."

"Oh, that is too bad. I hope he won't have to do that. I do not want to be the one to bring misfortune upon my friends."

"I believe your friends is trying to support you against Kane."

"That will do no good. They only hurt themselves. Kane is too strong. He can't be hurt."

Again Woodson's and O'Fallon's eyes met. "My friend here and I don't seek to be mixin' in private matters," Tommy went on. "We have rivers of our own to cross. But Johnson said something publicly, and you'd best know of it. He told Sheriff Parker that he knew that the reason Kane wanted you run out was because of Kane's ungentlemanly conduct toward your dotter there."

Helen Two Bear gasped. "Oh, Father!"

"Calm, child. Mr. Kane and I did have words. He feels everything in that valley belongs to him, including the women he finds charming. I don't believe this is the first time he has behaved improperly. Others may have just accepted and gone on trying to live here. I don't know. I faced him with it. In the end he accused me of being on his land and said that my cattle did not belong to me, but to him. He sought to disgrace me, and he did a good job of it. He has the law on his side. If I had stayed, I would have been burned out or killed, probably at night by those who would leave no trace. Helen would have been harmed, too. I have been brought up a peace-seeking man. My village, though it was Sioux, never warred against whites. My father, from his earliest years, preached it. There could be no way to win. He managed to live out his life without resistance or battle and still kept his pride, and so far I have. So has Helen. Except for resisting this Kane. We are more white than Indian. Indian by birth, white by belief and way of life."

"You stand accused of rustling," Woodson said. "That's why they're after you. But why, if he wanted you out of his territory, does he make such a big issue over a few head of cattle? He insists you have twenty of his beeves. I see only ten or so head here."

"These are mine, legal," Two Bear said. "Kane has no right to them. He adds numbers to my herd to put teeth to his claim that I am a rustler. By his rustling charge he further disgraces me with my friends. As to the land claim, I am confused. He may have arranged to have the records altered. All the time I understood my land claim was on open range. That was another reason I left. Being Indian, I will have fewer rights under white man's law to enforce my claim."

Woodson and O'Fallon scowled at each other, both angry at the unjust treatment of this Indian by Kane. O'Fallon spoke. "Parker and Wheatley and but a few hardcases with them talk of lynching on the trail or the hangin' you'll get if you're brought in."

Two Bear smiled. "If I escaped them so far, I will continue, even if they are up in this country. But now I have the problem of you two." Two Bear's smile lifted one side of his face again. "I have never fought white men, nor threatened nor so much as held a gun on any man. Now look at me!"

Now it was Woodson who spoke up. "It can be worked out, Two Bear. Tommy and I won't see you hang, out here by a vigilance committee nor in town by a judge and jury."

"But you ride with Sheriff Parker's posse."

"Ah, booshwah the posse," O'Fallon said. "We just quit, didn't we, Frankie, m'lad?"

Woodson looked again at O'Fallon and then back at Two Bear and Helen. "I never gave my oath to nothing. I'm ridin' through and managed to get caught up with a bunch of men comin' this way."

Two Bear studied Woodson. "Is your name Kane? You look like Kane."

"So I've been told. No, it's Woodson. Frank Woodson. This is my partner, Tommy O'Fallon."

"Thomas Aloysius O'Fallon, Mr. Two Bear. My friend resembles our Mr. Kane sufficiently that nine years ago he went to prison for a crime Kane likely committed, or so we think."

Two Bear studied both of them, and as he did his hold on the Sharps relaxed. "Then you're here for revenge, Woodson."

O'Fallon spoke before Woodson could answer. "Not revenge, really. I am also looking for a man who matches Kane's description who shot and killed my brother in the same part of the country where Woodson here got into trouble, and at about the same time."

"Nine years is a long time," Woodson said, "for either Tommy or me to do anything against Kane. To try to prove anything, to go seeking revenge, would only get us deeper into trouble, and grief."

"Then why are you here? Your Bible says an eye for an eye, yet neither of you says he is here for revenge. Why then? In Kane's country. Why are you on this posse, aiding him? Why didn't you ride past and forget it?"

Woodson and O'Fallon again looked at each other. "We both been trying to figure out the same thing," O'Fallon said. "We met but yesterday. Both just curious, I suppose. Then we got caught up in this thing about you. I guess we both want to see justice done, for us and for you. But Kane is a mighty power."

"Powerful enough to drive me from a home where I had hoped to spend the rest of my days and leave something, more than I was left in this life, for Helen. And her man."

"Helen has a man?" O'Fallon said.

"No. I mean her man in the times ahead. Now Kane has succeeded in putting even me to flight."

"Will you accept, Mr. Two Bear, that we are friends, interested in your problem with our Mr. Kane, and wantin' to see no harm come to you?"

"Many of the white man's ways are good, just as many of the Indian ways are good. I tried to live a life that took the best of both. Until now it was working. That is, until I came under the influence of Cletus Kane. There are good and bad whites, just as there are good and bad among Indians."

"You'll accept what we say, then?"

"My judgments of white men in the past have usually not proved untrue. Most who appear good at first will prove out. Kane was the exception. His ways are like the smoke—sometimes pretty to look at, but when it gets in your eyes it stings."

O'Fallon looked at Woodson. "I think the man is saying he accepts us and our story."

"We must eat and then talk. The sun grows low, and soon it will be late, too late for cooking fires," Two Bear said.

"Tommy, I don't think we ought to hang around here. I think we ought to get back to Wheatley and the night camp."

"But what of Two Bear and Helen?"

Woodson looked around the hiding place Two Bear had selected and made for himself and Helen.

"By staying away we'll only build suspicion. They may come looking for us in the morning, and that wouldn't do. I think we should get back and report no sign. As for me, I don't think I found a cattle-rustling Indian, and I'm willing to report that in good faith. What I really think I found is up to me and my own conscience. Two Bear and Helen are safe here, particularly if we tell Wheatley we poked up every canyon in this part of the country and found no sign. Besides, we didn't find Two Bear. He found us, remember?"

"But what of them? They can't stay up here forever."

Woodson figured he knew more about Indians than Tommy O'Fallon. He asked anyway. "Can you make it a few days up here, Two Bear?"

The Indian grinned, this time broader, showing nearly every tooth. "I told you I have taken to myself the best of the white man's way and the best of the Indian's way. Only you will know where we are."

"It would give us time to work something out. I don't know what yet. But, Tommy, maybe I've found a reason for us to be in Medicine Springs. To see that Two Bear and his daughter get fair treatment."

"Aye," O'Fallon said thoughtfully. "The ranchers would appear to be friendly to Two Bear. But what of Kane? He swings a mighty shillelagh."

"I don't know, and that's why we need time. If we can persuade Kane and Parker that we found nothing, all this may settle down, and they'll think Two Bear has made his escape to parts unknown. Kane and Parker are only going to spend so much time and money hunting. They'll have to give up sometime and get back to business as usual. Things like this sometimes have a way of dying a natural death."

"Aye. What do you think, Two Bear? You're the man in the middle. You can wait here awhile and see if Frankie and me can work out something for you. Or you can move on if we can do you no good."

"My home was in Medicine Springs. My friends are in Medicine Springs. I have no heart for running like a whipped dog."

"Yet you ain't particularly partial to sticking your neck in a noose neither."

Two Bear's acknowledgment was again in his knowing grin. Woodson was struck by the fact that under more normal circumstances John Two Bear probably flashed his toothy grin a great deal. Suddenly he felt that he had found another friend, at least a kindred spirit when it came to being tormented.

"There's more to my story," he said. "Before Tommy and I ride on to Wheatley's camp. Best that you know. I was sent to prison for a stage robbery that may have been done by Kane years back. I looked like the actual robber, and that was enough then to get me sent away. The clincher is that Tommy's brother was shot and killed in an argument in the same area at the same time by a man who looked like Kane. We believe it was Kane. Still, at this late date there really is no way of proving it. That's why we say we can't be here for revenge. I was from Texas and was coming back from a cattle drive to Montana. I was going home to be married. My best friend was also there. Yesterday, when I rode into Medicine Springs, I saw both my former best friend and my once-intended bride— but they didn't see or recognize me."

Two Bear gave Woodson a quizzical look.

"My best friend of years ago is Sheriff Parker. I'm sure he thinks I'm dead. The woman I planned to marry before I unjustly went to prison is his wife."

"Will they know why you have come to find out about Kane?" Helen Two Bear asked, speaking for the first time since her gasped exclamation. She had a pretty, dove-like voice. Woodson studied her, feeling strange, almost-forgotten urges building within him. Despite her rough clothing, Helen was a beautiful woman who spoke and carried herself with dignity.

"I'll have to see and talk with them, yes, Miss Two Bear. To clear up the past and to talk with Sheriff Parker about where he stands on the problem of your father and you. But not, of course, revealing that I've seen you. I hope, too, that I'll learn more about Kane from Sheriff Parker."

"But you do not seek revenge on Parker for taking your woman?" Two Bear asked.

"No. That, like the Kane thing, is too far in the

past. But Parker may help me better understand what's going on here."

"I believe, after all, I do not know the white man's way," Two Bear said. "Both of you have been wronged by Kane, and you, Woodson, wronged by Parker. Yet neither of you holds ill will."

"Nah, we don't. We cherish revenge—don't we, Frankie?—but of a different sort. No suffering of another man—Kane, however guilty he might be, nor, in Frankie's case, Parker—would atone for the suffering both of us have endured for these ten years. Direct vengeance against Kane would only be misunderstood under white man's law, Two Bear, and would land us both in trouble. Frankie and I know that. We've suffered enough. But"—O'Fallon paused for effect—"if we could in some way bring Kane to account for the miseries he's inflicted on you and your fine young dotter there, and maybe others in Medicine Springs, I believe Frankie Woodson and I could ride on satisfied that our suffering had not been in vain. Am I right, Frankie Woodson?"

Woodson stared at O'Fallon a long moment, the truth of his words sinking in. "Yeah," he sighed. "You're right, Tommy. By your leave, John, we'll be getting back to Wheatley's camp to see what can be done."

✵ 12 ✵

Woodson and O'Fallon made an easy ride of it out of the long, ragged slash of canyon that hid the Two Bears and their cattle. They rode silently, following the maze of tributary draws back toward the pass meandering its way down to the Medicine Springs basin.

Coming into this desolate country earlier in the day, they'd been shown the region of Wheatley's proposed night camp. As they rode for it the giant wafer of orange sun, darker somehow at its base as it seemed to approach the horizon, perched beyond their left shoulders, slowly dipping behind the helter-skelter of buttes and prominences to the west. Under other conditions Woodson would have reveled in the beauty of a spectacular sunset.

Though their minds were full of the problems of the Indian and his daughter, the time was a quiet and comforting one. With the sun waning and long shadows filling the land around them, the heat quickly began to moderate with the deepening grayness down close to the land. Over them a sapphire sky still held its gleaming brilliance; this day would be long in dying.

The absolute stillness of the air that had lent a furnace-like feel to the day stayed with them even as the land cooled. Sound carried like a whisper in church, and Tommy knew it.

"We'd best not talk about our friends back there anymore," he said softly. "Unfriendly ears could be anywhere." Woodson nodded in acknowledgement. That was uppermost in their minds, so the rest of the ride was done in total silence.

As they rode a broken, craggy land incapable of supporting little more than chaparral, coyotes, and jackrabbits, the race of Woodson's thoughts slowed to a more reasonable pace, and he sifted through his options. I've got the advantage now, he told himself, of my own good time before I need to come out in the open with Jed and Nancy. To find the proper way to ease the shock, and shock it surely will be. He shook his head in wonderment. Thank heaven for Hughie Kelso and Tommy O'Fallon. He wondered what his reactions might have been before the understanding he'd found in their friendship and the stability the two of them had coaxed back into his life.

Around them the buttes and frowning rimrock drove long, dense shadows over the broken country and canyons they traveled. The sun had disappeared, sinking into a distance hidden from view. Trails, he thought, looked different in reverse; he hoped they found the right passages through the maze of canyons and outcroppings. For a half hour they rode the darkening land.

"This here's the place, ain't it?" O'Fallon asked, his soft voice bringing Woodson out of a mood of deep thought. He looked around, sensing what he thought were familiar signs.

"Wheatley said it was this draw to the west, if I'm not mistaken, Tommy."

They reined their horses up the broad coulee flanked by high tableland, a fresh lilt of air coming down it fed by the cooling approach of night. It was like walking out of a hot day into the soothing air of a cave or a mine shaft.

This air now held a thirst-quenching tang to it. After a long day in the saddle, followed by some warm food, Woodson thought, this would be a good night to sleep. He was ready. The fatigue of a day on horseback was enough in itself. He sensed the added exhaustion of a day with a mind tight with the problems of John and Helen Two Bear, the questions about Cletus Kane, and the coming confrontation with Jed and Nancy Parker.

Instead of the bunched-up gang from the posse, as expected, two men squatted by a small fire in a grove of aspen carpeted by thick grass, indicating water somewhere close by. It occurred to Woodson that before rolling up for the night he'd replace the brackish stuff in his canteen with the refreshing clarity of whatever was offered at this spot.

One of the men at the fire he recognized as Gus Shepard, with whom Wheatley had spoken earlier in the day down in the basin. He had Shepard pegged as a friend of Wheatley and thus in league with the Parker-Kane faction. There would be no discussion with Shepard, he knew, of the unjust treatment and chase of the Two Bears by Parker's posse.

He and O'Fallon walked the horses in slowly and got down, tying their mounts to convenient aspen limbs. They ambled to where Shepard and his companion crouched by the fire.

"You're Kelso and Harris, ain't ya?" Shepard asked, flatly and without hospitality.

"That's right," Woodson said.

"You're the last to come in. Where the hell you been?"

Woodson looked around. The last to come in? No one else was in sight. O'Fallon caught Woodson's eyes, and his brows arched. The same question was on his mind, judging from his expression.

Woodson saw no point in tact, since Shepard showed little. "Well, where the hell we've been was conducting the job of this posse. Hunting for John Two Bear and twenty head of Kane's cattle."

"Well, he ain't up in here. Hannibal and them rode over to join up with Mr. Parker west of here. They found sign. By now they prob'ly got Two Bear and his kid and them cows. Hannibal, he told us to wait till you-all come on in and hustle on over there."

"They found Two Bear's trail?" O'Fallon's voice was so querulous that Woodson thought he might give away what he and Woodson knew.

"Well, they was hot enough on it that Parker sent a man over here to fetch Hannibal's crew," Shepard said. "That's how come nobody's here. They left an hour ago."

O'Fallon looked at Woodson, his face Irish deadpan, but there was an unmistakable grin around his eyes. The posse had found what it considered sign miles from where Two Bear was hidden.

"Well, m'lad, so you took me on another wild goose chase." His eyes flicked back on Shepard and his companion by the fire. "That country we rode through most of the day didn't have one bear, much less two, and would have trouble supportin' a coyote. It's a bit late, ain't it, Mr. Shepard, to be ridin' out and j'inin' up with Mr. Wheatley and Mr. Parker?"

Shepard was obviously put out at having had to wait for Woodson and O'Fallon.

"Well, a half hour ago it wouldn't've been, if you two had got back here. You'd best fix some grub here, catch some sleep long's it's dark, and we'll ride out with first light. As it is, we'll prob'ly find Two Bear and his kid strung up in a tree over there with the buzzards and the varmi'ts havin' 'em for breakfast, and Parker and Wheatley and them'll have them rustled cows back in Medicine Springs and be havin' a couple drinks with Mr. Kane in the Silver Concho. And all because of you two lollygaggin'."

Woodson's eyes flicked on O'Fallon and then back on Shepard. He was ecstatic. It was Jed Parker who was leading the wild goose chase now, and some time had been bought—some real time—for John and Helen Two Bear. The same thought was on Tommy O'Fallon's mind. The grin was still smeared in the stubby Irishman's eyes. In spite of himself, O'Fallon had to bait Shepard.

"You're probably only mad because they'll all have some fun with that little girl before they string her up, and you won't be there, Shepard."

Shepard glared at O'Fallon. "You're the one that'll be missing out there, Harris," he said. "Harris don't sound like no Irish name. But you sure as hell sound Irish."

"Me grandsire was a travelin' man," O'Fallon said patronizingly. "What's on the bill o' fare for this evenin'? Me and my crony here is eager to fill our bellies and roll up in our soogans."

"Wheatley didn't leave nothin', if that's what you

mean. It's every man for himself." Shepard glanced at his companion. "We already et."

"A tarnal shame," O'Fallon said. "Kelso and me got a fine brisket o' beef we was going to roast while we boiled some spuds and carrots and such. A shame you both have eaten and wun't be able to j'ine us."

Knowing he was only being baited, Shepard clamped his mouth shut and glared at O'Fallon. He was eager to be with Wheatley riding down the Indian rustlers, Woodson thought. It stuck out all over him.

Still, Woodson wondered at O'Fallon's constant verbal poking at Shepard. Probably, he thought, it was only because O'Fallon knew that in the morning all traces of Parker and Wheatley's posse would be out of this country, buying time for them to do something for the pair of exiles hiding up a canyon to the south. All he and O'Fallon really had between them was a good-sized tin of beans, bacon, some coffee, and the quart bottle of O'Fallon's "auld monsturr" Woodson had bought the night before.

O'Fallon eased off. "I was only funnin' you, Shepard. What's your mate's name there?"

"Ganderson."

Ganderson looked at them and said howdy. He was only a boy.

"Well, Shepard," O'Fallon said, "we'll have us a bite, roll up for a few hours, and ride as soon as we can see to. I think I'm safe in assurin' you they won't be lynchin' Two Bear and his child till you get there, at least. Don't worry none about missin' out on the festivities. Them redskins over that way'll be hard to find in the daylight and next to impossible at night."

"For an outlander, you sure know a lot about our

Indians, Harris. As for them two, I ain't anxious to see 'em strung up, if that's what you mean," Shepard said.

"You could've fooled me," O'Fallon said, getting up out of an awkward crouch and heading for the food in his saddlebags.

Daylight came on as a thin flare of gray in the east as the four possemen rolled up their gear and made ready to ride out. The light came up fast, promising another hot day. Though he could hardly see what he was doing down close to the ground, Woodson felt the air drying around him. This one would be another scorcher.

By now they had slept and breakfasted together, and some of the tension between the two sets of strangers had abated. O'Fallon, though, was still testy.

"She's gonna be hotter'n a fryin' pan before we know it," Shepard acknowledged, working the thong hitches of his bedroll behind the saddle. "Let's mount up and ride while we can still make good time in the cool." Woodson could see Shepard had appointed himself leader of the tiny group, and he let the man have his head.

O'Fallon was still rolling up his gear on the ground, carefully brushing away burrs and tiny chunks of dirt and pebbles from his blankets. His tone was impatient. "As you can clearly see, I'll be ready in a mite," he said. "You don't have to wait on me. I'll catch up."

Woodson surveyed the scene. Shepard and Ganderson already stood by their horses, waiting. "Yeah," he said, "if you want a head start, that'll be okay. Harris and me'll be right along and catch up."

Young Ganderson stared at Shepard, trying to read his feelings.

"Just shake a leg, Harris," Shepard said in an ill-tempered growl. "We'll wait."

Even when they mounted up and started, Shepard took a quick lead, with Ganderson riding beside him when he could, or a mare's tail behind. Woodson and O'Fallon trailed them by a score of yards, also riding side by side or in close single file when the land dictated it.

"If I know Jed," Woodson said guardedly to Tommy, "he'll have rousted 'em out early, earlier than us, and have 'em in the saddle long before now."

O'Fallon's voice was even softer. "But Jayzuss, they'll be riding all day following whatever sign it is they think they got, and all they'll be doin' is chasin' their tails."

"This day's going to be interesting, that's for damned certain."

"This crew ain't brought enough gear to stay out too long, Frankie. They'll head for the barn tonight or first thing in the mornin', sure."

"If they don't find more solid sign of Two Bear, they may figure he made his escape clean and forget it. Maybe all Kane wants now is to have Two Bear out of Medicine Springs."

"If Parker comes back sayin' they tracked him a respectable distance and they didn't find him, they'll figure he was lightin' a shuck out of the territory. Maybe Kane'll figure Two Bear has left for parts unknown and forget it."

Shepard guided them out of the mountain's cleft and along the fringes of the Medicine Springs basin to the opening in the hills that had been taken by Parker's wing of the searchers. By midmorning they were well through the mountains again and moving into country much like what Wheatley's band had scoured the day before. They rode the baking, sterile land only a short time before Shepard began to slow his horse's pace, following fresh sign that a gang of horsemen had ridden that way. He allowed O'Fallon and Woodson to catch up.

"They came this way," he said with a haughty self-assurance that bordered on the pompous. He pulled at the front of his shirt against the blossoming heat. The horses were beginning to get lathered, and Woodson figured it was time to start slowing down.

"You're right, Shepard," O'Fallon said in a goading tone. "Don't take much to see that. There's been turds along here for two miles that's hardly dry. And in this weather you got to know that's recent." O'Fallon obviously had little use for Shepard, still taking him for one who harbored visions of lynching Two Bear on the trail.

"You know so much, Harris, you come up here and do the trackin'." The growl was still in Shepard's voice; the blistering sun would bring any man's anger to full boil. "All you done since last night whenever you come in was prod. I'm gettin' a little sick of your mouth."

Shepard had twisted back in the saddle to look at O'Fallon as he spoke.

"Well, Shepard, me b'y, you may not have to put up with my mouth long. And it just may be that your responsibilities for leadin' us to Wheatley and Parker is about over. Looks like them returnin' yonder."

Woodson looked from O'Fallon and Shepard out into the scarred, rutted infinity of landscape they were approaching. The country ahead of them, supporting only minimal chaparral, sloped away gradually, deeply etched by washes and draws, the only relief to the eye being small but craggy buttes and mesas. From behind one of the taller of the dun-colored prominences a body of men, specks in the distance, rounded the trail into view a good three miles away. They were strung out but clustered together in bunches of two, three, and four riders. Over the wavering vision of the heat Woodson could make out Jed Parker and Hannibal Wheatley riding at the head. His breath choked in his lungs despite the heat that was making it hard to breathe. His moment of confronting Jed was probably at hand. He was in a small group now, one that Jed would see immediately. There was no way to avoid his old friend seeing him.

He could try to be inconspicuous until he chose to reveal himself. He ran his hand over his chin. His beard was nearly two days old, and with the grit and dust of the trail his face was probably well disguised. He pulled his hat brim down to cover his forehead as best he could. And it had been nearly ten years. That, along with the fact that Jed had lived those ten years with the notion that Frank Woodson was dead, worked in favor of his not being immediately recognized. Maybe, just maybe, he could identify himself without Jed first finding it out and being taken totally by surprise.

"We'll wait here," Shepard said. "No point in latherin' these horses more."

"Wisht to hell there was some shade, Uncle Gus," Ganderson said.

Ganderson, Woodson realized, was Shepard's nephew, and now he understood why the youth stuck so close to the older man.

"Well, there ain't, Billy, so jes' simmer down."

They got down from the horses and squatted in the sparse shade afforded by the animals' bodies, clutching the reins. The horses appeared grateful for the rest and for having the weight off their backs. This was cruel country and rough treatment for a horse, Woodson thought. They were docile now in the heat, winded, thirsty, and hungry.

For an eternity, it seemed to Woodson, the long queue of riders twisted and dipped through the country, approaching the four men and horses waiting on the rise of ground along the trail. At last they came close enough for the four waiting men to hear the murmuring of voices, the tired clop of hooves in the searing gravel, and the soft squeak of saddle leathers as men's haunches rocked rhythmically with the animals' gaits.

Suddenly Woodson remembered another posse coming up to him, smaller than this one, and the abrupt and drastic change it had made in his life. A shiver jolted his frame; this one was going to produce some dynamic changes as well.

"Hannibal!" Shepard shouted as the sheriff and his chief deputy plodded past, riding point for the strungout body of hot, tired riders. "Find 'em?"

Wheatley looked frazzled from his long hours in the saddle. He was equally tight-lipped, his hawk-like face drawn and pinched by fatigue and the heat. "Uh-uh. He's gone. Good riddance. Tell ya about it in town. Git mounted and come on."

Woodson had stayed crouched in the thin gauze of shadow beside his horse, hoping this, too, would shield him from Parker. Jed rode past not twenty-five yards from Shepard's small group. His tight-lidded glance at them was cursory, and his eyes flicked back to the trail ahead. There wasn't so much as a hint of recognition or question as his gaze swept past Woodson and O'Fallon beside their horses. Shepard and Ganderson had gotten up and led their horses closer to the group of riders filing by, watching, eager for information that none seemed willing to offer. The heat and the long hours on the trail had beat the starch out of these riders.

Parker's face, too, had an exhausted, defeated look about it. His mind was probably too full of disappointment to pay much heed to the four possemen he was passing. He'd have to go home and tell Kane that Two Bear had eluded him. Woodson thought about it. It didn't look good for Jed Parker. A bunch this large couldn't track down and bring back an aging Indian and a girl with a bunch of tired, thirsty cattle holding them up. Woodson suddenly felt sorry for Jed, even though he didn't know what kind of a relationship he had with Kane, or how Kane was likely to react.

Shepard stepped up, heaved himself into the saddle, and got ready to take his place in the line plodding back toward Medicine Springs. "Come on, you fellers," he shouted at Woodson and O'Fallon. "Let's go home."

O'Fallon, still in a crouch in the shade, was close to Woodson. "Well, what you gonna do now, Frankie?"

"It's not the best time, but it is a long ride back to town. I'm going up front and have a talk with Sheriff Parker."

"We're in this pretty deep, Frankie. Be careful."

"I know. I don't want to get our hand tipped to Kane. Either of us. But better me than you. That's why you've got to stick with the Harris name. Our story is that I'm the only one who changed my name because I wasn't ready to have Parker know I was here. Something like that. We got to back each other up on that. If the name O'Fallon comes out, we could both be in deep trouble. As it is, Kane probably has no idea of the name of the man who went to jail for him. As for the facts, I'll probably have to be very careful about that."

"Just the word Jimtown'll blow it all into a cocked hat."

"It's not going to be an easy story to tell—to be truthful with Jed and Nancy and not have Kane find out who I am."

"In a nutshell."

They were up now, the rear guard of the posse filing past them. They checked their horses for the long ride into town, swung into the saddle, and urged the animals into the line of march for Medicine Springs. The other riders, hot, sweaty, and tired from being in the saddle since before daylight, paid them little mind.

"Best we split up for a while," Woodson said softly to O'Fallon. "I'll see you in town. I'm going up to the head of the column and have a little talk, if I can, with the sheriff."

"Godspeed," O'Fallon said.

Woodson touched the spurs to his horse's flank and took up a faster gait, riding past the other possemen.

❯❯ 13 ❮❮

Woodson urged his horse at a reasonable canter, well outside the long line of dusty possemen, toward the head of the strung-out column. Inside him was a heartthrob of anticipation and anxiety at confronting Jed Parker; maybe some fear, he was willing to acknowledge to himself. He still had no idea how he'd handle it, or how deeply he'd get into his possible connection with Cletus Kane. He only knew that it had to be done.

It seemed a matter of heaven-sent convenience that as he moved along the line of march Hannibal Wheatley had pulled to the side, had gotten down, and was tightening his saddle cinch. Woodson rode to him.

"Mr. Wheatley?"

"Sir? Oh, yeah. Let's see. It's Kelso, ain't it?"

"Kelso, yes, sir."

"We didn't find the Indian and the girl, if that's what you want to know."

"No. I know that. Heard the others talking, heard

what you had to say when you came by me and Shepard and the others."

"Damned snipe hunt, all it's been. Miserable hot one to boot. So whattaya want, then?"

"You been riding with Mr. Parker."

"He's the boss. I'm the chief deputy. That's where I'm s'posed to be."

"I wonder if you'd ask him if I might have a word with him."

"Mr. Parker's got a lot on his mind, Kelso."

Damned deputy's playing like a mother hen, Woodson thought. Protecting the high and mighty, in his eyes, from the commoners. He decided not to let his impatience show.

"I think he'd like to talk to me, Mr. Wheatley."

Wheatley kept at the protectiveness. "Is it important?"

Woodson let an edge creep into his voice. "I'd be obliged if when you go back up to him you'd tell him an old friend from Texas would like to palaver a bit."

"That's right, you said you know him. I'll ask him, Kelso, but I ain't sayin' he'll do it."

"Well, I'll appreciate your askin', Mr. Wheatley."

The dusty deputy cocked a leg tiredly and levered himself slowly into the saddle, bringing his horse into motion as quickly as he settled his rump against the high cantle. Woodson lagged back, watching as Wheatley urged his mount to the head of the line to rejoin Parker, who still rode facing straight ahead.

Woodson kept his horse at a fast walk that brought him closer to the head of the line as he saw Wheatley ride up next to Parker. They spoke briefly, and he saw Parker's head pivot and his gaze center on Woodson in the distance as he rode slightly outside the line of march. He swung his head back to watch the trail ahead and said something to Wheatley. The deputy turned toward Woodson, flung up his hand, and waved him on ahead.

With that motion, like a flick of fate, Woodson questioned his judgment, his heart dropping. He was about to disrupt lives that by all outward signs had made proper peace with his absence.

"No, dammit!" he thought. "I didn't lose all those years and come all these miles to slink away. My own conscience will find proper rest when this is over and done with."

Resolve poured back in with his thoughts. It was now or never. Woodson spurred his horse to the head of the line.

The impressions he'd gained two nights before about Jed swirled back. His face was older, seamed with more trouble now as Woodson approached him. Some of the haggard look he saw was carved there by the futile Two Bear chase. There was no instant recognition in the eyes as Woodson rode up; only questions as to why this newcomer needed to talk.

"Mr. Kelso, is it?" Jed asked as Woodson pushed his horse closer, edging Wheatley and his mount away.

"No, Jed. Not Kelso. You don't recognize me, and it's small wonder. It's been a long, long time."

"Wheatley said something about Texas. . . ." Awareness and recognition slowly dawned in Parker's still-flashing eyes. The flinty gray of them that Woodson remembered from years of etched memory hadn't been dulled by the passage of time. Realization bloomed slowly in the eyes and in the expression.

"Wait," Parker said. "It can't be. Your face is so

familiar, but you can't be. Frank? Frank Woodson?"
Jed almost shouted the name.

Waves of new, hardly understood emotion swept
over Woodson. Words tried to come, but they stuck
in his throat like a fish bone. He sensed his eyes mist-
ing over. He shoved out his hand. All he could muster
by way of words was a soft "Yep." He was tight
with emotion.

"Holy Mother of God!" Parker shouted, pumping
Woodson's hand from horseback. "Frank Woodson!
But what . . . We thought you were dead!"

"I'm sorry, Jed. I've got a lot to tell you. This isn't
the time or the place. I only wanted to say howdy and
let you—"

"The hell it isn't! Frank! For Lord's sake!" Parker's
eyes searched Woodson's as if trying to call back the
missing years. He turned to Wheatley, who now rode
outside the two. "Hannibal!"

"Yes, sir."

"Keep at the point and take the men in. If you need
me, I'll be back down the column. Frank, c'mon." Parker swung his horse away from the trail and motioned
Woodson to follow. Clear of the dust churned up by
the riders, Parker swung around and got down, a new
eagerness and vitality in his movements. Woodson followed suit.

"We'll wait here to let them pass, then we'll follow
up. My Lord! I can't seem to get it through my head.
Where in the devil have you been?"

Woodson was pleased that this first encounter had
gone so smoothly. Parker was surprised and bewildered, but his initial shock had passed away quickly.
He seemed genuinely thrilled to see Frank Woodson
alive.

"One thing at a time, Jed," Woodson said, more in control than Parker was. "It's been a long time for me, too."

"But my Lord, man, there was no word. We were sure you were dead. I hardly know what to say. Where to begin. We—that is, Nan ..." Parker stopped. "There's something you've got to know, Frank. Right off."

"I already know. You and Nancy ... she's your wife. I saw her from a distance when I rode into Medicine Springs day before yesterday. That night, when I was asked to join this posse, I learned that you were the sheriff here. It didn't take much to put two and two together."

"Oh, man, so much I've got to tell you. Nancy won't know what to say. Oh, Frank, we both waited and hunted for you for so long. Two years it was. Two years after Nancy wrote me about you. We waited, Frank. We waited a respectable time. In two years we never gave up hope, either of us. Our worry about you brought us together. Then we simply had to conclude that you were dead. I still can't believe it. Here you are, in the flesh."

"It's true. I'm here. Not dead."

"So much to think about. So much to remember. So much to tell you."

"How is Nancy?"

"Fine. Fine. But where were you? When you didn't come back after the cattle drive she got in touch with me." Parker now spoke almost breathlessly as his mind darted from thought to thought. "Frank, you've got to understand. Nancy and me."

Woodson said it hoarsely. "I think I do. I understand, Jed."

Parker seemed to have a need to apologize, to explain.

"We truly waited a respectable time, Frank. She was your promised. I was your best friend. First I went up to see her, to find out more about what had happened. The Merrills—everybody at the ranch—were so concerned. I went back to Abilene. Quit my job."

"You what?"

The tag end of the posse was thinning now. In a break in the bunches of riders Tommy O'Fallon rode slowly by, saw Woodson and Parker a few yards off the trail, and rested his eyes on Woodson's, questioning. Woodson's only sign to O'Fallon was a slight nod of the head that everything was all right. O'Fallon acknowledged the subtle message with an almost imperceptible nod back at Woodson. O'Fallon swung his gaze back to the trail and rode on.

"Quit and spent most of a year on the trail to Montana and back. Look, Frank, the last of the men are going by. Let's head out. We can talk as we ride."

"Fine with me." Woodson stepped into the saddle and, close together as they had been in the old days, he and Parker walked their horses back to the trail, keeping a moderate distance behind the last of the possemen and the dust churned up by their horses. As it was in this windless air, the dust still lay thickly and head-high over what passed for a road through this near-barren desert.

"But tell me about you, Frank. Where were you all this time?"

There was no credible lie that would substitute for the truth in Woodson's mind. "I can explain it all later, Jed. Maybe. I've been in prison. For something I didn't do."

"Good Lord. I didn't know. But you could have made contact. You could have written. We'd have gotten you out."

"It's a long story. If only I could have written. I wasn't allowed. Seven long years."

"In heaven's name, why?"

"It was a stage robbery I was sent up for. I wouldn't ... couldn't tell them where the loot was hidden. The price I paid for my bullheadedness was that I was forbidden to make any outside contact. That was my reward if I'd opened up: I could get in touch with friends and family. If I'd had any notion where their damned money was hid, I'd have told them in a minute."

"That's unnecessary cruelty. We'd never do such a thing in Texas. Nor here. Then you got out. What? A year ago?"

"Two."

"Why didn't you go home?"

"It was a different man came out of prison, Jed. Too much time had gone by. I knew things would have to be different with Nancy. I knew she'd have given me up for lost and probably married. It would have been wrong of me to have tried to barge back into her life at that point."

"Yeah. While you were rotting in prison, at least part of that first year, I was riding to Montana, hunting for some trace of you. Tuck Merrill grubstaked me. I'd have gone whether Tuck backed me or not. I thought I rode every possible inch of ground. Thought I covered every hill and dale, asked all kinds of questions."

"Maybe not the right questions at the right places. I don't know."

With the words, some of the troubled waters in Woodson's mind cleared. He really had nothing to fear in telling Jed the truth, even mentioning Jimtown. He'd only avoid mentioning any suspicion of Cletus Kane. The area around Jimtown was remote enough, it seemed, that even Parker, in scouring the land for some word of Woodson, had missed it.

He would also conceal any knowledge that the man who had done the robbery resembled him. His and Kane's similarity, if it was mentioned, could be but an amusing coincidence. He surely had nothing to lose with Jed. Even if Jed carried the story to Kane, the town strongman wouldn't be dumb enough to tip his hand to Parker that it was he, and not Woodson, who had robbed the Jimtown stage. That would be between Woodson and Kane if it ever came to a head.

He had been fearful as long as he had been in this neck of the woods, and now realized he had nothing to fear. So what if Kane knew Woodson was the man who had been unjustly imprisoned for Kane's crime? Kane couldn't come out in the open about it. Kane was a powerful man, but not all that popular. Something might yet happen to upend Cletus Kane's applecart.

"So many things to talk out, Frank," Jed said. "We've still got a lot of time on the way in. I'll have to report to Mr. Kane. About the posse, I mean. You've heard of Cletus Kane, haven't you?"

Woodson smiled across at Jed. The lawman's excitement at Woodson's sudden appearance was simmering down. It was that about Jed that had made Woodson like him nearly twenty years ago. He could be excitable and enjoy the life the excitement brought. But when it was time to be serious Jed Parker could be all business. Woodson realized that it was possibly the same things about Hughie Kelso and Tommy O'Fallon that had attracted him to them.

"A man can't be in Medicine Springs more than a few minutes without hearing Mr. Kane's name." Woodson fished for a reaction from Jed. "I was sitting right behind Honus Johnson in the meeting night before last."

Jed's face reddened slightly. "You were there? Well, of course you were. Otherwise you probably wouldn't be with this posse. Any town, Frank, is going to have its factions. Mr. Kane is a powerful man. He's bound to have his enemies. This Johnson is one of them."

"I gathered that."

"That's not important now. What is important is that you're here. You've come back to us."

Woodson sensed delight in the way Jed phrased it. Parker's attitude paved the way for Woodson's reunion to be a good one.

"Of course I'll want you to come by the house, Frank. But I'd better see Nancy first. Not that we have anything to hide, mind you." Parker paused as though thinking through the statement. "But just better that I break it to her before you come by. She'll want to see you, but there could be complications if we just went bolting in."

"I understand. But you've been asking all the questions. Now it's my turn. What brought you to Medicine Springs?"

"Like yours, it's a long story. As I said, I left Abilene and spent most of eight months hunting for you. When I went back, well, at first Nancy and I were together in our concern for you. I felt some obligation.

Oh, I don't know, Frank. Nothing noble, and certainly nothing nasty. I wasn't waiting to move in on your territory."

"Jed, I understand. Stop apologizing."

"Berdan needed a chief of police, so I took the job for a while so I could be near the Merrills. I got awfully close to Tuck and Amy."

Remembering again swept over Woodson. "Good old Tuck. And dear Amy. How are they?"

"Amy died in '75."

"That's too bad. She and Nancy were close."

"More than maybe you know. Her mother was a strong anchor for Nancy in the things that happened after you disappeared."

"Yeah." Woodson's thoughts were full of those days. There was no resentment in the thought that he, too, could have used someone to anchor to during those first horrible days and months.

"Tuck's fine. Ten years older, of course. Haven't seen him in a while, but he writes to Nancy a lot. Raised cattle for a few more years and then switched to horses. He's one of the best horse breeders in that part of Texas. He's got quite a reputation, even up here. That helped bring us to Medicine Springs."

"Tuck'd be good at anything he tried."

"Six or seven years ago Mr. Kane went to Berdan. Went to see Tuck, actually. For horses. You know, Mr. Kane looks a lot like you, now that I think about it. Or did then. He's changed a lot, too. It gave Nancy quite a start when Mr. Kane rode out to the TM spread. I met him one night when Nancy and I were out to have supper with Tuck, and we got to talking. He asked me to come up to Medicine Springs and work at keeping the law here. Nancy and I talked it over. She loved Berdan and the TM Ranch. But there were also bad memories of everything that had happened. She and I both thought it would be a great way to start new, away from everything there. And it has worked out. Generally."

"Generally?"

"There are unusual problems being the law in a town that's controlled for the most part by one man."

"I guess I'm glad I'm just a cowpoke and a drifter. I owe nothing to any man."

"I don't either. Really. I've tried to keep my integrity, but sometimes it hasn't been easy."

"But you stay."

"It's a great country, Frank. It's treated me well. Been a fine place to be with my family."

"Family. Hell, I didn't even think. Of course you must have kids by now."

Woodson saw Parker's face visibly cloud over, and his eyes seemed to be searching the distant range of tableland that announced the pass down into the Medicine Springs basin.

"We've got three fine children, Frank. Little Tuck, our youngest, was born here. He's four. Amy was born in Berdan just before we left Texas. She's six now."

Parker paused as if there were more, but he was hesitant. When he spoke his voice was determined. And definite.

"Our oldest is Cindy. Well, actually Cynthia Frances. She's nine. Soon going to be ten."

Woodson's mind clicked with quick arithmetic. Jed and Nancy hadn't been married long enough. It wasn't like Jed to make mistakes about such things.

"She's a wonderful little girl, Frank. For a lot of

special reasons, maybe I love her even more than I love little Amy and Tuck."

"That's ..."

"Frank, I won't do anything to change that beautiful little child. And I won't have your being here change her either."

"What? I don't get it. What's my being here got to do with it?"

"Her middle name is Frances. Nancy named her after you. Cindy is your daughter, Frank."

❋ 14 ❋

Woodson's face reddened and felt hot. His body turned ramrod-stiff in the saddle. The rear guard of the posse and the country around the pass leading to Medicine Springs reeled and swam in his vision.

My God, he thought through shock and total astonishment, there was more disgrace than just mine. I've suffered. But I caused Nancy Merrill to suffer so much more than I ever did.

Again he sensed his thinking whirling and swirling in a kind of rolling weakness and helplessness deep inside him in the wake of Jed's revelation. A man, he thought, can haze half-wild cows out of rugged country, and he can survive cold camps and heat and sweat and dust. But no old trail boss nor good saddle pard could ever teach you how to handle your feelings when something like this happened.

Damn! What a fool thing to have done to that fine woman! There was no way he could ever atone for having created such a mess. He had fathered a child out of wedlock. That was disgrace enough in itself.

Leaving the mother to make her own way with a bastard child was unforgivable.

It was almost too much to handle, even for a man who thought of himself as having grown tough in his prison ordeal. Too many things were happening too fast. The reunion with Jed and Nancy was going to be difficult enough. And now this. He looked at Jed watching him.

"Jed, I don't understand. I mean, I do understand, but I don't understand. I'm not making sense."

Parker smiled, a smile intended to put Woodson at ease. Good old Jed, he thought. Never one to make things too tough on anyone else, if he could help it. Even if it meant shouldering the other fellow's burden. Great God, Woodson thought, that's exactly what he's done. For me!

"You and I can't have any secrets at this point, Frank. I'm married to the woman you once loved. I know just about everything that happened during your courtship. I wasn't prying. We honestly thought you were dead. When Nancy and I began to get serious about each other it was important for her to tell me everything."

"Then you know. About that afternoon before I left." Jed nodded. "Those things happen fast, don't they? I never thought. We were both just kids. First time for both of us. And that had to happen! Jed, if I had known I wasn't coming back to marry her, I'd never have let it happen. I hold women in high regard, and Nancy the very highest. God, how I've disgraced that woman. And you."

"Ah, take it easy, Frank. Whatever you do, don't let it eat you alive. A few people are aware of it all, but they're in Berdan, Texas. That's another reason we were eager to come to Medicine Springs. Up here that little girl is Cindy Parker. When people ask how long Nan and I have been married we're purposely evasive. We don't lie, nor do we say or do anything to darken Cindy's character, or that of her natural father. For all the world knows, I'm Cindy's father. Around Berdan they know that Cindy is Frank Woodson's child. But Berdan's a long way from here."

"You're certainly more her father than I am. I left things in a hell of a mess in Texas, didn't I? I ought to ride out here and now and not disturb things by bringing up the past any more than I already have."

"Frank, quit beating yourself over the head. You didn't have any control over what happened. Besides, the years heal, my friend. It's all back there in the past. Beyond our poor power to add or detract, as Old Abe said." Jed reached across and slapped Woodson on the shoulder in a consoling, reassuring way. "If Nancy were to find out you'd been here and hadn't seen her, she'd never forgive me. It will be all right once I talk with her. She thinks you're dead, but she's a strong girl. Once she gets over the fact that you are indeed alive, she'll adjust. We've all suffered a lot out of this, Frank, but we're all grownups, and we can adjust."

"That's good to know."

"There's been no shame or disgrace. If there was any, it was long ago. True, there've been some awkward moments. In her heart Nan remembers that Cindy is Frank Woodson's child. And she treasures that memory. But that's as far as it goes. We both secretly know. And now you do. To all outward appearances she is Cynthia Frances Parker. She's my child now, Frank."

"I know. And you know I wouldn't do anything to change that. It's still hard to get hold of, Jed. But then you ... you married Nancy. You dignified the whole rotten situation by marrying Nancy and giving my baby a name."

"Nothing rotten about it at all except what comes out of the mouths of gossips and fishwives."

"But men ... men don't do that, Jed. They don't marry disgraced women with bastard children." Woodson was still full of emotion over what he was learning.

"At first, long before I had true feelings for Nancy, I got into it out of my concern for you, old friend. I suppose then my concern for Nan and Cindy came in there someplace. At first I was drawn to her because we both had a stake in what had happened to you. Then I began to respect her pluck in trying to go on without you—God, she was brave about it, Frank. There she was keeping her head up, trying to adjust to the mystery of what had happened to you and raise Cindy as a normal youngster. In a year or so respect got to be love, Frank. I deeply love and cherish the woman."

"I know that. Jed?"

"Huh?"

Woodson looked squarely at Parker. They had slowed their horses now and trailed the posse by as much as a quarter mile. He reached across for Jed's hand, which came up. Jed's eyes carried a questioning look.

"Thank you, old friend. Thank you for taking on my responsibility."

"Believe me, Frank, I didn't do it as 'taking on your responsibility.' I had feelings for Nan the minute I walked through the door of Tuck's house and saw her standing there with the baby. She was my best friend's intended, and never for a moment did I forget that. I got busy trying to find you and bring the two of you back together. At first that's all I wanted."

"I understand, Jed."

"That's why I have to talk with Nancy before you come to the house. And I won't have anyone blurting out anything to Cindy. I intend to take that one up myself when the time is right. As it stands now, she feels she is one hundred percent our child, and I mean to keep it that way until it's time to tell her."

"You can trust me, Jed. She'll never know anything from me."

"I always could trust you. We were together a lot of years."

"The war. Yeah, and after."

"Save the reminiscing for later. Let's get hopping to town. I've still got a job to do."

Jed led Woodson past the tail end of the posse at a fast canter. They were started well into the pass leading down to Medicine Springs. Woodson stayed with Parker even as they rode past Tommy O'Fallon. The stubby Irishman watched the two riders going by with questions in his eyes.

As if to underscore the turbulence and the passion Frank Woodson felt over the events of the last two days, the weather turned from the scorching hot of his two days with the posse to an insufferable heat that even went so far as to make breathing difficult.

The day after their return from the futile posse chase Woodson and O'Fallon hung close to their hotel rooms, keeping as cool as possible. Keeping cool, however, was not possible, as the heat confined in their second-floor rooms seemed even closer than it was out on the street.

Out there nothing moved. Woodson had expected to hear from Jed Parker about a visit with Nancy and the children, but with the heat keeping everyone from moving around, Woodson was not upset.

It was hard for him to remember days as hot as these. The white-hot light of the sun, a contrast to its normally yellow and balmy light in this country, seemed to invade everything. Nowhere was it cool.

Activity in Medicine Springs ground to a virtual standstill, people doing only what was absolutely necessary. Still the incessant heat blazed down in a baking fire that sapped the energies of man and animal alike. Pastured horses and cattle did the best they could to find shade.

The town's stray dogs, normally yappy at anything that moved, dozed in the shade of the raised board sidewalk, awake and alert but dulled by the heat. They, too, watched and waited patiently for the hot spell to pass, their long pink tongues actively panting and dripping.

The heat abated some at night, and men came out of their daytime hiding place in houses and barns, saddled up, and rode into town for a drink and to talk about the weather. Encouraged by the relief brought on by darkness, O'Fallon would drag Woodson across to the Silver Concho.

In a silent corner of the only slightly warm saloon Woodson related to O'Fallon what he had learned in his long talk with Jed Parker.

During the day, however, with little to do to break the monotony of long, dull, and hot hours, Woodson and his Irish friend spent long spells once or twice a day in Wong Chun's bath emporium, their tubs filled with the coolest water possible.

As if impervious to the hot spell, the Chinaman still wore the shiny black clothing of his native country—the long sleeves of the coat still at the wrists, the collar buttoned tightly at the throat, and a black skullcap with a silken carmine tassel on his head. The fires of his heating stove, however, were out, and he sat patiently on a bench beside it, his face shiny but not perspiring.

Wong Chun took the heat with great patience, the happy, patronizing grin never leaving his face.

In the tub beside Woodson, O'Fallon lay immersed, relaxed and relatively cool, working on a cigar that he chewed at the same time he smoked it. His small flask of the "auld monsturr" perched on the bleached wood floor beside his tub. The water in it was clear and cool, and O'Fallon lay back against the canted and smooth sheet-metal back. His eyes were half closed as he drowsed, enjoying his relief from the oppressive heat.

"Tommy," Woodson said, and the Irishman opened his eyes and looked at Woodson in question. "How much money have you got?"

"What a question to ask a man. His financial status ought to be his own business."

"Be serious."

"Me roll is in me trousers hangin' there. A bit under thirty dollars."

"I don't mean ready cash. I mean what are you worth?"

"I sense you have a reason for askin', Frankie Woodson. I believe at last tally I had the better part of four hundred and fifty dollars to me name, in a bankin' institution up north of here."

"What's it worth to you to give Kane his comeuppance?"

"My four-fifty would never in this world buy him off. Nor would it atone for Paddy O'Fallon's murder."

"What if we at least expose him and drive him out of Medicine Springs? When I went to prison I had three hundred in a bank in Berdan. Interest ought to have brought it up a bit."

"What are you thinkin', Frankie?"

"Something my mother used to say. About bearding the lion in his den."

❧ 15 ❧

"**I**f we're to get a rise out of Kane, we'll have to step out boldly," Woodson said.

"Why would you care to get Kane to rise to anything?"

"What we both came here for. To get even. But on our terms. I want it now more than ever when I think he was the one, too, who was responsible for Nancy's suffering with my bastard child. That's even harder to swallow than the years in prison. He kept me from my rightful place as Cynthia's father. We still don't have any evidence that he was the one. But, Tommy, he had to be. As I see it, we've got to get him to make new mistakes, this time in his own territory and in his own time. We've got to make his knowledge of his own guilt bring him down."

"I don't get you."

"He's craftier here than he was ten years ago up around Jimtown. Everything he's doing here is perfectly legal and honest. But much of it is still unjust."

"And what can be done about that?"

"Depends on how much you want to risk. All of your money. Maybe even your life."

"I'd have to consider those risks very carefully. Especially the latter."

"I don't think we'll lose on the financial investment I have in mind. And I don't think the risk to life and limb is that great."

"Pray continue."

"How about this: We pool our money and go into partnership in a ranch here in Medicine Springs."

"You want to settle in Kane's country? Even if I believed you wanted to, I think we've both been drifters too many years for settlin' down to ranchin', Frankie."

"Oh, we won't. At least we don't have to. We move someone on the place as a tenant-manager. And you know who I'm thinking of."

"John Two Bear. Who else? Ain't you the crafty one, now? Craftier'n Kane."

"Now you're following my line of reasoning."

"But what of Kane? And your friend Parker?"

"Jed may appear to be under Kane's thumb, but he's got grit of his own that maybe he's not showing much of these days. This is an excellent setup for Jed under the circumstances. His job is secure, and he's probably making a good living doing Kane's bidding. He's got respect here, generally, I suppose. There's certainly less danger and dirt than in a trail town. As for Kane, when he arranged his takeover of Medicine Springs he did it well. Sad to say for our cause, he has probably put as much back into this town as he's taken out. Our job will be tougher because we aren't taking on a complete blackguard. Medicine Springs is a good town in a good country; you can't dispute that.

Kane has seen to it. Aside from being under his control, people around here seem generally content."

"And Parker?"

"He's suffered enough because of me, but now I mean more than ever to bring Cletus Kane to account for the past by bringing him up short in the present. Jed and Nancy may feel a bit of the pinch of our making. But I believe they'll see it's more a case of Kane lying down in his own bed."

"You would seem to be making decisions for a lot of people, Frankie Woodson."

"Maybe it appears that way. I don't intend that it should. I intend that Mr. Thomas O'Fallon and Mr. Frank Woodson become honest, hardworking ranchers in the Medicine Springs valley. If as a result of that certain people in this country make conclusions and act on them in certain ways, it really won't be our responsibility."

"I still don't get you."

"First of all, we shed the aliases. As soon as we can get our money telegraphed to us we file papers of partnership and see what can be done about buying a likely site for a ranch, or a ranch already established."

"Kane knows everything that goes on in this town. What's he going to think when he sees O'Fallon on a deed of property? And how do you know he's not aware that the man who went up for him was named Woodson?"

"I hope he is. I said it's his own guilt that'll trip him up. He'll put two and two together that these two are coming at him out of his past in the Jimtown territory."

"That what you mean about risking our necks, Frankie?"

"Look at it realistically, Tom. What's he going to do? Order Parker to shoot us down like dogs? Or drive us out? What really went on in Jimtown is a secret only the three of us share—you, me, and Cletus Kane. To get someone else—in this case, Parker—to do his dirty work will mean exposing his criminal past. As long as we conduct ourselves on the up-and-up, he'll have no reason to ask anyone to force us to move on. Nor will he dare take any action himself. Maybe he keeps an eye on the doings of everyone in this basin, but the people here also have their eyes on him."

"Stands to reason. You'll tell Parker? About Jimtown?"

"Why not? That still would be no admission that I suspect Cletus Kane. On the face of it, with the people in this country, including Parker, we just like it so well here that we decided to stay and go into the ranching business. I think I can set it up so that it won't bring more discomfort to Jed and Nancy, despite my miraculous return from the dead and from a sad past. As for the convicted robber of the Jimtown stage being in Cletus Kane's country, well, that man will have to draw his own conclusions."

"And him bein' partners with an O'Fallon'll give our Mr. Kane a great deal of food for thought." Tommy O'Fallon was now getting caught up in the intricacies of Woodson's conspiracy to bring down Kane.

"*If* he knows the name of the man he killed."

"My information indicates he does. I talked with a Mr. Brown in Jimtown. He thinks the killer at least knew Paddy's name."

"Kane will feel he has to do something about us.

Meanwhile, we merely set ourselves up as honest, hardworking ranchers. I have special reasons for settling here. Old friends. Jed and Nancy and their family. I can work it out. You about done bathin', Tommy?"

"Any longer in here and I'll look like a shriveled prune. Let's go."

As Woodson and O'Fallon emerged from Wong Chun's bathhouse into the hotel lobby Hannibal Wheatley was coming through the door toward them. His face was beet red from the heat. The redness and his hawk-beak nose made him resemble a turkey buzzard.

"Hey, there, uh, Mr. Woodson! Hah-dee."

"Howdy, Wheatley. How you standin' the weather?"

"Ain't no way to stand it. You jus' got to suffer it. Hah-dee, Mr. Harris."

"Top o' tha marnin', Wheatley."

"What brings you out in this weather?" Woodson asked. "No rustling or crime going on in this heat, is there?"

"No, sir, and I ain't really here on official business neither. Just you might say on an errand for Mr. Parker. He'd like you to come by this evenin', 'long about six when it commences to cool."

"If you see him, tell him I accept."

"He says he'll be expectin' ya. Mrs. Parker, she wants you to dinner."

"That's mighty kind of the Parkers."

"It's a treat. They've got a nice 'dobe out south of town about a mile. You can't miss it; on your left. Cool in there as a cave. Snug in the winter, too. Wisht

I had me a 'dobe. My place is a frame shanty, and it'll be hotter in there than hell's firebox."

"You oughtter go back and take advantage of old One Hung Low's bathhouse," O'Fallon said. "Nothin' like a cold tub a his water."

"Might jus' do that. Mr. Parker and his missus'll be expectin' ya about six."

"I'll be there."

"Yessir. So long." Wheatley started for the bathhouse door, taking O'Fallon's suggestion as good advice.

"Much obliged for coming out to tell me, Hannibal," Woodson said.

Wheatley turned, smiling apparently at Woodson's familiarity. "My pleasure." Wheatley disappeared into the bathhouse.

"Well, Tommy, this is it. I'll be seeing Mrs. Parker at last."

"How do you feel about it?"

"As nervous as a sinner in church."

"You need a drink. Shall we go over to the Silver Concho? I need one just on general principle."

"One only. I'll need to be on my best behavior this evening."

"Agreed. Let's go."

The sun was a long way yet from setting when Woodson saddled his horse at the livery stable and headed south for the Parker place. He could sense a slight cooling trend in the air, but it wasn't much. He was thankful, though, that the intense heat had also baked most of the moisture out of the air so that at least he wasn't sweating. Still the heat pressed in on him like some kind of weight and dried his nostrils.

Neither had the two small drinks he'd had earlier with O'Fallon helped much to slake his thirst. In fact, he seemed to feel even drier. Over it all, he was thankful he wouldn't meet Nancy Parker dripping wet.

Out of concern for his horse he started early enough so he could make the mile or whatever it was to the Parker home at a slow walk. The horse had been in the relatively cool darkness of the livery stable for two days and certainly wouldn't take to being lathered up in a fast gallop.

Woodson also felt he needed as much time as possible to think it through, though he'd been over it enough in his mind and had visualized this first meeting time and again, working it over a hundred different ways.

Still, no matter how he turned it around in his thoughts, the jumpiness in his stomach didn't go away. His insides leapt and fluttered when out of the dusk the ample adobe house took shape against a graying land. Light pouring through several windows was beckoning and welcoming.

A well-polished hitch rail stood in front of the home's long veranda with a shaped ripple-tin overhang. He tied up his horse, stepped to the door, caught a deep breath, and knocked.

❧ 16 ❧

The door swung open easily, as if someone had anticipated him. The fullness in Woodson's chest squeezed him to the point of near suffocation. The years had done nothing but enhance the beauty that had attracted him to Nancy Merrill in the first place. She had been a sweet and gentle girl brimming with compassion; none of that, it seemed, had diminished.

"Frank!" she said, her voice choking on her emotion. "Come in." Nancy was smiling as she stepped back to let him enter, her face reflecting a host of new and strange feelings.

She reached out and caught his lower arms in hers, holding him at this distance, her eyes probing his as if to call back the lost years. He allowed her to take the lead. "Frank, Frank, Frank, let me have a look at you! Dear God, I was so certain I'd never see this day!" Woodson was aware of the movement of other people in the big main room of the house, but his eyes feasted only on Nancy's face. He sensed himself grinning broadly at her, but his words refused to come.

"Lord, let me have a look at you," she said again, the breathless catch still in her voice.

Finally his words came. "It's been forever, Nan. I'm sorry for all you've suffered on my account."

For a long moment she held him by his arms, looking deeply into his eyes. Then with a gasp she arced her arms to hug him by the waist. His arms encircled her and they hugged, a warm but friendly embrace. It would be wrong, he knew, to kiss her, so he only allowed her head to rest against his shoulder in the welcome embrace of reunion. She was trembling.

In the soft light of several lamps around the white-walled room Jed stood a few feet away, grinning in approval and looking tanned, robust, and happy. His expression beamed joy at the reunion of the two most important people in his life. Woodson blinked, trying to focus on Jed and the room, but his vision was clouded by the panorama of the past and the years of suffering that had brought him to this moment.

Almost as suddenly as she had embraced him, but in a movement that registered neither embarrassment nor apology, Nancy stepped back. "All that is past, Frank. Now is now, and you can't know how pleased I am to see you."

"Me, too," Woodson said. "I only hope there's time to tell it all ... and to find out about you."

"There will be. There will be. Come in, Frank. Sit down."

As the first strong wave of emotion passed, Woodson stuck out his hand to Jed. "Thanks for having me, old friend."

"Glad you could make it." Jed's handshake was firm and sincere. Thrills continued to wash over Woodson. It was good to be back among the living, with these two people he had thought of almost constantly for ten years. The Parker home was well-lighted. Around a doorway to another room he could see two round and impish faces watching the scene in the living room with timidity but compelling curiosity. Little Tuck and Amy Parker had obviously been told quite a bit about the evening's visitor. Now they watched him from afar and from the childish protection of another room. Their eyes were bright and alert as young squirrels.

Woodson's eyes took in the rest of the room as he grew more comfortable in the surroundings and being close to Nancy.

The sensations, the fullness in his chest, and the unsettled activity in his stomach wound down from a gallop to a trot. They quickened again, however, as he saw the little girl, soon to be on her way to young womanhood, sitting demurely in a chair in the far corner, a part of the room he hadn't seen as he entered. Her ankles, encased in gleaming high black shoes neatly buttoned, were crossed, her hands clasped lightly in her lap. Her long light blue dress had recently been washed and starched and ironed. Her hair was piled high, and at the back of her head he could see a large bright blue bow. Cynthia Parker's eyes gleaming on him were a deep blue that radiated intensity as well as intelligence. Already her features were taking on the strong lines of the handsome woman she would become. Still, there was very much of the little lady about her.

"Cindy," Jed called, "come here and say hello to Mr. Woodson." There was no timidity or reluctance in her movement as the little girl pushed herself out of the chair and crossed the room to her parents and their guest. She had only stayed in the background until summoned. "Amy, Tuck," Jed called to the other two, "come out here now."

R. C. HOUSE

Cynthia sidled close to her mother, watching Frank, waiting to be spoken to. Woodson was immediately struck with the thought that Jed and Nancy were doing a beautiful job with the upbringing of this child that was rightly his responsibility. She made a light curtsy. "Hello, Mr. Woodson," she said. Her voice tinkled like a delicate bell.

Woodson looked at Nancy and Jed for some sign. They only smiled.

"This must be your Cindy," he said, looking at his child. He bowed slightly. "Mighty nice to make your acquaintance, Miss Cindy." She smiled at him politely. Tuck and Amy, clutching their mother's skirts and half hiding behind her, stared at him with wide eyes. He dropped to a crouch to look at the two pint-sized kids. "Howdy, Mr. Tuck Parker," he said with a manly authority he thought would appeal to the boy. "Proud to know you. They tell me you're four years old now."

Tuck grinned sheepishly and, as if he had been coached, stepped forward and stuck out a fat little hand for Woodson to shake. "Hello, Mr. Woodson." His tongue darted out in a lisp on "Mithter" and "Woodthon."

"And Miss Amy," Woodson said. "You look well." Amy kneaded her little hands in front of herself and looked at Woodson, tipping her head with the kind of shy, childish pleasure that only a six-year-old could show. She giggled. It was obvious to Woodson that he had been the topic of a lot of talk in the Parker household for several days, and his visit was much anticipated by the adults. The same anticipation had been communicated to the children.

Trying not to be obvious, he studied Cynthia even more. He could see little of his influence in her, and

162

that was a blessing. She more favored the Merrills; he could see traces of the grandparents, Tuck and Amy, and much of Nancy. Little Tuck and Amy Parker tended to favor their father's side of the family. Tuck looked the way Jed must have at that age. It was easier to see in the little boy. He had first known Jed Parker fifteen or twenty years ago, when he was still growing out of his own adolescence.

"She's a beautiful child, Nancy," Woodson said openly and pointedly. "And your little ones are about as delightful as young colts."

"Thank you, Frank," Nancy said, but there was an absentminded ring in the words. Her thoughts were evidently on this first reunion. She seemed not to be able to look at him enough, to study him, to probe in her mind to try to find explanations for all that had happened. Jed, however, had obviously told her as much as he knew about Woodson.

It was Jed who broke the minor tension of this first meeting. "How you standing this heat, Frank?"

Woodson advanced into the room. "Tol'able, I suppose. Well as can be expected. Thank God for that Chinaman's bathhouse at the hotel. I swear, you could heat brandin' irons in the middle of the street in town."

"Fry eggs, anyway."

"You'll excuse me, Frank," Nancy said. "I better get out to the kitchen and finish supper. Cynthia, come help Mommy, please." She turned to hurry to the back of the house, then turned back and again took Woodson by the forearms, gripping them tightly and emotionally. "Frank, I'm so happy you're with us again. Promise you'll stay until we can really get acquainted again. And I hope tonight you'll stay so we can talk. I believe I have a half million questions."

"I promise, Nan," he said, smiling at her. The three children tagged after her as she disappeared into the back of the house. "At least this place is cool, Jed," he said.

"Yeah, and easy to keep warm in the winter. Adobe's the only thing in this country, but everybody wants frame and siding on their places. Traditional, I suppose, the way it was back home where wood is plentiful. But the people who lived in this country hundreds of years ago learned the best way to do it. And that was adobe."

"Well, it's sure a nice place. You fixed it up so homey."

"Thanks. Care for something before supper? I usually have a brandy after my meal, but it's good before, too. This is a special occasion."

Woodson thought a drink might put both of them more at ease. "Don't mind if I do."

From a simple but sturdy buffet Parker pulled a crystal decanter filled with a rich, reddish amber and two cut crystal glasses that gleamed and reflected the lamplight. "Have some good cigars for after dinner, too."

"I don't smoke much. They took away my makin's before the trial, and much as I pleaded for a smoke, they wouldn't let me have one. Prison pretty well cured me of the weed. Seven years in there can change a lot of your ideas."

"Oh, Frank, that was an awful time for all of us. But this is a joyous occasion. Let's not dwell on the past now."

"Well, I sure don't want to."

"I never did drink brandy or smoke cheroots until I came here and went to work for Mr. Kane. He has a fine taste for such things. He's the one who keeps me in brandy and fine cigars. It's part of the good life we have here, Frank."

Yeah, Woodson thought, at the expense of people like Honus Johnson and John Two Bear. His brief flare of mental anger was directed at Kane, not Parker.

"Mr. Kane runs a good town here, Frank. I'm fortunate to be working for him. He's tough, no mistake of that. And sometimes he's a bit arbitrary. He has to be. With his firm hand running things this town is taking shape, becoming something."

Woodson took the glass from Parker and studied its contents. The color was rich and appealing. He took a tentative sip; the brandy had none of the harsh bite of hard whiskey. He could see how a man might take to this tangy, mellow flavor. Another man, maybe. But not Frank Woodson. If Cletus Kane liked it, that was enough reason for him to steer clear of it as a regular thing. He didn't comment on Jed's remarks. He was a guest in Jed and Nancy Parker's home, and this was his first time with his own child. He was not going to mar it by getting into a debate about Cletus Kane. At least he was getting closer to settling all this hash; drinking Cletus Kane's brandy at least seemed to bring him nearer to the man he meant to get revenge on.

Jed, unaware of Woodson's thoughts, rambled on. "We have a good and active church here, and a school that will improve as time goes on. Just now it's taught by some of the mothers, but one day we'll have our own full-time schoolmarm. A lot of good things are taking shape here. Through the church. Nancy is president of the Medicine Springs Ladies' Culture League. They are trying to get a town band started, among other cultural and uplifting things. As soon as the school gets going good there are plans to start a town library in a small way. Good things are happening. This fall, as soon as the weather can be depended on, we've contacted a traveling players' group to give some performances here. That's quite a bit of progress for little Medicine Springs."

Woodson sipped his drink and eased into a russet-covered horsehair sofa with an ornate and curved walnut frame. He looked around him. The Parker adobe home was ample and nicely furnished, but not pretentious. The place felt like a home.

"We're expecting someone from the theatrical troupe through here any day now to meet with Nancy and make plans for several performances in the fall."

"Uh-huh." Woodson was only half interested that Kane's town was going to put on a play. "I've a favor to ask of you, Jed."

"Anything anytime, my good friend."

"You worked in Berdan awhile."

"That I did."

"And got well acquainted."

"As well as any public servant could."

"You remember the banker there? The name escapes me."

"Bell. Vaughn Bell."

"That's it. Vaughn Bell. A big man, wasn't he?"

"Taller and broader than most. And a streak of decency in him as big as he was."

"I had three hundred dollars with him before I left. Now I need that money. But I don't want to have to ride all the way there to get it. I could wire for it and get a letter of credit here, but I'll need some verification, I'm sure, particularly since everyone in Berdan thinks I'm dead."

"You want me to wire Vaughn a verification?"

"Would you mind?"

"I'll attend to it first thing in the morning."

"And I'd prefer you keep my financial standing confidential."

"We've shared secrets before, Frank. Did I ever let you down?"

"That wasn't the point. It will be a favor to me if it doesn't become public knowledge."

"Say no more. Well, Frank, what do you think of her?"

"Nancy?"

"Well, yes, but I was thinking more of Cindy."

"You both are marvelous parents for her. Since God, or somebody, decreed that she would not grow up as my child, I'm glad she's with you. It's awfully strange, Jed. A strange feeling. Until two days ago I didn't know she existed. I can't say it's love, but already I do feel a strange, close bond with her. Your other children are beautiful, and I'd like to get to know them better as long as I'm here. But there is something special about Cindy. And like you, I mean to see her protected from the truth as long as it's necessary, and to shield her from nasty gossip."

The little girl in question burst into the room from the kitchen carrying a bowl of steaming food. "Supper's ready, Poppy and Mr. Woodson. Come to the table." Her voice was eager. From across the room the supper table beckoned, bathed in soft light from an ornate china and brass hurricane lamp suspended on delicate chains. Woodson gulped the last swallow of his brandy, truly enjoying its rich, mellow flavor, and looked at Jed.

"The festive board is spread. Our long-lost friend's homecoming dinner. Glad to have you back with us, Frank." His voice had an appropriate gaiety and joy. Jed was obviously pleased that Woodson was back, despite all the complications that his homecoming presented.

"I'm glad to be here," he said. Quietly, inside him, Woodson vowed to do everything possible to avoid harming Jed and the Parker family in his plot to bring down Cletus Kane. He might be the instrument of Kane's undoing, but it would be Kane himself and his guilt that would bring it about.

Cynthia slid her bowl onto the table as Tuck came in carrying some of the things for the supper. Nancy was right behind him with a large serving tureen from which vapors of steam and the rich aroma of well-cooked roast beef curled. Amy, too, carried something—a platter of sliced, fresh-baked bread. That delicious smell also came strongly to Woodson's nose.

"Mr. Woodson, you are to sit here," Cynthia said, indicating a place at the opposite end of the table from the armed chair reserved for the head of the household.

"It would be all right, Cindy, if you called him Uncle Frank," Nancy said. "Wouldn't it, Frank?"

"Nothing would pleasure me more."

Cindy looked at him, delight showing in her eyes. "Then you sit here, Uncle Frank. Poppy, would it be all right if just for tonight I sat beside Uncle Frank?"

Woodson saw a glance dart between Jed and Nancy. It was one of disguised pleasure. "I think that would be fine, my darling," her mother said. "Jed, would you ask the blessing?"

⇒ 17 ⇐

The meal was a delight to Woodson. The table conversation was given over to small talk, the adults wisely steering away from the topic closest to their minds, the ordeal of Frank Woodson. They talked about the monstrous weather since Jed had come back from the Two Bears' pursuit. Woodson quietly let that one alone. They talked about the children, with each of the kids being involved in the conversation in a small way. It was evident to Woodson that the Parkers didn't believe the old axiom that children should be seen and not heard.

Jed and Nancy seemed to respect their children's right to independence and individuality. Cynthia, as well as Tuck and Amy, knew this, but none of them dominated the supper table discussion, threw tantrums, or spoke loudly. In the same regard, the parents did not preach, coach, nor scold the youngsters about table manners in front of their guest. Maybe that went on at other times, he thought, but not now.

Woodson's respect grew for Jed and Nancy's handling of their brood. Even when little Tuck dropped an oversized bite of potato loaded with gravy down the front of him, Nancy was quietly strict. Tuck was allowed to get down and get the dropped morsel, take it to the kitchen, and clean himself up before returning to the table. The lad was not made to feel guilty or unduly punished for this infraction of table manners. His own embarrassment was enough. Jed and Nancy acted as though this was part of being a child and growing up. The attitude seemed to be that such things happened, so why make a fuss?

Through the brief, well-handled experience little Tuck learned and grew. He'd obviously be more careful the next time and not take such a big bite.

Frank found himself growing envious of Jed and Nancy's family and their experience of learning and growing with their young children. He wondered when, if ever, the circumstances of his life would put him in this kind of a situation. Ah, well, he thought, in time, in time.

Cynthia sat close to Woodson, speaking to him as "Uncle Frank." Though she didn't fawn over the guest she was allowed to address as uncle, the child was attentive and interested in him. Woodson tried with all his might to keep from studying her every movement and adoring the beautiful person this little child of his was becoming. His life suddenly had a strange—and bewildering—new dimension.

The meal over, Nancy and the children cleared the table and disappeared into the kitchen to clean up. While Jed went for his decanter of brandy and their glasses and his box of cigars, Woodson against studied the pleasant home they had established. The walls had been plastered and whitewashed, giving the main living room, at least, a clean, bright look. There were a few pictures and splashes of color here and there. Clean lace curtains at the windows added a homey touch. He imagined the rest of the house must have this same well-cared-for appearance.

His attention was attracted to the kitchen doorway. Although he couldn't see Nancy and the children at their chores, the impish face of Tuck Parker appeared around the door frame, grinning at him. Woodson caught the boy's eye and grinned back. Tuck giggled and disappeared. He was quickly back again like a fly on a slice of bread. Woodson purposely ignored him, watching the boy out of the corner of his eye.

Abruptly he swung his look at Tuck and stared at him intently, going along with the little boy's game. Tuck's glee was a peal of childish laughter as again he darted out of sight into the kitchen. Woodson ignored him longer this time, purposely directing his attention to the room he was in. When he swung his gaze back at Tuck the little fellow was nearly beside himself with anticipation. Woodson grinned and pointed a finger at Tuck, whose gales of compulsive laughter now filled the house as he darted away. Woodson was delighted.

Jed came back, carrying their glasses of brandy and his box of cigars. "You got to watch that Tuck," he said. "He's a bad actor."

"He's a marvelous kid, Jed. All of them are. I can't get over it. Your whole family is a delight."

"I claim no credit. Nancy's the one. I'm gone so much. When I'm here I do whatever I can to support her in raising the kids. Cigar?"

"I guess." Woodson took a cigar from which Jed had clipped the end, as well as a big wooden lucifer match with a blue head. He scratched the match on his boot sole, and the air around him filled with the strong odor of sulfur. He touched the fire to his cigar, driving away the sulfur fumes with tobacco smoke. He didn't smoke anymore, but the cigar added to the mellow feeling he had with a full stomach of fine food and being here with people he really loved after all. He swirled the brandy in his glass and took a sip of the fine stuff, alternating it with puffs on the cigar. Jed sat down. "Well, by God, friend, it's good to have you here. So good."

Woodson figured the kitchen work must have been nearly done when little Amy flounced in and quietly crawled into Jed's lap. The little girl was sleepy and merely lay totally relaxed in Jed's strong arms, regarding Woodson solemnly.

"It's getting close to your bedtime, young lady," her father said.

"Yes, Poppy. In a few minutes."

"All right. When Mommy says."

"I will, Poppy."

Cynthia and Tuck came in, followed by Nancy. She was flushed from her work of cleaning up after the meal and directing the children in their chores. She radiated happiness and contentment in her home, her husband, and her little brood. It hit Woodson suddenly that perhaps she was happier than she might have been with him; there was no way of knowing. At least he was consoled that despite all that had happened, Nancy had coped with it and, indeed, had found the happiness she so richly deserved.

"Bedtime for the little folks," Jed said, and there was quiet authority in his voice. "Cindy, Amy, Tuck, say goodnight to Uncle Frank."

The children came to him, saying goodnight and

looking into his eyes. There was such innocence there, he thought. How soon they'd learn the viciousness and brutality that existed in that big outside world away from this strong sanctuary of home and family. But with Nancy and Jed's upbringing, these three would be ready for it.

Cynthia was tall enough to get on tiptoes to give him a goodnight peck on the cheek as he sat at the table. He was glad he'd shaved in Wong Chun's emporium before coming out to the Parkers'. The brush of her little lips against his cheek was delightful and meaningful. He sensed the fullness of some kind of joy coming into his chest again. He caught Nancy's eyes as Cynthia stepped away from his chair. There was a pleasure in Nan's expression that Cynthia had gotten on so well with her natural father in this brief evening of being together.

"It's still warm tonight, so I won't have to tuck you in," she said as the three skittered for their sleeping rooms. "I'll be in in a few minutes to say goodnight and hear your prayers."

"All right, Mommy," Cynthia said as they finished kissing their father goodnight.

"How long do you think this hot spell will last, Jed?" Woodson asked after the youngsters had gone.

"I give it five days total, if I know this country at this time of year."

"Sure glad to hear that. Ought to break then in a day or so."

"You can depend on it. Then it'll be good for a week, maybe two, maybe longer. Then we're due for some storms. Seems to work that way."

"Rain?"

"And wind. In this country at this time of year we get real gully-washers."

"Not a good time to camp in a draw, I take it."

"Not unless you're overdue for one hell of a bath."

"You don't have to go soon, do you, Frank?" Nancy asked. "I'd like the children to get settled. I've so much to ask you."

"Little pitchers have big ears, is that what you mean?" Woodson grinned at Mrs. Parker.

"That's just what I mean. Excuse me. I'll go hurry them along."

With Nancy gone Woodson turned to Jed. "It's been awfully good being with you and Nancy tonight, old friend."

"The pleasure was ours in having you, Frank. Remember, now that you're back, this is your home, too. You're welcome anytime."

"What if I decide to stay in Medicine Springs?"

"Nothing would please me more."

Even as he heard Jed's words of assurance Woodson sensed a reserve in them.

"Are you sure?"

"Are you really thinking of staying?"

"For a while, anyway. That money I spoke of. I'm thinking of getting some property here. A ranch."

"You could do worse. This is a fine valley."

"I know ranching. Heaven knows I've done enough in the past two years. I've seen some places that were run well, and a lot more that weren't."

"There's only one thing that disturbs me about it, Frank. Anybody that comes in has to know that he'll be dealing with Cletus Kane."

"I figured on that. I reckon I'll be dealing with him

soon enough. Do you know of any places that might make a good start?"

"Some get tired of bucking what they call the Kane machine. There may be one or two around. Really, before you spend a lot of money here, Frank, you ought to get to know Mr. Kane and the way he does business. It might not be the absolute right place for you."

"You suggesting you might think twice about having me here permanently?"

"That's not it and you know it, Frank. It's just that people here have to learn to deal with Mr. Kane. He calls the tune, and I just don't know if you'd like his brand of music."

"I'm prepared to take that chance."

"Three hundred dollars won't buy much. Land, maybe, but not breeding stock and buildings and fencing and such."

"My partner's got money, too."

"Partner?"

"O'Fallon. Tommy O'Fallon. The man I ride with."

"O'Fallon? I thought you rode with that Harris."

"Until we got the lay of the land here we decided to use other names. You remember I called myself Kelso."

"Because you didn't want to reveal yourself to me too soon. I can understand that. But what's this O'Fallon hiding?"

"It was strictly my doing. When Hannibal Wheatley enlisted us for your posse and asked our names, I simply said Kelso and added Harris for Tommy."

Parker's instinct as a lawman surfaced. "Is there something you're not telling me, Frank?"

"Not really. I'll tell you just about anything you

want to know. There are some things about the last ten years I'd just as soon forget."

"I mean about this O'Fallon."

"You ever heard that name before?" Now, Woodson suddenly realized, he'd find out how really close Jed Parker was to Cletus Kane.

"Not that I'd recall. Is it on a Wanted poster?"

Jed came up with a passing mark; he certainly didn't know about Kane's past. That's it, Woodson thought. Give a lawman an alias, and the wanted man suspicion rears up. "If you find it, let me know. I'm preparing to go into business with the man."

Jed smiled. "All right."

"What's all right?" Nancy spoke as she re-entered the room, closing the hall door.

"Man talk," Jed told her.

"Well, I'm ready to sit down and talk with Frank. You men want anything? There's still some coffee."

"Sit down, hon," Jed said. "Frank and I are having our brandies."

"Jed said you told him you'd been in prison, Frank. How positively awful. And you weren't allowed to write any letters."

"Like I told Jed, the deal was I could write if I told them where I hid the money. I could hardly do that, so they kept me . . . I think the word is 'incommunicado.' "

Jed got up and refilled Woodson's glass as he began to relate the long, sad story to the woman he was returning to that tragic day nine years before. Conveniently, he left out any suspicion of Cletus Kane and their resemblance. He let it go that as a lone rider in the country of the robbery he seemed to fit what the posse was looking for. His wages from the cattle drive, he said, composed the circumstantial evidence that pinned him to the robbery as far as the jury was concerned.

He dispensed with the details of the seven-year stretch behind bars as easily as he could, not wanting to bring Jed and Nancy further anguish. He told them of his two years as a drifter and the lone hand he had played, as well as the bitterness he'd experienced in those early months until he met Hughie Kelso. He spoke of that tragic loss of the one man who had truly befriended him and whom he had come to trust. It was Hughie, he told them, who really started to bring him out of the hard shell that he had grown around him during the prison years.

He tried to stick as close to the truth as possible, avoiding Vern Griffin's remarks about the close resemblance Frank Woodson bore to Cletus Kane. His story was about as straight as he could tell it without getting into that. In the wake of Hughie's death he couldn't bear any longer to work on the Ham Tyson spread, and so he rode away, drifting down to Medicine Springs. He did tell Nancy about seeing her at a distance on the street, being enlisted for the posse, and putting two and two together about Jed and Nancy Parker.

"I could see the night of the meeting at the church that Jed had his hands full and would have for several days. It seemed hardly the time nor the place to come back from the grave," he said. "I thought it was just as well, too, that I rode with Wheatley's division."

Jed grinned. "If you'd come forward about then, it would have been a hard complication to handle," Jed said. "I think you picked the right time and place. I was surely disappointed that even following that hot lead didn't turn up anything. I was so sure I was just about to nab the two of them."

"Will you go out again after Two Bear, Jed?" Frank asked.

"I doubt it. Mr. Kane is well satisfied that the Indian has finally left these parts. Mr. Kane just can't let people go riding out of this valley driving off Kane cattle, that's all. Let one get away with it, and they'd all try it."

So that's it, Woodson thought. Hang the Indian and strike terror into the hearts of everyone in the valley. An object lesson, he thought they called it.

"Hannibal and you fellows who went up the main pass didn't find anything. We found sign of two horses belonging to someone running about twenty head, and all the signs were that they were traveling at about the right time to be Two Bear and his girl. We sent a courier to Hannibal and started out. The trail went cold about the time the sun heated up good and proper. There was nothing left but to turn back. That's when you came in."

Jed grew thoughtful. He picked up his brandy glass and took a sip. He looked at his cigar and, seeing that it had gone out, thought better of relighting it and put it back in the saucer he was using to hold the ashes.

"But that's not why we're together. To talk about the sheriffing job in this valley. We've still got ten years of catching up to do."

Woodson looked at Nancy. "Well," she said, glancing at Woodson, but with a faraway look, "Jed knows what we felt for each other, Frank, and how Cindy came about."

"We've no secrets, Frank," Jed added. "It had to be that way."

"God, I'm so sorry for all the grief I've caused both of you."

"None of us had anything to do with it, Frank," Jed said. "Really, it was that hardcase who actually held up the stage that you got blamed for. That's the one I'd like to throw a loop around!"

Woodson kept quiet. It was hardly appropriate to talk of suspicions at this point. If Jed only knew, he thought.

"Jed was so kind in those first years," Nancy said. "The people in Berdan never quite understood my having Frank Woodson's child. Everybody knew. It was difficult, even with those who said they understood. Still, it was never quite the same for me."

Jed spoke up. "I've told you most of that, Frank. My trip to Montana and back trying to find you, or some trace of you. I was through in Abilene. When I got back I'd gotten close to the Merrills in our common concern for you. Hell, I didn't plan it that way. Because of the baby the Merrills lost a bit of esteem around there. Not much, but enough to be noticeable. I had a pretty good record from Abilene, and when I got back there was a lawkeeping job in Berdan if I wanted it. I decided I wanted it."

"Jed was there when we needed him, Frank," Nancy said. "Dad liked him, and they talked. Constantly. Mother seemed to transfer the love she felt for you to Jed. She was always after him about dressing warmly and getting enough sleep, and worrying that he might take a bullet or something."

"Dear Amy." Woodson sighed, remembering the pudgy white-haired woman that he, too, had come to love.

"In two years it was totally apparent that you

weren't coming back. For whatever reason. We never once thought you might be in prison, did we, Jed? In time Jed's proposal of marriage seemed to be the most natural thing in the world. I'd come to love him as much as Mom and Dad had."

Woodson sensed the fullness coming into his chest again.

"And in doing it, Jed, old pard, you gave that child a name and a chance for a decent life. For that one I'd take any bullet intended for you."

A long silence reigned at the Parkers' dinner table.

❧ 18 ❧

This time when they rode into Two Bear's camp, Woodson and O'Fallon approached it boldly, talking loudly, hoping to alert the old Indian and his daughter. They made it all the way to the rope gate at the open end of the box canyon, and still they had seen neither Two Bear nor Helen.

The scene before them was much the same as it had been more than a week before when they were here supposedly upholding the law. The small herd of cattle grazed, scattered over the grassy apron below the sheer face of the canyon end. The great granitic cliff towered upward as though trued up by a carpenter's square.

This time the Two Bears' saddle horses and pack animal mingled with the cows.

Woodson got down and untied the rope gate. O'Fallon led Woodson's horse through and toward the shade of the trees. Woodson retied the rope and strode to where O'Fallon was securing the horses.

"What do you make of it, Frankie?" O'Fallon said. "They're not here."

"They're here."

"If they are, they can't be far."

John Two Bear materialized out of the brush at the base of the canyon across from them. Helen stepped out of a similar dense copse at the head end of the canyon. Both carried their guns and had concealed themselves at right angles to each other. This way, if there had been gunplay, they wouldn't catch themselves in their own crossfire.

"Mr. Woodson, Mr. O'Fallon," Helen called cheerily, sounding relieved and happy to see them. Her voice—to Woodson—carried the silver tinkle of a songbird.

"Hello, Helen!" Woodson called. "John! Good to see you."

John Two Bear cradled his big Sharps rifle easily in his arms as he came up to them, smiling, radiating pleasure at their return. "Good to see you." There was warmth in his words and assurance in his lithe movements. Woodson felt better that it was all working out as he and Tommy had planned. "We heard you coming up the arroyo. Voices carry well in this canyon. I went to see, though. I was practically beside you the last quarter mile. I still must be on my guard, even with you."

Frank and Tommy grinned at each other. "Told you we couldn't sneak in here under that unerring rifle," Woodson said, grinning at his companion. "Has it gone well for you, John?"

"The heat was bad. I hunted small game to keep us in meat. Meat and water's about all we had. Also some plants most white men don't know about that are good for you. Usually, though, they taste awful!" Two Bear grinned again at the visitors.

"You're getting on to the white man's ways, John," O'Fallon quipped. "Can't stand Indian grub anymore."

"We've gotten along fine," Helen said, her eyes locked on Woodson, as though reporting only to him. He was struck by the brightness of her eyes and by the freshness of the skin of her cheeks. The yearnings he had known the first time he'd seen her surged into him again.

"We brought plenty of food from town," he assured her. "Some beans and other things in airtights. Fresh vegetables. Coffee. We've got bacon and flapjack flour for in the morning. Brought some beef with us, thinking you probably hadn't butchered any of 'Mr. Kane's cows.'"

Helen smiled at him, understanding his reference and enjoying the light banter that surrounded and brightened the welcome return of Woodson and O'Fallon.

"We've a couple of loaves of good bread, and in a tin box on Tommy's horse there's a fresh-baked apple pie."

"I'll have the pie first," Two Bear said, grinning; the wry amusement Woodson saw in John's face assured him that Two Bear found ease and comfort in his new friends, a closeness growing among all of them. A strange and free urging that Woodson felt told him that his attraction to Helen had much to do with his own feelings. If he had started to crack through a shell built up over seven years behind prison walls, her appearance in his life pried it open more. Though reality dictated guarded behavior, Helen somehow renewed a youthful zest he had abandoned at the gates of the jail. Accepting his responsibility for little Cynthia and the Parkers' unreserved forgiveness lessened his burden of guilt and allowed him to begin to give his feelings free rein.

"We've much to report," O'Fallon said. "Figured the best way would be over a fine meal. Me and Frankie'll fix it."

Two Bear glanced at his daughter. She got his message and spoke—though she really hadn't needed her father's prodding look. "If you unpack it, I'll make supper. You men need to talk," she said, still reserving her eyes for Frank Woodson.

"We thank you for bringing food," Two Bear said. "Helen is right. You are guests in our camp. If we don't have the food ourselves to feed you, we can at least make the meal from yours."

"Fair enough," O'Fallon cheered. Frank got busy rooting around in their saddlebags and packs for the food they'd brought.

"Do you ever take a wee nip o' the auld monsturr, John?" Realizing he might be misunderstood, O'Fallon added, "Whiskey?"

"Not often, but I have been known to. This is a good time, if you have some. Unfortunately, I have none."

"We got plenty."

"Let's sit over here in the shade," Two Bear said.

Woodson gave Helen a hand getting the food to their campsite, feeling good and comfortable with her now. Being near her sent old familiar cravings creeping into him, making themselves known in small stirrings in his chest—and in his loins.

Not far away O'Fallon unlimbered his flask and handed it to Two Bear as the two of them settled under a spreading cottonwood. "I don't drink much of the stuff," Two Bear said. "A bit before supper with friends, though, surely makes everything brighter."

He took a small sip, ground his sleeve against the bottle top, and handed it to O'Fallon. Woodson mumbled something awkwardly to Helen about letting her get to her work but to call him if she needed help. He joined the Indian and the Irishman and took the flask for a short draw. After the several hours' trip up through the pass and across the desert, the sip of O'Fallon's fine whiskey was bracing.

Feeling good about himself and about the release of some of his insecurities around women, and especially with Helen Two Bear, he glanced at her, busy with her chores. O'Fallon and Two Bear made small talk he chimed in on occasionally. He found himself sneaking glances at Helen as she worked. She moved about with a grace that heightened the beauty he saw in her. Woodson sensed that the food she prepared, even over the open fire in these rude surroundings, would have all the makings of a feast. Her touch, he thought, would improve anything.

"You say you have news?" Two Bear asked.

"In-dayd," O'Fallon responded. Woodson noted that most of the time Tommy spoke like a native-born American. Now and again, though, the broad pronunciations characteristic of the Irish came through. "Where do we start, Frankie?"

Woodson glanced at Helen; she was close enough to hear the conversation—and needed to. "In the beginning. What happened after we left here."

" 'Twould be wrong of me to make light of Frank's friend, Sheriff Parker. . . ."

Two Bear turned his gaze to stare into Woodson's

eyes as if to plumb his feelings; what, the look seemed to say, were Woodson's loyalties to Kane's sheriff— the man who posed a real threat to himself and his daughter?

"Maybe under other circumstances it would be something to laugh about," Woodson said, trying to reassure Two Bear. "They hustled us over west—miles from here—the morning after we were here with you. Some of Jed Parker's division found what looked like positive sign of you and went galloping off on a real wild-goose chase. Tommy and I were happy that it took the search away from around here." He looked at Helen to make sure she was listening as she moved about the fire and her chores with skill and ease.

"That was pretty much it, John," O'Fallon added. "The sign played out about the same time as the men and the horses. The heat started to come up, and they lit a shuck for town to get out of it. Back to the cool places and the thirst-quenchers."

"You've talked with your friend, Sheriff Parker, Mr. Woodson?" Two Bear asked.

"Drop the 'Mr. Woodson,' John. Make it Frank."

Two Bear grinned broadly. "All right . . . Frank."

"And I'm Tommy," O'Fallon said.

John's grin flashed again. "Proud to know you, Tommy."

"Yeah, I saw Parker," Woodson said. "Talked to him first on the trail after the posse gave up the ghost. Later I went to his home. Saw his wife and family. We had a fine evening."

"Forgive me for saying it, Frank," Two Bear said. "I don't mean to insult your friendship with Sheriff Parker. In my eyes he bears watching. He is at Kane's beck and call, has been for many years. I won't tell you how to live, but my life and my daughter's life are in danger from those men. Forgive me if I don't share your feelings for Mr. Parker."

"It's a sticky situation to be sure, John. Tommy and I are trying to handle things in your best interests ... and Jed's."

"I have seen you twice now, Frank. I believe I can rely on your judgment. But be careful."

"Thanks. My quarrel is with Kane, not Jed. Somehow I'll keep it that way."

"The best is yet to come, John," O'Fallon said. "Frankie and me pooled our resources. Gone into partnership, you might say."

"I ... don't understand," Two Bear said.

" 'Twas our life savings. But it will turn out to be worth it. It was nigh nine hundred dollars together. Do you know the old Hollingsworth place far out in the southeast quadrant of the Medicine Springs valley?"

"I sure do. Hollingsworth died two years ago. A brother, I think, in England, was left the property. Six hundred acres or thereabout. Damned near a section. The brother's done nothing with it. It's laid fallow since. A good basic house on the land. A barn and some corrals. But now they need work."

"Would you be interested in helping fix up the place?"

"Again I don't understand, Tommy. I'm a fugitive from the law in Medicine Springs. How could I possibly have any interest in the Hollingsworth place?"

"Because, my good friend," O'Fallon said, looking at Woodson as if for permission, "it's not the Hollingsworth place anymore. It's the Circle TW Ranch."

"I don't know that name. That brand. And what's this got to do with me?"

Woodson now chimed in. "The T in Circle TW stands for Two Bear. The circle is the O in O'Fallon, and the W for Woodson."

"But ..." Two Bear protested, questions in his dark eyes.

"Let me tell you. You'll handle your side of the partnership by managing the ranch for us. It'll be your place. Six hundred acres is a good spread. When all this current fuss is over, if Tommy and I decide to stay, there's plenty of room for us to build places of our own. Otherwise you can manage it, and wherever Tommy and I are, you can send us our rightful thirds."

By now Helen was devoting only about half her attention to the meal. She listened intently. There was a sparkle of great interest in her eyes. And one of spunk. In no way had she relished being run off their land. This now seemed to be a chance to fight back; her anticipation was mounting by the minute. Woodson was suddenly glad it was working out this way. If he pulled it off—if they pulled it off—he'd be close to Helen Two Bear, and the prospect didn't displease him one bit. Seeing Nancy Merrill as Jed Parker's wife had somehow released him to take a new interest in women.

"It's risky, sure," Woodson said. "You know that Tommy and I are here because Kane all but destroyed our lives years ago. We have no way of knowing how he'll react."

"But we're figuring to be right square with the man," O'Fallon said. "We've got the Hollingsworth place all properly deeded and recorded. Kane can't touch us on that. Our prospective brand, too, is registered."

"When we're ready—and we're here to see if you're interested or not—we take the cattle, and you and Helen, and go straight to Kane. Right up to his front door."

"You make a clean breast of it with him, John. Right there at the moment of his greatest surprise. By this time he probably knows we're here and has an idea who Frank Woodson and Tommy O'Fallon are. But he can't make a move against us without having to reveal to someone why or how he knows."

"And he can't very well do that," Woodson said. "Jed Parker, I think, would side with me completely if he learned that Kane was responsible for putting me behind bars. But I don't want that to happen. I'm hoping Kane will trip himself up."

"And there's the murder of me dear brothurr, the sainted Paddy O'Fallon."

"You go to Kane with your hat in your hand. Tell him it was all a great misunderstanding on your part. You truly meant to leave the land he claims is his. You no longer contest it. If he feels the cattle are justly his, then here they are. You clearly confess to having made a mistake, and you ask him to forgive you."

"But I didn't make any mistakes."

"Of course you didn't. You may have to lie a little. Swallow a bit of your pride. Are you going to let ten measly steers stand in the way of your becoming a respected citizen of Medicine Springs again, or of keeping you off the fugitive trail? Very soon they'll probably mount another posse and get back to hunting you down for a hanging. The heat was the only thing that held them back before."

"Kane's going to be careful the way he handles me and Frankie," O'Fallon said. "As we see it, he'll have to do the politic thing and drop the charges against you. If you're on our place as ramrod, you'll have our personal protection. I'm telling you that Kane'll walk mighty lightly where me and Frankie are concerned until he can figure what our game is."

"I think you put too much faith in a man of Kane's nature," Two Bear said.

"He's got too much at stake in Medicine Springs to act rashly," Woodson said. "Our necks—mine and Tommy's—are more in the noose, really, than yours. All he wanted before was to have you out of his hair, to insult and humiliate you. When it dawns on him who we are, his only instinct will be to see us dead."

"Trust us, Two Bear," O'Fallon said.

✦ 19 ✦

The Kane mansion was a pale blue and stark white towering two-story frame palace of gingerbread, scallops of fish-scale shingle siding strangely out of context in this ocean of rolling grass. Kane held title to miles and vast miles of rangeland surrounding his place, oddly isolating himself within its boundaries. The place had a huge barn and adjacent corrals cleverly hidden downslope from the house and shielded by it from the approaching road.

With John and Helen Two Bear riding point, and Woodson and O'Fallon at drag, the small queue of cows plodded obediently up the lane toward Cletus Kane's mansion.

Despite everything he had told himself about the sure ground he was on, Woodson felt his heart in his throat as he and O'Fallon attempted the first move to confront Kane directly on his own ground. "Bearding the lion in his den" was the way he had put it to O'Fallon days before.

Kane's place was fenced for about an acre in horizontal white-painted planking, the grass inside it cultured and somehow cropped short. Kane had had a few trees planted around his large yard, but they appeared stunted and slow-growing as they struggled for survival. Beside Kane's front gate stood a small cast-iron statue of a black livery boy, one hand extended, holding a ring to which to tie up the reins of a visiting buggy or wagon. At the north side of the house, the part that would almost always be in the shade, a long hitch rail had been set for the horses of Kane's visitors.

Woodson noted with a spear of shock that one horse was tied beside the house. It belonged to Jed Parker. He hadn't anticipated this.

He was in too far to turn back. Surely the approach of this large bunch of men and animals had already been seen from the house. They circled up the stock on a gradual hillside below the front fence. While Woodson and O'Fallon and Helen rode slowly around the cattle, John Two Bear, his face tight with apprehension, broke from the group and rode to Kane's front gate. He tied his horse to the statue's ring and headed up the flagstone walk toward Kane's veranda. It was shaded by a broad and long overhang roof and supported by tall pillars attractively turned and fluted, enhanced by intricate white-painted fretwork.

Two Bear had been anticipated. Cletus Kane came out through the front door that was ornate with geometric glass designs in the upper half. Jed Parker appeared behind him.

It was but a short distance to where Frank Woodson sat his horse and watched the developing scene, keeping another eye on the stock. Jed's eyes met his, and there was question and a hint of resentment in Jed's expression. Kane only surveyed the scene and the big Indian approaching him with amazement.

So this is Cletus Kane, Woodson thought. There was a resemblance between them, but at this distance, Woodson thought, the similarity was a strained one. Kane's hairline and hair and skin coloring were about the same, as was height and breadth of shoulders. Not much more. He couldn't make out Kane's scarred eyebrow. If anything, Kane was the heavier of the two.

Kane had his trousers tucked into his boot tops. He wore a deep blue and elaborately brocaded smoking jacket, the material glistening in the midmorning sunlight. The jacket had wide plush velvet lapels in a rich russet color, the jacket secured at the waist by a tasseled blue belt of the same brocaded material and looped casually at the front. Kane smoked a cheroot much like the one Woodson had smoked at the Parker home. Kane was well-groomed.

As Two Bear approached the pair standing at the edge of the veranda Kane waved a small gesture at Parker, slightly behind him, indicating that he would handle it.

"John Two Bear," Kane called in a voice that sounded nothing at all like Woodson's. "What is the meaning of this?" His words had an accusing tone.

"An apology, Mr. Kane," Two Bear said, playing out the script he had rehearsed with Woodson and O'Fallon. "There's been a misunderstanding. I come only to return the cattle that are rightly yours."

"But you rustled them, knowing full well they were mine."

"A misunderstanding, sir. It was not my intention to leave with anything that did not belong to me. These men with me, Mr. Woodson and Mr. O'Fallon, found me and explained that I was being hunted as a fugitive."

Woodson had been watching Kane, who visibly tightened with the names. He had no way of knowing Jed might already have told Kane, or what Kane knew about his and O'Fallon's purchase of the Hollingsworth spread.

"I'm sorry, Mr. Kane," Two Bear said, "for having spoken harshly to you some time back." Woodson knew this statement was a truly tough one for the Indian to make. "I ask your forgiveness. I relinquish all claim to the land I was on, and to these cattle. I return them to you hoping you will understand that my actions were not intended to break the law. I hope that you—and Mr. Parker—may understand and forgive me."

It was clear that Kane didn't know which way to step. He looked at the small herd of cattle milling practically on his doorstep, and at the three riders keeping them in check. His eyes, particularly, centered first on Woodson and then on O'Fallon, wondering at their motives in being there. He knows why we're here, Woodson thought. It's just that he doesn't know what he's going to do about it.

"This is highly irregular," Kane said, making a grand understatement, in Woodson's opinion. The whole thing was going to turn out to be irregular in Kane's scheme of things, he thought. "Are you giving yourself up? You know there is a warrant for your arrest."

Two Bear was alert and clever. "I had hoped that by coming to you and explaining as I have and returning the cattle that the charges against me and my daughter could be dropped."

Kane was confused and at this moment of confrontation was not willing to show any weakness by confer-
ring with Parker on the legality or the implications of
all this. He was handling this one himself, and it was
clear to Woodson that enough questions were spinning
around in Kane's head that he didn't want to act im-
pulsively. Yet action, right now, was called for. Still
Kane equivocated.

"Leave the cattle here," he said. "I'll have my men
take care of them. Where will you be, Two Bear?
We'll have to see what is to be done."

Two Bear responded as if on cue from Woodson
and O'Fallon. "My daughter and my friends and I will
be at the old Hollingsworth place."

"I knew they'd be there, but not you," Kane said.

"He's with us," Woodson called across the short
distance. Jed Parker was regarding his old friend
coldly. Woodson shrank a little inside. He was putting
Jed on the spot. The time was fast approaching when
Jed might have to decide between Kane and Woodson, and Woodson had truly hoped to handle it without putting Jed in that position. He owed him better
treatment than that. Still, there was that old score to
settle with Kane—for both his and Tommy O'Fallon's sakes.

"We will be in touch," Kane said, eyeing Woodson
with suspicion. That, as far as he was concerned, finished it. He pivoted, veered around Parker, standing
behind him, and disappeared through his front door.
Parker took another look at Two Bear, the cattle, and
the three riders and turned to follow Kane. "Come
on, John," O'Fallon called. "Our work here is done."

They were a half mile down the road and still hadn't
recovered enough to talk of their reactions when

Helen yelled at Woodson that they were being followed. Woodson turned back to see Jed Parker coming after them at a fast gallop.

"You ride on," he called to the others. "I'll catch
up. Head on over to the place. First thing we've got
to do there is make it reasonably livable." O'Fallon
touched his hat brim in acknowledgment and turned
to ride on as Woodson suggested, Two Bear urging
his horse alongside Tommy's. Helen paused. She was
near Woodson.

"Be careful, Frank," she said.

Woodson smiled at the concerned tone of her
words. There was sincerity in it. But maybe something
more than sincerity. Call it deep personal concern,
Woodson thought. Her attention gratified him.

"I appreciate your concern, Helen," he said. "Don't
worry. Jed's an old friend. Nothing will happen. Go
ahead with your father. I'll see you at the place." She
was close enough on her horse that he could reach
across and grip her hands, clutching the reins against
the saddlehorn.

A look passed between them that spoke volumes.
Woodson was suddenly aware within himself that he'd
pull off everything exactly as planned—or hoped. But
now, almost abruptly, there was another motive, another dimension to all this: Helen Two Bear.

He swung his horse around to ride out to meet the
fast-approaching Jed Parker, feeling a new glow of
resolve. Jed's face was knotted with questions as he
rode up. It was flushed with anxiety and frustration.

"Frank, what in God's name are you doing?!"

"Helping Two Bear clear his name. Anything wrong
in that?"

"Whatever you're doing is all wrong. Mr. Kane is

furious. And I don't know why. Maybe you're moving too fast in this country. I don't know. I'm confused about Mr. Kane's behavior. You've been here a few short days. Already you and your friend have bought land and have put yourselves smack-dab in the middle of a local squabble. There's something about all this I don't understand. Some of the pieces are missing or don't fit. But why in hell are you taking sides in this?"

"You forget, Jed, that I'm no stranger to injustice."

"You found Two Bear. Or he found you. Too much there to be coincidental. And too soon. You knew where he was when you met me on the posse, didn't you?"

Woodson dropped the fat squarely into the fire. "I did."

"Mr. Kane figured that. Why, Frank, why? And why in hell didn't you tell me that day on the trail? That right there is a clear violation of the law."

"Everywhere I turned those two days, Jed, I saw nooses. I didn't think Two Bear was guilty of anything to be strung up for, and I still don't. I'm trying to help him clear his name. As a matter of fact, I was told to look for a cattle-rustling Indian. I can say in all honesty I didn't find one."

"Frank, Frank, you know so little of what goes on here in Medicine Springs. You've charged in here, and with next to no knowledge about what's going on you've sided with a known land-grabber and a rustler."

Woodson stiffened. "Jed, do you really believe that? Is that what Kane's done to you? That harmless old Indian? Come on. He was harassed into abandoning his land, land he thought was rightly his. He took cattle he had rounded up as mavericks or raised from calves. That's rustling? And by the way, there were ten, not twenty. Now, against his will, really, he's been persuaded by O'Fallon and me to turn them over to Kane and ask forgiveness. This is the hardened owlhoot you want to dangle from the nearest tree?"

"You have so little knowledge about what goes on in this valley."

"Seems I heard you tell something like that to Honus Johnson one night not long ago. Kane is the only one in this valley intelligent enough to make the decisions, is that it? And for looking after people incapable of taking care of themselves, Kane extracts what he considers his due, is that it?"

"The people in this valley owe Mr. Kane a great deal for making this a decent place to live."

"Again, something they couldn't do for themselves, I suppose. Cletus Kane, the noble protector of the downtrodden."

"Frank, you're on a collision course with serious trouble in this country. I heard—even though you yourself wouldn't come and tell me—that you'd invested in a ranch here—"

"Kane told you."

"I had to hear it from him, yes. He asked me a great deal about you. And this O'Fallon. More pieces that don't fit. I'm looking at all this through some kind of haze. At first I was delighted to hear you'd decided to stay. Pleased for Nancy's sake, too, and Cindy's. But now you drag in a common criminal, siding with him."

"We brought Two Bear back to live at the ranch and manage it for us. Tommy O'Fallon and I don't know for certain that we'll stay. It was an opportunity

for us to help Two Bear and at the same time benefit ourselves."

"Without ever consulting me. You know my position here. Frank, I tell you, I'm disturbed. You know
you could be charged with being an accessory to the
crime of rustling, or at least of obstructing justice."

"Is that what Kane plans to do?"

"Mr. Kane and I hardly had a chance to talk. I had
to get out here ... to catch up with you to find out
what was going on."

"That's what was going on. We talked Two Bear
into bringing back the cattle and asking Kane's forgiveness for any wrongdoing, intentional or otherwise."

"And set him up with a ranch."

"And set him up with a ranch, yes. As our
foreman."

"Helen Two Bear wouldn't have anything to do
with your acting this way, would she? She's a beautiful woman."

Woodson tightened at Jed's tone. "Jed, if you
weren't my friend, I might be inclined to knock you
out of the saddle for that one."

Parker neither acknowledged Woodson's remark
nor apologized for a low cut. The slight lodged uncom-
fortably somewhere deep inside Woodson.

"I better be getting back to Mr. Kane. I'll see what
I can do to get him calmed down and make the best
of this difficult turn of events."

Woodson couldn't avoid the bitter retort. "That's it.
Make it easy on yourself, Jed. I think opinion in this
valley will be on our side. Kane had better know that.
He may have done a lot of good around here in your
eyes, but there's plenty of ill will. Don't ignore the

fact that John Two Bear has friends and supporters in this valley. Let's not have a range war."

"If it comes to that, I don't want to have to ride over you to get to John Two Bear, Frank."

"If Kane gets heavy-handed, you may just have to do that, Jed."

"You put a man in a hell of a spot, Frank Woodson. Setting him up to choose between his duty and his best friend."

"I don't want it that way, Jed. I have no intention of hurting you or Nancy or any of your family. I'm only doing what an old lawman friend of mine in Abilene used to do."

"What's that?"

"Seeing that justice triumphs."

Parker's eyes told Woodson that that one cut deeply. Jed gave spur to his horse's flank, reefed him around, and headed back for the Kane ranch.

※ 20 ※

When Sheriff Parker got back to the Kane ranch his boss was, in words Jed's wife would use, fit to be tied.

With Parker in a side chair beside Kane's big mahogany desk in the sprawling front room, Kane strode up and down behind the desk, his cheroot glowing in angry puffs. He alternately shoved his hands in his pants pockets and clasped them behind his back. He often looked at the ceiling as if to find help there.

"Who the hell are these people, these friends of yours, Parker?"

Jed sensed that, under the circumstances, his words emerged almost apologetic.

"The one is Frank Woodson. He's the friend of mine. The other is a fellow named O'Fallon. Thomas I think it is. I don't know him. Never saw the man before."

"This friend of yours, did he ever go by the name of Fred Whitsun?"

"No, sir. Not that I ever heard. Why?"

Kane calmed. He seemed to be pulling back. "Nothing. I just seem to remember the name." For a moment Kane was deep in thought. "Woodson was the one you told me about in Berdan when I first met you, wasn't he?"

"Yes, sir, Mr. Kane. He didn't come back from a trail drive to Montana in 1868. He was betrothed to Nancy."

"Now he's come back from the grave, so to speak. Hmmm. You said he'd been in prison?"

"That's what he told me."

"Where'd he pick up this O'Fallon?"

"I think they rode into Medicine Springs together. I don't know when they met. Maybe worked together on some ranch. I don't know."

"Isn't it your job to know these things, Parker? What do you propose to do about them?"

"That's why I'm here, Mr. Kane. To talk about it with you. This is touchy. They seem to feel that by bringing in Two Bear to apologize and hand over the cattle that you'll see fit to have the charges dropped."

"We'll do nothing of the sort. I wonder what their game is."

"I don't think it's a game, Mr. Kane. Frank and this O'Fallon have gone into a ranching partnership. They've bought the old Hollingsworth spread fair and square. You know that. It sounds as though they are putting Two Bear in charge over there."

"I want them out of here."

"I don't understand."

"Of course you understand, Parker. I don't care how it's done. I want them out of this valley. Not only want, I demand!"

"Mr. Kane, they have every legal right—"

"Stop quarreling with me!"

"I simply don't see how it can be done."

"Well, you get busy and find out. There's got to be a legal technicality. Some loophole. The man they are putting on their payroll is still a fugitive from justice. There is still a warrant outstanding for his arrest, is there not?"

"Yes, sir, but—"

"There's your case, Parker. This Woodson and O'Fallon are accessories after the fact or accomplices to rustling. Something. As such, they are felons. They have no legal right to the Hollingsworth place. It was bought under false pretenses. It's a fraud. That ought to be enough."

"Mr. Kane, first of all, Frank Woodson is my friend. I can't do that to him. I believe he's acting in what he considers to be a just way."

"I don't care if he's got God Almighty on his side. I want something done to get him out of here. I refuse to drop the charges against that Indian. He trespassed for years on my land. That's on the record. When he left these parts he took along with him cattle he had rounded up and bred from my stock. That still makes him a rustler. Bringing them back here and asking my forgiveness was just a shabby, hollow dodge. They are trying to call my bluff. I don't bluff, Parker. I want Two Bear in jail as soon as you can get over there and serve the papers. And I want to take action to declare this Woodson and O'Fallon's purchase of the Hollingsworth spread null and void. If they choose to contest it, then I want them in a cell right along with Two Bear."

"Mr. Kane. Let's reconsider action like this—"

"We'll give Woodson and O'Fallon the choice. That's it. Get their money back to them. Tell them if they leave peaceably and don't ever come back, the charges will be dropped. Otherwise they may stay and stand trial."

"That puts me in a terrible spot, Mr. Kane. Don't you see?"

"I only see the welfare of this valley at stake. They sheltered this Two Bear knowing full well he was a fugitive. Didn't you say they had been duly deputized to serve on the posse?"

"That was the understanding, yes."

"Then it's perfectly clear. And see that you have no further truck with this Woodson yourself. Nor this O'Fallon. Send Wheatley out with your message. You're too close to all this. That's it! Let Wheatley and some other deputies go out and get Two Bear and his kid. And give the message to Woodson and O'Fallon. I want you to avoid personal involvement. Do I make myself clear, Parker?"

"Mr. Kane, I still don't understand."

"Have I made my wishes clear in this, Parker?" There was an almost feverish urgency in Kane's words, and in his manner. *I've never seen him quite this way,* Jed thought. *But I can't knuckle under. Not with Frank Woodson involved.*

He decided to try again to reason with Kane. "It's perfectly clear, Mr. Kane. But don't you see we'll be dipping our hands into a hornet's nest? I told you how Honus Johnson disrupted the posse meeting."

"You did. And I want that man out of this valley, too, if he hasn't gone already."

"There are a lot of men in this country who will side with Two Bear. And Woodson and O'Fallon."

"A collection of mere pip-squeaks. You can handle them. That's your job. That's what I pay you for. Show them your strength, Parker. Strength. Guts. They also know that we can make it tough on those who run counter to some of the policies around here."

"Mr. Kane, don't get me wrong, but just this once, let's let it roll by. Woodson and O'Fallon have bought the land, yes. As an investment. They're sympathetic to Two Bear, so they've set him and his daughter up on the land to manage it. What's the harm in that? Frank has more or less indicated to me that eventually both he and O'Fallon will ride on. They'll be . . . absentee owners. All this will calm down in good time if we don't stir it up. The cattle have been brought back. I really see no reason to pursue this issue of the rustling."

Kane stared incredulously, the raving glint still in his eyes. "I don't believe this. You've been given your orders, Parker. There's nothing more needs to be said than that you carry them out."

"I beg you to reconsider in this case, Mr. Kane. All this puts me in a very awkward position. Frank Woodson was my best friend. I can't—simply can't—be a party to seeing him dragged in like a common criminal."

Kane ignored the intensity of Parker's plea.

"You said he'd been in prison. Unjustly accused, he said. My friend, that's what they all say. He won't want to go back. Wave the prospect of going back to jail at him and he'll pull out, no question. Just do it. And by the way, your personal life is no concern of mine. If we let this Two Bear off, we will be showing our weakness to everyone in this valley. Everyone will think he can bluff us. No, Parker, the law is meant to be enforced. Bring in Two Bear to answer the charges!"

"It's much more than my personal life being involved, Mr. Kane. Sentiment is running high among the ranchers favoring John Two Bear. Despite what you or I may think, he has considerable respect."

"Among that bunch like your Honus Johnson. Pipsqueaks! Mere pip-squeaks! Johnson and his stripe are sodbusters, not heads-up cattlemen. Face up to it, Parker. We're building this valley for men, not felons and rustlers and pipsqueaks! I run this valley, and you are my enforcer. No ifs, ands, or buts. It's as simple as you getting out and doing your duty."

"Mr. Kane, there's a lot about all this I don't understand. I have some feelings that I can't put meaning to. I've been with you here better than five years and have tried always to act in the best interests of you and the people in this valley. Now I don't know. Something strange is going on. My friend Frank Woodson taking up the cause of John Two Bear. He and his friend O'Fallon. Somehow there's something that's not square about all this."

"All you have to do is your job. And I absolutely prohibit you from talking with this Woodson again. If you're doing a lot of thinking about all this, so am I. And I'm thinking this Woodson is a bad influence on your law-keeping, Parker."

"You have a reputation for being tough, Mr. Kane, but your reaction to all this puzzles me. It's not like you. It's like there's something more to it that I can't see."

Kane again drew himself up in anger. "You continue to defy me! All that's required of you is your duty."

"If I bring in John Two Bear after word gets out about what happened here this morning, some of these 'pip-squeak' ranchers, as you call them, may get up in arms."

"Oh, no, they won't! Their tallies will be called at the mercantile and at the feed store and at the mill. A few mortgage foreclosures will teach them some sense. My good man, you don't need a gun to enforce the law. A man's stomach and the welfare of his family are the greatest persuaders of all."

"Mr. Kane, economic pressure, like guns, amounts to cruel and unjust harassment. If a man is hardworking and law-abiding, that's enough. If he breaks the law, he ought to be brought in and dealt with. But punishing a man for the way he thinks, that's . . . that's . . . well, it's not fair!"

"I thought you'd been around awhile, Parker. Not much in life is fair. How long will it take for you to learn that?"

"I only know that for the first time since I've been here I'm faced with an action I can't at all agree with. Like I'm fighting with one hand tied behind my back. You're not telling me everything, and I don't think Frank Woodson is, either. I've had to do things around here from time to time that were disagreeable to me, but I did them with the full knowledge that it was for the betterment of Medicine Springs. I don't see the merit in this one. And it may be because I believe someone somewhere is still holding some aces up his sleeve."

"Well, don't be accusing me!" Kane's voice again approached a raving screech. "It's cut and dried. I've got other work to do, and so have you. I'll see you when you're ready to give me a report on all this, Parker."

Jed got up to leave, words forming in his mind, but

as fast as the thoughts came he dismissed them as futile. Cletus Kane had his objectives, and he had his reasons.

"I'll do that, Mr. Kane," Jed said, hearing resignation and fatigue in his own voice. He grabbed his hat and headed for the door.

There was a solution to all this. Kane couldn't be reasoned with. Frank Woodson could be. It was against Kane's orders, but it would have to be done. He'd ride out and have a serious talk with one of the partners of the Circle TW. It would have to be done if he was to see his duty clearly and carry it out. Frank Woodson, too, was hiding something.

✳ 21 ✳

As Jed Parker might have imagined, his wife was delighted to learn that Frank had invested in a spread in the Medicine Springs valley. He, too, had been pleased. Until the scene with Kane. Still, there were elements about it, when the problems were solved, that were good—nay, excellent, he thought. Gradually, slowly, when he felt Cindy had matured enough to be taken into his confidence, she would learn the identity of her real father. By the time he broke the news to his oldest daughter she would know Frank Woodson for the kind, gentle man he truly was. It was probable, too, that some sort of realistic and long-lasting relationship could build between the daughter and her natural father.

Jed was also certain that this would in no way threaten or undermine his and Nancy's role in Cindy's life. Knowing Frank as her natural father—that she had been created in love—could make her a stronger woman.

These thoughts were on Jed Parker's mind as he rode off from his home, perhaps for the first time in his association with Cletus Kane, flying in the face of direct orders from his boss. Jed had done a great deal of thinking, and this now seemed the best course. He was riding to the old Hollingsworth place, now the headquarters of the Circle TW Ranch, to have a long—and, he hoped, heart-to-heart—talk with his old saddle pard.

With Jed gone, Nancy busied herself with her daily chores around the Parker home. Her heart was light, her mood expectant. A representative from the traveling thespian company was due to arrive on the stage this very morning to discuss with her the plans for theatrical performances a few weeks hence. This would give a real send-off to the Medicine Springs Ladies' Culture League. Maybe enough money would be made to have a start for the town library. The library's beginning was the major task Nancy had set for herself in her term as president of the league.

With their chores finished Tuck and little Amy were out behind the house playing around the stable. A huge tree grew in back of the barn. It was their favorite place to play, climbing the tree or digging in the dirt around its roots.

Cynthia was just enough older that she didn't care to join in the childish play. She hung around the house, helping her mother or reading. A regular little bookworm when reading material was handy, Cindy was as eager as Nancy to see the Medicine Springs Library get started. She also took a great interest in her mother's affairs with the "League," as Nancy had come to call it. Cindy knew someone from the theatrical troupe was due this morning. It was an event she wouldn't miss for the world. She had put on her best dress especially for the occasion. Now, as Nancy made another tour of the house to make certain everything looked just right for "company," Cindy went out to the shade of a tree at the front of the house. To try to keep her excitement and anticipation in check, and to make the time pass, she got her nose, for the third or fourth time, into Louisa May Alcott's *Little Women*.

Nancy made one more trip to the kitchen to check the plate of cookies under a freshly pressed napkin. She made certain her teapot was filled and ready to boil to serve her anticipated midmorning guest.

From the kitchen she heard the front door open and heard Cynthia call, "Mommy?"

"Yes, honey?"

"There's somebody here to see you."

"Is it the lady from town?" Nancy asked, taking a second to check everything again. "I'll be right there."

"No, Mommy. Mr. Kane is here."

Nancy felt a pang of apprehension thump in her chest. Kane seldom called at the Parker home. Anything that had to be done between him and Jed was conducted in Jed's office in town. In the front room she found Cletus Kane had already hung his hat on the hall tree. He stood in the center of the room, impatient and strange-acting, looking at the room's furnishings, but in a fidgeting, nervous way. Nancy's mind raced; what was this all about?

"Mr. Kane," she said. "I'm sorry. Jed isn't here. He's out someplace. Said he would be gone most of the day. Did you go to his office in town?"

Kane's manner suddenly changed, but it didn't make Nancy any the less jumpy. His smile turned benevolent, and if he had been more of a stranger,

Nancy would have sworn she caught the glint of a leer in his eye.

"It's you I've come to see, Mrs. Parker. Can we talk?" He swung his head in the direction of Cindy, standing beside the front door watching.

"Don't you have some reading you're doing, young lady?" she said.

"Yes'm," Cindy said politely, stepping back and closing the door behind her.

"I'm expecting company later this morning, Mr. Kane. I have some things set for tea and cookies. May I offer you some?"

"Obliged, Mrs. Parker ... Nancy. No. Thanks just the same. Do you know where Jed is this morning?"

"I think he was going to ride out to see his friend— uh, our friend—Mr. Woodson."

Kane's expression changed, darkly. "I imagined so. Damn!"

"Is anything wrong, Mr. Kane?"

"Ah, no. No, nothing at all. Nancy, I'll come right to the point. I am a little concerned about Jed, and perhaps you can help. I'm not a married man, but I know that husbands and wives confide in each other a great deal."

"Jed and I have few secrets, if that's what you mean, Mr. Kane. Quite naturally, the things he tells me are not for common knowledge. I'm not a gossip, if that's what concerns you. For obvious reasons he doesn't usually want to bore me with every little detail of his work." She had never felt totally trusting of this man Kane. "Is something wrong?"

"No. Just that lately Jed and I have been having our differences."

"He said nothing to me about it."

"Ah, that's good. Well, it hasn't been differences, really. You know I like Jed, always have. He's an extremely fine man at his work. A genuine asset to Medicine Springs and what we're trying to accomplish here. And so, I might add, are you."

"Why, thank you, Mr. Kane. I'm glad to hear you say that. But what of these differences? Is there something I should know about? I didn't think you drove all the way in here for a purely social call."

"I thought perhaps you might be able to talk with him. Not to tell him I was here. It would be better coming from you. You're his wife. You know what a great investment Jed has here in Medicine Springs. And you have. A fine home here, a fine family, a stake in the people and the future here. Surely you don't want all that jeopardized."

"Is there a problem, Mr. Kane?"

"Jed's attitude. Lately he's been—well, fighting me. I have an even greater investment here. Jed and I, well, we've built this country. There is no one in whom I put stronger faith and trust than in your husband, Nancy. It's important to me that Jed and I have a good working relationship, a progressive one. We need not have it eroded away by—well, insubordination."

"Jed has been insubordinate?"

"No. It's just that lately we're not seeing eye to eye on some things the way we usually do. He's taking strong issue with some of my positions on things."

"And you want me to help in some way."

"Yes, in your conversations with him. Simply impress on him the importance of your lives here. How important Medicine Springs is to you and the children."

"Jed knows that without my having to tell him."

A gleam came in Kane's eye that frightened Nancy, already on edge in this confrontation. "Nancy, if Jed has ridden out to see this Woodson, just now he is acting in outright defiance of my expressed wishes. We have a problem with this man, and because of Jed's obvious sympathies where he's concerned, I thought it the better part of wisdom that Jed not see him for a while."

With the door closed and their attentions focused on each other, neither Kane nor Nancy was aware that a buggy had pulled up at the front of the Parker home. A woman stepped down and walked with stately grace to where Cynthia stood near the front door, almost breathlessly, trying to act ever so grown up. The woman all but glided over the hard-packed earth, impressing the waiting Cynthia.

"My dear," Christine DeLong said. "Is this the Parker home?"

There was elegance in the woman's words. To Cynthia she appeared like a romantic figure out of one of the books she'd read.

"Yes'm. Mommy's expecting you. She has another visitor. But I'll go and tell her you're here."

"That's a good little lady."

Cynthia opened the door just enough to slide through. Her mother and Mr. Kane were intent on a conversation across the room and hadn't seen her come in to stand silently against the door, watching. Something in what was going on alarmed Cynthia.

"Don't you see?" Kane said, his voice rising. "I gave that man a direct order. Don't you see what he's doing?! I insist you take a hand in this, Mrs. Parker."

"Mr. Kane, you're not acting rational. I think anything you have to say to Jed should be taken up with him. Leave me out of it! I would ask that you leave my home. You are welcome here, but not on such a mission as this."

Kane grew more animated, waving his arms, leaning close to Nancy to screech at her. "I mean to have this Woodson and O'Fallon out of my country. Your husband is showing total disregard for my wishes!"

"Mr. Kane, what you ask is altogether irresponsible. It is not my place to direct Mr. Parker in his job in any way, shape, or form!"

In their preoccupation with their talk neither saw Cynthia beside the door, waiting for an opening to announce her mother's guest.

"Well, don't get so high-and-mighty with me, Mrs. Uppity Lady," Kane said loudly, his voice thin and reedy in his absolute impatience. "I think you'll do as I ask. Do it or, so help me, you and your husband and your family won't find Medicine Springs a fit place to live any longer!"

"Mr. Kane, I insist you leave this instant."

Kane's face was tight and splotchy with rage. "Oh, sure, order me out. How would you like it if I was to let this valley know who really is the father of your oldest child?"

Nancy gasped, stricken with a paralysis of shock at Kane's words.

"I spent some time in Berdan. I asked around about you and this Jed Parker. And I found out about Woodson, the supposed father of your Cynthia. Yes, and maybe he wasn't the father. Maybe it could have been any drifting saddle bum. It surely wasn't Sheriff Parker, from what I was told in Berdan. What do you say to that, Mrs. Jared Parker?"

Nancy's attention was diverted by a scream at the doorway. Cynthia stood there, her face ashen, her body rigid, her mouth a small O of shock.

"Oh, dear Lord, Cynthia! My child!" Nancy screamed, starting for the girl, who shook with emotion, her eyes wide in terror and bewilderment. Seeing her mother coming at her, Cynthia spun the door open and disappeared. Through the opening, though she hardly noticed it, Nancy saw a buggy tied at the front and the woman who must be representing the theatrical troupe waiting expectantly. There was surprise in her eyes as well.

Nancy forgot all thought of leaving Cletus Kane in her living room in her mad dash to get to her child, to explain, to console her. "Please," she screeched at the waiting woman, "please wait. I ... I'll be right back." She darted at a run after Cindy, disappearing in a fast, hysterical flight across the fields surrounding the Parker place. Even at a distance Nancy could hear Cynthia's hysterical sobs.

Still raging, Kane hauled his hat from the hall tree, jammed it on his head, and strode for the door. At the front he nearly bowled over the tall woman standing there bewildered. There was something vaguely familiar about her.

"You!" Christine DeLong screamed. "You! You're the man who killed Mr. O'Fallon!"

❋ 22 ❋

The standoff was an awkward one for the two old friends.

Two years had raised hob with the ranch house of the old Hollingsworth place. The less fortunate in the Medicine Springs valley, or maybe drifters, had invaded the place like harpies in the night and hauled off most of old Hollingsworth's furniture. Likewise, they had stolen the glass from the windows. Now a breeze, suggestive of an approaching storm, moaned through the raw gray wood of the vacant frames and mullions. The winds of eight changes of the seasons had strewn the floor with dust and debris.

The only occupants had been owls and packrats who had filled the place with fragile little bones from their meals and with nesting materials of sticks and cactus needles and all manner of cottony stuff and feathers. The place was a shambles, Jed thought as he and Woodson opened a door that sagged on its hinges. His old pard and his friends had their work cut out for them.

The three men and the young woman who now

lived here so far hadn't accomplished much by way of cleaning up. There simply hadn't been time.

Jed stood in the midst of this desolation and faced Frank Woodson squarely. He had asked when he rode in that Two Bear, his daughter, and Frank's partner, O'Fallon, leave the two of them in this semblance of a house to talk alone.

In the subdued light of the abandoned living room of the vacant frame house Jed studied his old friend again. "Frank, we've never kept any secrets from each other. But you're doing it now."

"Jed, the last time we talked I thought it might be the last time ever. I don't know what you came out here for. As for secrets, no, we never did."

"I had a lot of things on my mind the other day. Still do. I went back to see Kane. He wanted to have Wheatley come out here and take Two Bear in."

"Over my dead body. Wheatley or you."

"For Lord's sake, Frank, pull in your horns. I'm here to avoid that kind of nonsense. Kane specifically forbade me to come. I'm disobeying strict orders right now. But I've got to get at the root of this thing, Frank. There's something you're not telling me. And until I find out what it is, I have no way of judging if I'm doing right or not."

"Did Kane say anything about me? Or Tom O'Fallon?"

"Plenty. After seeing Two Bear behind bars I'm to offer you and O'Fallon two choices. Both of you. Either sell this place and move on or stand charges for being accessories and accomplices to rustling, and for obstructing justice. He insists that under the law you two were felons when you bought this, so the deed is fraudulent."

Woodson turned angrily cynical. "Some choice he gives us."

"Frank, you know darned well I can't do either. I'm still in a hell of a spot. And I'm in the dark about a lot of this. I've still got Kane on the one side, giving me orders. Impossible orders, but he expects me to carry them out. On the other is my friendship with you. And all that's happened. Either way, this is going against my grain."

"Well, I'm sorry you're in that spot, Jed. But you're the one who'll have to deal with Kane. I'll say for my partners out here that we find none of the alternatives acceptable. We stay here, all of us. Peaceably, I hope. If you and Kane want to force the issue, you'd better bring up some strong persuasion. I mean lead. And men. Kane won't drive us from here like he drove Two Bear out. The Indian has rights here. Tommy and I have seen to that."

"I don't want you run out, Frank."

"We only want to be left alone. We won't stir up Kane if he doesn't stir us up."

"That's not enough, Frank. What are you keeping back? What's Kane keeping back? Neither you nor I was born yesterday. I know there's something more. What are you hiding? I have a hunch it has to do with Kane."

"Jed, if I tell you all of it, you'll be in an even tougher spot. Then you really may have to choose between me and your boss."

"I can take making that decision. It's trying to operate on half the truth that is destroying me."

Woodson decided now was the time to come out in the open. "Has Kane ever mentioned a place called Jimtown?"

"No, but you have. Is that it? That's where all this nasty stuff started for you, wasn't it?"

"Yeah. And just now I'm only playing out a hunch. So's Tommy. Neither of us wants trouble. We've both had our share. If Kane sees evil in what we're doing, then he may very well be the guilty party after all."

"What in the everlasting hell are you talking about?"

"You said the other day how much you'd like to get a loop on the man who put me away for seven years."

"I did. And I still do. For you. And for Nancy and Cindy. You think it's Kane?"

"It's possible, Jed. I was put away because I resembled the man who robbed the Jimtown stage. The scar over the eye, the general coloring and build and such. They had nothing more than that to pin on me. You yourself said that when Kane showed up in Berdan you and Nancy were amazed at how much he looked like me."

"Not much to go on."

"Of course not. Only suspicion. It's a big world, Jed. Or a small one, as our getting together after nearly ten years proves. It's likely that Cletus Kane was never within a hundred miles of Jimtown, then or lately."

"What's O'Fallon got against Mr. Kane?"

"Nothing. Same as me. His brother was shot and killed in a barroom fight in Jimtown a few days after I got put away. All Tommy knows is that the murderer matched the description of the man who robbed the stage. Except by that time they had behind bars the man they were convinced robbed the stage."

"Still not much proof."

"Tommy and I both agree with that. We came here separately, though, to check it out. We met quite by chance in Medicine Springs a week or so ago. The day before we joined your posse."

"And there's been no one else discovered who was responsible for the stage robbery nor for the killing of O'Fallon's brother, right?"

"Right."

"And you think Kane was the one. You think it so much that you're prodding him, baiting him, trying to get him to expose his hand—whatever his hand is—so that you can nail him with the robbery you got blamed for and for the O'Fallon murder still unsolved."

"You make it sound like we want to see Kane sent up, Jed. We don't want that—not if he's innocent. But he has been heavy-handed in Medicine Springs. What it boils down to is that we've both been victims of injustice, Tommy and me. When we came across Two Bear up in the badlands and heard his story, after what we'd heard Honus Johnson say, we decided maybe we could see the injustice he'd suffered some-how turned around."

"And in the process get me into a great mess of trouble."

"That was not my intent, Jed. By the way, do you have any idea how Kane got the stake that got him started in Medicine Springs in the first place?"

"He was a big man here before I came on the scene. He'd bought much of the land at a price that has since gone sky-high, thanks to his efforts. The country was loaded with unbranded mavericks. He had them rounded up, ran his brand on them, and he's gone on from there."

"Then he had to have had a good-sized stake."

"Well, yes. He didn't come here penniless."

"So he's never said where his money came from."

"No, I don't guess he has. I always figured that was his business."

A commotion outside distracted their attention. A rider had galloped in. Woodson and Parker heard shouts, muffled by the distance and the vacant walls as the rider was met by O'Fallon and Two Bears.

Pounding feet approached the house, and the bulk of John Two Bear filled the doorway. "Frank, you better come. There's a man here from town. There's been trouble. It's Mr. Wheatley."

Woodson and Parker headed for the door together. In the rutted, weed-infested ranch yard Hannibal Wheatley was jogging toward them, with Tommy O'Fallon close behind. Helen Two Bear, clutching the reins of Wheatley's horse, began leading the animal toward the cluster of men in front of the house.

"Mr. Parker, you better get to town right away," Wheatley said, the eyes over his beak nose glinting with urgency. "There's been some trouble."

"What kind of trouble, Hannibal?" Parker said.

"Your wife. Your daughter. Cindy. Oh, they're all right. But something happened."

"They've been hurt?"

"Oh, no, sir, nothing like that. It was Mr. Kane. He was there."

"Make sense, Hannibal!"

"I don't know it all."

"Well, what then, man?!"

"Your daughter ran off. Mrs. Parker can't find her."

"Oh, my God," Parker said. "What happened?"

"Mr. Kane was there, I think, talking to your missus. They had an argument. He said something to her about Cynthia not being your real daughter. I think Cynthia heard him say it, and she ran off."

Parker turned to Woodson, terror and pain frozen in his expression. "How in the hell did he know?"

Woodson, too, went stiff with the news Wheatley had blurted out. "You'd better get to him and find out. Where's Kane now, Wheatley?"

"Gone. Nobody knows for sure where. They said he went back to his house, got some stuff, and rode off. They don't know. There's something else, Mr. Parker."

"What?"

"A lady was there. You know, come to town to talk to your missus about the shows."

"Well, yes, Nancy was expecting a visitor this morning. What's that got to do with all this?"

"Was her came back into town to tell me about your daughter running off. She claims she knows Mr. Kane from some time back. She's acting a little wild herself. She was there, she says, years ago, when Mr. Kane killed a man named O'Fallon. But ain't that O'Fallon there?"

"Saints presarve us!" Tommy said. His face, too, reflected a jumble of emotions, mostly shock, at Wheatley's spewed-out tidings. "The man killed was Patrick O'Fallon. I'm Thomas O'Fallon, Mr. Wheatley."

"Kin?"

"Me own dear brothurr."

Woodson looked at Parker and found Jed studying him closely.

"I'm sorry, Jed. It sounds like Kane let the cat out of the bag."

Parker's face was set, the muscles around his jaw twitching. "All deals with that bastard are off," he said hoarsely. "I'll get him for all this. To hell with the job. To hell with Medicine Springs. To hell with everything. Somehow he knew about Cindy. Maybe from Berdan. Waiting to use it against me, and he figured now was the time. Damn him! I'll get him for it. That's just . . . just . . . obscene! What an awful thing to say to that child, or even in front of that child, Frank."

"If he's been exposed as Paddy O'Fallon's killer, you'd better take it slow, Jed. Kane's apt to act like the wild man he really is," Woodson said. "I'll ride with you."

"You will like hell. This is a matter for the law. My clear duty. I'll get into town and talk with this woman. If Kane is a murderer, it's my job to bring him in. Mine and Wheatley's."

"Then deputize me, too," Woodson said. "I have as much at stake in this as you. There's not much doubt now that Kane was also the robber of the Jimtown stage. I need to talk to him about that."

"No, Frank, you stay here. Stay out of it—for now. Whatever you do, don't go to see Nancy just yet. Let me handle this. Come on, Hannibal. As soon as I decide what to do I'll be back, Frank. I promise you this—I won't ride after Kane until I've come back here to see you."

With that Parker raced for his horse while Wheatley took the reins of his from Helen. Wheatley swung up and was but a few lengths behind Parker when he wheeled out of the Circle TW yard and headed out the road to Medicine Springs.

Watching them go, O'Fallon spoke. "I thought I'd rejoice when Paddy O'Fallon's killer was finally exposed." His tone was sad. "The feelings ain't nearly what I thought they would be. I hope that woman, whoever she is, stays in town till I can get in there to talk with her."

Helen, standing near her father and the two partners, spoke up. "Frank, what was all that about Cynthia Parker and her father?" There was compassion, not suspicion, in her voice.

"I guess you'll all need to know it sooner or later," Woodson said, appreciating the concern for him Helen was showing. "I'm Cynthia Parker's real father."

Helen gasped, and Two Bear gave him a strange look.

"I can tell you all about it in good time. Let it go for now that Jed wanted to wait until everything was right to tell her. When she was older. I was going back to Texas to marry Nancy Merrill—the woman you now know as Mrs. Jed Parker—when I was railroaded and sent to prison. Now Kane's spilled the beans. The poor child! Sounds as though she's run away from home."

"If Parker doesn't get Kane, Frank," Two Bear said, "we will. He was impolite to Helen—that's putting it mildly—so I've got a score to settle with him, too."

"Jed asked us to stay here. He'll be back. For now we let him handle it. Kane'll get what he deserves, John, have no fear."

A burst of muted gunfire came to the group in the yard. The sound was a long way off, down the road Parker and Wheatley had taken. Woodson identified the sounds as several bursts from six-guns.

"What the hell was that?" O'Fallon said, his voice rising.

"Trouble," Woodson said. "Let's mount up. John, you and Helen wait here!"

Woodson and O'Fallon sprinted for the stable,

which they had cleaned up enough to house the five horses belonging to the Circle TW remuda. It took them scant minutes to saddle and bridle their horses. The two thundered out of the ranch yard as fast as Parker and Wheatley had done a short time before.

They were hardly out of sight over a hill north of the ranch when they saw the two riders coming back. Wheatley rode close to Jed Parker, helping him keep his seat in the saddle. They came at a walk. Parker was hunched over in pain, clutching the saddle horn for balance. In his pain his riding posture was stooped and ragged.

As Woodson and O'Fallon approached the two lawmen Woodson's mouth gaped in shock. A crimson blot the size of a saucer stained the left shoulder of Jed Parker's shirt.

※ 23 ※

Gently, their minds full of questions, they eased Jed down off his horse. Supporting him as best they could, Woodson and O'Fallon got him into the house and into one of the rooms that had been planned as sleeping quarters. This room was slightly tidier than the living room, thanks to Helen Two Bear. At least it had a bed frame to which a broad mesh of rope supports had been tied. They had found a mattress bag of sturdy ticking, aired it out, and filled it with clean straw from the stable.

While the men slept in the stable on some musty old hay, Helen's first night on the Circle TW Ranch had been spent here.

They helped Jed into the room. With the crude mattress covered by some of their soogans they laid him there.

"You men get out," Helen Two Bear ordered. "I'll look after Mr. Parker's wound. Mr. Parker, if you'll allow me . . ."

His face twisted in pain, Jed blinked his eyes in assent.

"I'll need some clean cloths for bandages," she said. "Father, see what you can find in our things. A doctor will have to look at it. First I have to clean around it and get the bleeding stopped."

"I've a clean shirt out there," O'Fallon said. "Get that, John. In my saddlebags."

As John Two Bear hustled out to the stables to rummage through O'Fallon's gear, Woodson and the other men went into the living room to confer.

"It was Mr. Kane," Wheatley said. "Never seen him like that. Like a rogue horse he was. A wild eye in his head. We seen him, Mr. Parker and me, right after we left here. Riding this way. He was coming for you, Mr. Woodson, he said. And for Mr. O'Fallon."

"Then he's still out there someplace," Woodson said.

"Right enough," Wheatley said. "Him and Mr. Parker, they had heated words. Mr. Parker, he told Mr. Kane to turn around and ride to town with us and they'd get it all settled there. But Mr. Kane said he was taking Mr. Parker's job away from him, and he was going to be the law here. He said he was going to start with you, Mr. Woodson, and Mr. O'Fallon."

John Two Bear hurried through the room with O'Fallon's clean shirt and some other things Helen would need to treat Jed's wound.

"They argued, and to make his point Mr. Parker pulled his belt gun. Mr. Kane had a hideout gun someplace and shot Mr. Parker. Mr. Parker fired once after he got hit, but not at Mr. Kane. More to scare him. I hauled out mine and let fly, too, but not at Mr. Kane. Just 'cause I thought I ought to protect Mr. Parker, seein's how he was hit. Kane lit out, and I got me and Mr. Parker headed back this way."

"Did Kane head for town?" O'Fallon asked.

"Didn't seem to. He took off west, along the range, like he was heading for the pass up to the badlands to get lost. Town wasn't the way he was headed. Neither was his house. I think he's making it out of the valley, if you ask me."

John Two Bear came out of the bedroom and joined the three in the disarrayed living quarters.

"I saw it," he said. "Drilled through the shoulder. Mostly through the flesh. No bones hit that I could see. Maybe a chip or two. Couldn't tell. The bullet passed through, so the wound won't have to be probed. He's in a lot of pain. I checked him, and he has the use of the arm and hand. Unless the mortification sets in, he'll probably come out of it okay."

"Wheatley," Woodson said. "As soon as Helen has him wrapped up, we've got to talk to him. Tommy and I are going after Kane."

"No, you ain't. It's rightly my job as deputy. I'm the sheriff now that Mr. Parker's laid up."

"That's why we've got to talk with Jed. I'm taking this one over, Wheatley. You go to town and look to attending to things there. Tell Mrs. Parker what happened. Get a doctor out here, and Mrs. Parker will want to come. Get somebody to stay with the Parker kids, things like that."

"Why don't you, Woodson?"

"I . . . we've got a score to settle with Kane."

"Well, just the same, I'm going to talk it over with Mr. Parker."

Helen came out of the back room. "He'll be all right. He needs a doctor, but he'll be all right till the doctor can get here. He may have some fabric from the shirt in there that could cause trouble. The doctor will know what to do."

"Helen wanted to be a nurse," Two Bear said softly. "They wouldn't let her."

"I think we ought to talk with him," Woodson said. "Is he awake, Helen?"

Her eyes swung on him, and there were a million messages and as many questions in her expression. "You're going after Kane, Frank?"

"I need to talk with Jed first."

"He's awake."

"Come on, Wheatley," Woodson said.

Jed Parker's face was ashen in pain and shock from the wound, but he was lucid. "It's come to that, Frank," he said. "We need to get Kane behind bars. He's a madman." Jed's voice was weak and hoarse-sounding. "If nothing more, he'll be charged with attempted murder."

"Here, maybe," Woodson said. "They may have other ideas in Jimtown. I thought Wheatley ought to go to town and tell Nancy, get her out here and attend to things there."

Despite his pain, Jed weighed the idea. "Frank's right, Hannibal. Do as he says."

"But he ain't the law here, Mr. Parker. Now that you're hurt, I'm the one ought to be out tracking down Mr. Kane."

"You're a good man, Hannibal. I appreciate your dedication to duty. But let Frank take it from here. You go on to town like he says."

"Yes, sir." Hannibal Wheatley was clearly disappointed.

"Get my wife to come out here. Get a rig. If Cynthia is there, bring her. Go. Now. I want to talk to Frank."

Wheatley studied his boss a few more seconds. "Yes, sir, Mr. Parker."

When Wheatley had closed the door behind him Jed's eyes centered on Woodson's. "Watch Kane, Frank. He's gone totally crazy. The world he created is gone. Now he'll shoot first. I know I should send Hannibal, but you're the man I want to bring him in. For Nancy and for Cynthia. And for me."

"Seems like I've waited nearly nine years for this, Jed."

"Try your damnedest to bring him in straight up. I know I can't anticipate what will happen out there. But let the courts have him."

"At least he won't be railroaded like I was. The evidence'll be strong against him. More'n it was against me. Still, no matter what he's done, I'm not about to shoot him down in his tracks. He needs a little taste of the agony I went through. And some of Tommy O'Fallon's grief."

"I know you won't hurt him unless you have to. And don't worry about Cindy. The word got to her a little sooner than we had hoped. But she'll weather it, and everything will work out. She's made of good stuff. I ought to know. With time this will all work out. You'd better get going. The storms'll be starting soon, like I told you. How's O'Fallon's stock of good whiskey?"

Woodson read between the lines. "He's got enough, I'm sure, to leave the poor cripple a dollop or so. He'll still have enough left for the trail."

Parker mustered a grin. "That's news I'm pleased to hear for a change."

"I'll have Helen bring you some. She and John can look after you till Nan comes."

"She's a fine girl, Frank."

"Nan?"

"Well, yes, but I was thinking of Helen."

"I agree with you on both counts, old chum. Be back soon."

"Take care, Frank."

Woodson wasted no time taking charge after he closed the door on Jed Parker.

"Tommy, see to your horse. Check your cinch. We saddled up pretty fast a while ago. Throw in whatever we'll need for a couple days. See if you've got a little nip you can leave for the sheriff. Don't forget your slicker. Jed says rain's due."

"Aye," O'Fallon said, eager now that the hunt for Kane was really on.

"It's coming, for sure," John Two Bear said. "I know this country. Up there in the badlands it'll come down like the wrath of God."

"John," Woodson said to Two Bear, who stood in the disheveled room with his daughter, "you and Helen'll have to stay. Tommy and I are going after Kane."

"I understand," Two Bear said softly. He would have been within his rights in insisting on going along, Woodson thought.

"Jed will need both of you until Mrs. Parker and the doctor get here. I don't know where that lousy Kane is. I don't want Helen here alone. Kane could come here. Besides, I'm going to have to take your horses for spare mounts. Kane has just the one horse. If we've got spares, we'll make that much better time riding him down."

"Good thinking," Two Bear said. "You commence

to think like an Indian, Frank. As for Kane coming here, I hope he does. I've got the Sharps and Helen's scattergun. Want to take the packhorse, too?"

"No. I don't want to leave you completely afoot. As a last resort, at least one of you can ride that mare bareback."

"Indian style," Two Bear said, grinning. Woodson grinned back and headed out the door.

In the stable, while Woodson and O'Fallon looked to their gear for the chase, Helen bustled around the meager supplies of the Circle TW, filling a coarse gunnysack with what provisions she could find.

"Easy there, Helen," Woodson called. "We don't plan to be gone six weeks, you know."

Somehow, despite all the tragedy of the past couple of hours, an excitement and an anticipation was coming over him. A great many years had been invested in reaching this moment. Now he was sure he was riding after the man responsible for his long prison stretch. This was the man, too, who had prevented him from marrying Nancy Merrill and being there to raise his daughter Cindy.

"You don't know how long you're going to be gone, Mr. Woodson," Helen said. There was an almost wifely tone in her "Mr. Woodson." "If I can't be with you, at least I can see that you have the things with you to stay warm and well-fed."

O'Fallon was ready first and led his horse out of the stable, leaving Woodson and Helen alone in its dusky confines. She came to him with the sack of provisions.

"I don't know what that was all about in there with the sheriff, Frank. But I know you. I know that if Cynthia Parker is your daughter, it was an unfortunate accident. You may look like Kane, but there's an important difference. I don't believe you'd ever take advantage of a woman."

"I only did once, Helen, and I've been eternally sorry for it. My love for her—years ago—overcame my better judgment. I was in love with her . . . Nancy. We'd planned to be married. But a prison stretch for me got in the way."

"Do you still love her?"

"Huh! That's a good question. I suppose not. Years have gone by. She's now my best friend's wife. I cherish a beautiful memory. That's not the same as love."

His response triggered something in Helen. Her eyes locked on his. "I'll be here when you come back, Frank." In her words, he thought, was no presuming on his feelings; a great many messages had already been sent between them with their eyes, with their actions, and in their veiled messages. He was certain now that Helen had clearly interpreted his feelings toward her.

"You make me think there'll be something to come back for."

"Find whatever you want in my words. I'll be waiting."

Woodson took the sack of food from her, looped it over the saddle horn, and began to lead his horse from the stable.

"Be careful, Frank," she said after him. "I don't want to have to treat another wound like Mr. Parker's."

Woodson looked back at her, his spirits soaring. "Don't worry," he said softly. "I feel so good just now that if Kane shot me, the bullet'd only glance off. I'll be back, Helen, and you can be sure it'll be in one piece." He thought a bit and added, "For you." He paused again, hunting for words; the right ones wouldn't come. He hated it when he got tongue-tied. He yearned to take her in his arms but decided that would come later. "I'd better git," he said. "Tommy's mounted up, and Kane's just getting that much more of a head start."

Helen Two Bear stayed in the darkness of the stable as he led his horse out into the bright sunlight and mounted up. O'Fallon was waiting. It was as though Tommy had known that Woodson needed a few moments of good-bye with Helen.

"Mr. O'Fallon!" Woodson called. "We have us a murderer to run to earth!"

"Well, what's keepin' you?"

They gave spur to their horses and galloped out of the ranch yard. Woodson looked back briefly to see that Helen had gone to join her father at the ranch door. Like dime novel Indians, they shaded their eyes with their hands against the westering sun.

Life had not held as much promise for him since his release from prison as it did at this moment. His torment over the Jimtown stage incident was about to be resolved.

Somehow a fine life would be waiting when all this nasty business with Kane was over. At last the future seemed to have some sort of promise. Woodson felt the anger and bitterness of the past lift off him like a heavy rock; and now Helen Two Bear was a strong influence.

❈ 24 ❈

The sky had developed a leaden quality by the time Woodson and O'Fallon rode over the mountainous pass and into the badlands beyond in pursuit of Cletus Kane.

A storm was brewing that would be—in Jed Parker's words—a real gullywasher. Up here the layered clouds hung low, gray and heavy as slate, pressing the two riders down into the vast and desolate land. For all the excitement that he should have felt at last being on the trail of the true robber of the Jimtown stage, Woodson felt an uneasiness and a depression flooding him. He chalked it up to the ominous change in the weather. Somehow, he knew, it was more than that. The good feelings of an hour before were beginning to fail him.

Tragedy of some sort was brewing; he could sense it coming. Heaven only knew what form it would take. Like Tommy O'Fallon, he should have been delighted about Kane being nearly in his grasp. Somehow he wasn't.

The land was cool with the approaching storm, a

contrast to the last time they had ridden to bring out John Two Bear and his daughter. An occasional gust of breeze broke around them, combing through the short and stubby-branched chaparral sufficient to move it.

All along they had known they were on Kane's trail. Hoof marks in the dust were unmistakable and recent enough to put the rider making them less than an hour ahead. The spread of the prints, too, suggested a man who wasn't sparing his horse. At least the indications were that he surely didn't ride at a relaxed gait.

It was Kane, sure enough. Through the jumbled maze of canyons and washes they followed his track. Kane obviously didn't possess the savvy to ride on hard rock or in areas where hoofprints wouldn't show. Woodson and O'Fallon, who hardly qualified as skillful trackers, had no trouble following the recent trail.

John Two Bear, Woodson thought, would be laughing in glee if he were along.

The two of them rode easily, leading their spare mounts. This very well could become a ride of endurance before they ran Kane to earth, Woodson thought. A little more time really didn't amount to that much. What mattered was having sturdy, reliable horses to get in there and back. As soon as Kane knew they were on his trail he'd push his horse fast, wear him down sooner; the tracks they had seen assured Woodson that Kane didn't have a spare. Everything was working in their favor.

"If he gets up one of these box canyons," O'Fallon said, "he'll have to ride back into us, or make a stand of it from ambush."

"And mind he'll shoot first," Woodson said. "But even then I don't think we have much to fear. He killed your brother close in with a hideout gun and apparently shot Jed with the same kind of pot-shooter. Maybe the same one. Also up close. He may be good at twisting the law and using his devilish disposition to work in his favor, but I don't see the man as much of a hand with guns. He let others, like Jed, do his dirty work. He's unused to it. I don't think he even owns a hogleg .44. I strongly doubt he has a rifle, or even knows how to use one."

"That's easy to say now when it's quiet," O'Fallon said. "But when the lead begins to fly it may be an entirely different story."

Woodson turned to look and grin at his partner, who rode close to him. "If you don't have the heart for the hunt, old friend, you have my permission to turn back right here."

"Not on your auld tintype," O'Fallon said, flashing his broad Irish grin back at Woodson. Woodson remembered the Irish grin from that first day in Wong Chun's bath emporium. So much had happened since then.

"And you can bet 'your auld tintype' we'll be breaking out our slickers before the hour is out. See that sky off to the north."

They paused to look. In this open country the view was almost without limit. "If it weren't out of season and in another part of the country, I'd say we're in for a good, old-fashioned blue Texas norther."

Behind them the heavens could not have been more sullen. The sky color verged on black, while below it in the vast distance great shaggy and ragged tendrils of gray clouds streamed down, carrying rain with them. Jagged, needle-like darts of golden lightning broke starkly against an ominous sky. Woodson and O'Fallon were too far away to hear the thunder.

"I don't relish the idea of hauling out the slickers," O'Fallon said. "That bright yellow will show from miles away."

"And make good targets, I suppose."

"That's what I'm thinkin'."

"Hey, pardner, I keep telling you. With that little peashooter of his he couldn't hit the side of a barn if he was standing in the shade of it."

"He hit Paddy, and he hit your friend Parker. That's enough of a record to make me want to hunch down in the saddle just a bit."

The wind picked up around them as they chased over the trail. It beat on their backs now, forcing them to screw their hats down tighter for fear of losing them.

"It'll be on us any minute," Woodson said. "I'm for getting on the heavy-weather gear." They stopped briefly and unlimbered their big yellow slickers. They were huge, voluminous things that completely covered a man from neck to ankle when he stood up. On horseback the skirts of the waterproofs flared out to all but serve as protection for a horse as well.

As they remounted they were pelted by large drops of rain. A bolt of lightning split the sky less than a mile from them, crackling and hissing in its downward electric race. The land around them filled with the crisp, sharp smell of air fried by the lightning's unfathomable instant heat. Before their horses had gone three steps, the sky broke with a drumroll of thunder that fairly jarred the ground under them.

With the thunder the barrage of raindrops picked

up in intensity, quickly assuming downpour proportions.

"We'll have to guess from here on the way he went," Woodson shouted over the rain's clamor. "There'll be no tracking him in this stuff."

"There's another advantage," Tommy hooted hack. "He'll probably have on his rain gear, too."

Woodson reached up to turn down the already sodden brim of his hat to distribute the rain. Upturned, it collected the rain, which ran squarely off the front curl, limiting his vision.

"There's much to be said for slickers," he yelled, prodding his horse down the trail. "He'll be as easy to spot as we are."

Woodson was thankful for horses that had been bred and raised in this country. Aside from little bursts of skittishness when the thunder pealed, both their horses and the remounts settled in easily to the dramatic change in the weather. The packed gravel and sand under them quickly soaked in the water, leaving firm footing for the horses. As he rode Woodson thought that some areas of the Medicine Springs basin would turn to mush with this amount of rain. He knew, too, that this was a storm that wouldn't be over soon.

Lightning arced out of the sky more frequently now. Thunder rumbled low in the distance, rising to a jarring crescendo as it clapped in violent explosions around and over them. The wind that had accompanied the first torrents of rain lashed the droplets and then moved on. Kane, wherever he was out there ahead, would have stopped by now to get his rain gear on. The wind, tearing along with the front of the storm, moved on past the two pursuing riders. Behind it the rain came down in a full and steady pour, drumming on their hats and raincoats and drenching the exposed hands clutching the reins.

Now they were in country where one wrong move could lose them their quarry. Buttes and mesas towered here, their rimrock all but obscured in the murky darkness of the hovering rain clouds. The low country that lay all around them was split with tributary draws and canyons, most of them leading nowhere.

In the plummeting rain something cracked through the air near Woodson, and he heard the far-off pop of a small-caliber handgun. Kane!

"There he is!" O'Fallon's voice leapt into his consciousness over the roar of the rain. Woodson blinked against the raindrops to see. A yellow-coated figure was out there. Despite the gray haze of limited visibility through the streaming cataract around him, he estimated Kane was no more than two hundred yards ahead. He had seen them, and he'd fired first.

Now Kane wheeled his horse and plunged away, quickly losing himself to their sight in the irregular land and in this midday twilight.

Woodson slowed momentarily to think through a plan of pursuit. He still believed Kane's gunfire to be ineffectual. What had gone by him at a considerable distance was a round from a small handgun, probably also of small caliber and short-barreled. If Kane was carrying a rifle, he surely would have used it at this distance. It was futility on Kane's part. Scare tactics.

All it would take now, really, would be to keep him in sight and to stay out of close range. They would have to wear down the strong man of Medicine Springs until either his horse pulled up lame or Kane ran out of cartridges for his little popgun.

Cletus Kane clearly was in trouble.

"Don't get too close to him. Let him run out his string," Woodson shouted at O'Fallon, who still rode close to him.

Tommy tipped a finger to his hat brim, which cascaded with water. He looked at Woodson as if for further orders. A thrill surged through Woodson.

"We've got him in our sights, Tommy! Remember, we have to take him alive." This time O'Fallon only nodded. Almost gaily Woodson remembered his old cavalry training. "Columns into line! Forward at the gallop! Hah-arch!"

Beside him Tommy O'Fallon gamely flicked the reins, touching his horse's flanks with his spurs as he did. O'Fallon's gray leapt like a true cavalry steed and was a half length ahead of Woodson just that fast. Now Woodson urged his horse on and nearly caught up with O'Fallon. Their spare mounts were a drag on their speed, trailing behind on long tethers, but they clung to them just in case.

Quickly they passed the area where Kane had paused to fire back at them. Woodson never for a moment thought of unlimbering his own six-gun to bring Kane down. Kane was not that far ahead, not that far out of their reach. There'd be no need, at this point at least, for more gunplay.

He didn't hear the zing of Kane's second bullet in their direction. Over the roar of the rain he again made out the distant popping bark of the gun's report. His eyes fought to find Kane in the distance, catching a quick glimpse of the yellow form on the back of his fleeing horse. Kane disappeared up a narrow wash bed. Woodson and O'Fallon followed in hot pursuit.

The going got tougher. The bed of the wash was

littered with small rocks and huge boulders, slowing them to a walk as the horses had to thread their difficult way through the rocky jumble. Kane was still a good two hundred yards ahead of them.

Dammit! Woodson thought. A hell of a place to track a man!

The deep wash narrowed to about twenty-five yards across, the lips of its banks higher than his head as he sat on horseback. Rainwater was beginning to course wildly down its boulder-strewn bed.

The draw they followed snaked in jagged, serpentine folds, at times almost doubling back on itself. At any moment they could round one of these loops and come face to face with Kane. Woodson looked up at the rim of the wash. It might be better going up there. He looked around him. There was no way up. He had seen a spot about a half mile back where a tributary arroyo came in that might have afforded a means to reach the high ground. It was too late for that now.

They rounded a curve in this tortured slash in the rain-beaten and desolate desert. They saw Kane clearly now, still about the same distance ahead, feverishly forcing his horse to race over the impossible footing of the wash.

"We've got him now," Woodson yelled. Preoccupied with his riding, Tommy didn't acknowledge Woodson. Woodson burrowed down inside himself and the rain, conscious only that within minutes he'd have Cletus Kane as his prisoner.

Over the scream of the rain around him he became aware of another sound, an erratic rumble growing in his ears. He couldn't be certain, but he could have sworn he felt the earth tremble beneath his horse.

Kane disappeared behind another hairpin twist in

the land, for the moment out of their sight. When they rounded the bend where they had lost sight of him they saw that Kane's horse had gone down. Kane was afoot in a straight stretch of wash, running away from them in a frenzied dash. His horse struggled to get to its feet.

The growl of sound out ahead had risen to a thunderous pitch. Reality cut Woodson like a lash. He hauled his horse to a stop.

"Tommy!" he screamed. "Flash flood!"

In one darting glance before wheeling their horses to escape they watched in horror as an avalanche of mud- and debris-strewn water beat its way around a bend and poured in a giant terra-cotta wall bearing down on Cletus Kane. He had turned to empty his tiny revolver at his pursuers. Over the gun's frequent pops Kane didn't seem to hear the raging torrent about to engulf him. Perhaps in his lunacy he was oblivious to it.

The cascade slammed Kane down and buried him as it rushed on to claim two more victims.

"Leave the horses!" Woodson screamed. "Come on!" He jumped down, turning loose his horse and the spare mount. O'Fallon, with sudden presence of mind, did the same. At the wash bank Woodson made a cup of his hands, fingers intertwined. Without a word of question O'Fallon stepped into Woodson's hasty hand-sling. With Woodson's hoist O'Fallon boosted himself to scramble over the top of the wash.

Now the wall of water bore down on Woodson in its furious intensity, its roar drowning out even the sound of the deluge of rain around him. On the lip of the wash, O'Fallon dropped to his belly and extended his arms down.

Woodson would have only one chance. He stepped backward for momentum and leapt for O'Fallon's outstretched arms. It was as though they had practiced it a thousand times. Their palms and fingers met, gripping each other securely despite the slippery wetness. Bracing his feet against the mud of the wash bank, Woodson dragged himself up with O'Fallon's help.

The wash, nearly full to overflowing, roared with a savage turbulence below them. Both men, exhausted by the chase, the fast action, and the narrow escape, flopped in the bank's mud, still hammered by the solid curtain of rain, their lungs heaving.

O'Fallon's breathing was labored. "You'll make a good ranchin' pardner, Mr. Frankie Woodson. You use your head."

"We wouldn't have had a chance with the horses," Woodson said, gasping.

"Kane never knew what hit him."

"No, and except for that woman in town who said he killed Paddy, we'll never know for sure about him."

"Ah, but we will, Frankie. We both do right now," O'Fallon said, grinding a muddy hand over his streaming face to rearrange the grime. "We've both been privileged to witness the final verdict against our Mr. Kane. We're the only ones that really matter. It was all set up to end this way."

"What are you trying to tell me?"

"The Bible, laddie, the Bible. Kane has been judged guilty and executed."

"I still don't get it."

" 'Vengeance is mine, saith the Lord.' "

❖ 25 ❖

Jed Parker had one of his cigars going and a snifter of his good brandy on the small table beside his chair in the front parlor. He was still hampered by a sling restraining his left arm as the shoulder wound healed.

While Nancy Parker and Helen Two Bear were busy preparing supper, Frank—declining a cigar—sipped a glass of brandy with his host.

Jed had a newspaper open on his lap. "Funny name for a paper," he said, chuckling. *"The Jimtown Jaw-breaker.* The editor there, though, a man named Douglas Grady, was quite helpful and cooperative about the letter I sent him. He mailed me a copy of the edition that carried it. It's all here. Editor Grady printed every word as I wrote it. Had a wire from him before they went to press. He felt that printing it as a letter with my signature and title as sheriff gave more validity to the facts about Kane and what happened there ten years ago."

"That was good of you, Jed," Woodson said. He

felt a little ill at ease around Jed since he had been responsible for the death of Parker's boss, Cletus Kane.

Woodson and O'Fallon had found the badly battered corpse wedged among rocks and desert debris a mile downstream of the tragedy. They hastily covered it with rocks and heavy limbs to discourage varmints. Three days later, after an exhausting trek on foot back to the ranch, they returned with Wheatley, Shepard, and young Ganderson to take Kane back to Medicine Springs for proper burial.

Jed's wound had kept him bedridden for more than a week.

"Doesn't bring back your lost years, Frank, or Tommy's brother, but at least your name is cleared in Jamestown and Batavia, for whatever good that is to you."

"Worth a lot," Woodson said. "Now I'm a totally free man. I did my time, but there was always knowing that those people over there held me accountable. Anymore, I've got no grudges or bitterness. There's too much to look forward to. A year ago—even a few weeks ago—I wouldn't have said that, Jed."

"Christine DeLong's statement and her identification of Paddy O'Fallon's killer is part of the letter, too."

"Tommy's mystery got solved. That's all he was after. He'd've liked it better if we'd been able to take Kane back there to face up to his past alive, but it wasn't meant to be."

Jed's eyes had a faraway look. "I suppose not," he said finally. "Where is Tommy, by the way? We thought he'd be with you and Helen."

"Oddly enough, since you brought her up, he's with

Miss DeLong. This is the last night of her play in town. Tommy's there. Afterwards he and this Christine are having a late supper. They've seen a lot of each other this past couple of weeks. Talking about Paddy. But he finds her quite a grand lady, as I guess his brother did."

"I suppose you left John Two Bear at the ranch."

Woodson brightened. "Somebody's got to stay and tend to the chores. Seriously, Jed, John's happy as a kid with a new pup ramrodding the Circle TW."

"We're glad Helen could come."

"Me, too," Woodson said laconically.

"She's a fine woman, Frank. The few times I've been with you two, I can see that strong feelings are there."

"Only time will tell, Jed. Only time will tell. I guess a lot of things look promising."

Cynthia, with little Tuck at her heels, came in from the kitchen, her face glowing with the excitement of having "company" for supper.

"Poppy, Mother says everything won't be ready for about twenty minutes. You and Uncle Frank won't have to hurry your talk."

Her sudden, intense look at Woodson was puzzled, but when she spoke she was astonishingly candid. "What should I call you, Uncle Frank? I call my daddy Poppy. Should I call you Daddy?"

Woodson looked at Jed helplessly; he saw mischief in his old friend's eyes. Clearly, Jed was going to let Frank work his way out of this one himself.

Woodson smiled at her, taking time to collect his thoughts. "Oh, I think you should just keep calling me Uncle Frank. Don't you think that will make things a whole lot easier? And probably better for Tuck there to understand, too."

"All right, Uncle Frank," she said. "But I think I'm a pretty lucky little girl. I have two nice fathers!" Cynthia spun around to dart back to the kitchen. "Tuck, come on. Mother wants us to set the table." The two disappeared.

"That's settled," Jed said, smiling.

"Her feelings—acceptance—about all this are very important to me, Jed. That she knows the truth and ... and is adjusting to it."

"Now don't you think for a minute she's not as important as life itself to me, too, Frank. Nancy's had long talks with her. And with Tuck. We've faced it squarely and honestly with them, kept it simple. I think you can see that the reaction has been favorable."

"That eases me greatly."

"There is something I've meant to get straight between us for years, Frank." Jed's tone was grim, but his eyes sparkled.

"What's that?"

"Do you remember Antietam in the fall of '62? I hunted high and low for you after the battle for three hours with my heart in my mouth. I've always remembered that you had a sheepish grin on your face when I found you in those woods. You never owned up to anything. I still think you were playing a trick on me. Now, how about it?"

Woodson paused to let it sink in while he searched for a response to fit the question. "I suppose now you don't remember, Sergeant Parker, hiding my shaving gear when a big inspection was due about a week before that." The two of them studied each other with sly, knowing smiles.

"So that was it! You really were funnin' me!"

"I'd never admit to no such a thing!"

For Frank Woodson, all guilt and uncertainty about his unfortunate past and the prison years had vanished. He was back among the living.